M. Dauphin

Just Go © May 2015 by M. Dauphin

This is a work of fiction. Names, places, characters and incidents are either the product of the author's imagination or are used fictitiously, and any resemblance to any actual persons, living or dead, organizations, events or locales is entirely coincidental. All sexually active characters in this work are 18 years of age or older.

This book is for sale to ADULT AUDIENCES ONLY. It contains substantial sexually explicit scenes and graphic language which may be considered offensive by some readers. Please store your files where they cannot be accessed by minors.

Cover design © 2015 Katie Lee
Edited by: Karen McVino
First Edition May 2015

In the end, we only regret the chances we didn't take.

To my grandma.

The old 'scutter'.

Just Go   M. Dauphin

Index

Prologue

ADAM

"Sir, are you sure you want to do this?" Seth asks, attempting to warn me from the situation.

"Shut the hell up and help me with these bags, Seth. I don't pay you to play mother hen," I growl at him as I haul my bags out of the hotel I've been staying in for the last few months.

That's right. A mother fucking hotel.

My ex-wife decided that our third wedding anniversary would be a fantastic time to introduce me to her boyfriend. Ever since I found him blowing his load inside of my wife, I've been living in a suite in the Thompson Chicago. I'm Adam Callahan. The price of this suite hasn't bothered me; it's the fact that it's been so damn far from my work that I've had double the travel time than I'd like just to get to work in the morning.

Today I finally get out. I'm a free man. Free from the hotel, free from my marriage, and free from the congestion of Chicago traffic. A high-rise downtown is the perfect place for me, and my penthouse renovation is finally finished. All I need to do is sign the papers, grab a few drinks, and celebrate the only way I really know how: booze, friends, and hot fucking sex.

Seth shakes his head at me as I dip into the backseat of the car, waiting to sit in traffic for yet another half hour just to get to the lawyer's office. He knows what I'm about to do; that I'm about to throw the preverbal brick through the window and shatter anything she thought she was getting from me. Since he's always been a huge fan of Dianne, he's tried talking me out of it for a month now. That's not what I pay him for though. I pay him to drive me to where I need to be, which he used to do very nicely until the divorce happened. I've wondered plenty of times about the two of them enjoying each other's company more than I thought they did, but I really don't care to know that truth. I just want Dianne and my marriage to her in my past, or as much of it than can be. Thank Christ this is the final time I'll be making this trip. My phone buzzes in my pocket but I ignore it. I'm sure it's my mom, trying to show me the comfort and support she thinks I need today. Really, I'm just done with all of this. If I could move away, I would, but being at the top of my game and owning my own company really makes it hard to relocate right now.

Just Go   M. Dauphin

The car starts to swerve in and out of traffic, trying to make it to the lawyer's office before Dianne, not wanting to give her any more reasons to bitch. I lay my head back on the seat and close my eyes, going over the last time we met in front of the lawyers. She's apparently not happy about the divorce settlement, but that's what happens when you get married young and sign a pre-nup that you never read without ever thinking divorce would come knocking. I smile to myself, knowing that she can't touch any of my money I've made since the start of our company, and look forward to seeing her reaction today when my lawyer hands her the final offer. She's going to be livid. Not that I care though. I did nothing wrong in our relationship. She's the cheating whore.

Finally we pull up in front of the building on North LaSalle and I wait for Seth to open my door, taking one final breath of fresh air before the Chicago city air hits me. Opening my door, I nod at Seth and walk towards the large glass doors one final time. A leggy brunette in a hot as shit polka-dot dress rushes in ahead of me, giving me time to admire the legs that don't seem to end and the shiny black heels that are screaming to be the only thing this girl is wearing. Her long hair cascades in waves down her back, and her bright pink bra strap makes my mind go to all kinds of places it hasn't been in a while.

Grinning to myself, I start to make my move, just as she speeds up her pace and throws herself into the arms of a guy in a cheap-ass, ill-fitted suit. Oh come on, I'm so much better than that douche. She's too hot for that guy. What has this world come to?

"Mr. Callahan?" I hear my name being called from behind me and, remembering why I'm in this building in the first place, replace my shock with a mask of impassiveness and turn to face Dianne's lawyer.

"Knightly," I say, and nod curtly at her. This one is ruthless. I've been a saint this whole divorce process, not once even having sex with anyone so they wouldn't be able to throw infidelity at me. Jesus, my hand can only do so much. If I don't find a piece of ass as soon as today is over, I may end up with blue balls for eternity.

"Right this way. Dianne should be here any minute," she states curtly as she turns and walks towards one of the conference rooms.

I smile inwardly, reveling in the fact that I am, for once, early to one of these pointless meetings. Not that I'm not taking this divorce seriously, but I have way too many other things on my plate to worry about making it to a divorce preceding hearing on time. I'm Adam Callahan. They can, and will, wait on me.

We walk into the room and I take my seat next to my lawyer, smiling and nodding swiftly as I sit. Once Knightly walks out of the room to wait for Dianne, my lawyer, Anthony, turns and glares at me.

"You aren't making my job easy today, Adam. Are you sure you want to do this?"

Why is everyone questioning my motives today? Of course I want to, or I wouldn't have had her sign the agreement.

"I'm paying you the best rates in the entire city of Chicago. I'm paying you to do a good job, not to have an easy one." I look into his eyes and he nods slowly. Accepting the fact that I'm not backing down, no matter how ugly this is about to get.

"Alright. You know she's going to flip a shit, though, right?" he warns and I smile.

"She shouldn't have been so stupid and should have actually read the thing when it was given to her. I can't wait to watch her reaction," I say honestly. "You think we should videotape it? It'd be great for YouTube."

Anthony laughs and shakes his head, "Yes, that's true. It'd also be terrible PR for your firm, and it's already taking a hit with the divorce of the founders. I'm not sure you want something else clouding up the already foggy future of your company."

I glare at him for a moment, and before I can tell him to fuck off, the door swings open and Dianne walks in with her lawyer tailing behind. Looking at her, I don't see any reason why I shouldn't ruin her day today.

Just Go   M. Dauphin

At one point, I thought I loved my wife. I thought I was happy. She was hot and I was horny. We fucked often and it was good, no complaints. She is smart in the business world and helped get our company to the place it is now, so I thought we were a good fit. What I didn't take into consideration, however, was the complete lack of emotion she's had towards this whole divorce. I was completely devastated when I found her in bed with someone else. I guess I thought we were partners for life. How I was wrong. The moment her eyes hit mine as he was finishing inside her, when she grinned at me while his orgasm ripped through him, unaware that I was even there, that's when I knew she never loved me. That's when my mind started working logically for the first time in years. My thoughts immediately went to my assets: *my car, house, and money.*

I realized then that I never loved her.

I'm not really sure what true love is.

And I'm not entirely sure I care to find out.

Chapter 1

Annaliese

8 months later

My head is pounding and even through the darkest tinted sunglasses I have, the sunlight is glaring at me, taunting me, reminding me how stupid I was to go out and party the night before the biggest test I'll ever take, and I haven't even left my apartment yet! I groan and throw back the aspirin left for me and swallow, enjoying the smooth taste of the most perfectly prepared coffee I've drank in a very long time. Being on a budget sucks the life out of my usual Starbucks trips.

I grab my bag and remember that my ID and a credit card are currently in the hands of strangers, thanks to the asshole that stole it last night. Jesus, last night was rough. Cursing to myself, I check the clock to make sure I have time before I have to leave, then log into my online accounts to cancel the number of the card that was stolen. Luckily, nothing had been purchased on it yet, but it still makes me wary that they would try. This also means I'm going to need to head to the DMV and get a new license. Just freaking great.

First things first. I need to ace this test.

Opting to walk to campus this morning, as much as I'd rather be lazy and take a cab, I throw on a pair of shorts, slip on my Toms, and grab my messenger bag. I need to clear my head from last night. I told Gabby that I really didn't want to stay out late because I had a final this morning and needed to go home before I got too drunk. None of that mattered in the end. She got trashed before I did and can be so hard to deal with drunk that I just kept on going so I didn't have the confrontation I knew would happen.

When it finally did, I gave up and told her I was going home. She was pissed, and the only thing that saved me was the beautiful man that walked onto that bus. The man who made me feel things last night I never thought I'd want to feel. Things I never thought I'd be able to feel. The beautiful man that left me coffee and a very mysterious note this morning on my counter. How in the world he knew I had a final this morning is beyond me. All the note said was 'Good luck on your final.'

What the hell is that all about?

I was drunk, but I'm pretty sure I never mentioned that fact that I'm still technically in college. Sure, graduation is next week so it's not like I'm a freshman. Though, something tells me a guy like him wouldn't typically take a girl home if he knew she was still in college studying to be a school teacher.

No, this man knew something I didn't. We met randomly when he kicked the ass of my attacker, then a few hours later when he walked onto the party bus ready to rip the driver a new ass for being in the way, our eyes met and everything around us stopped. I knew I felt something for him in that dark alley, but seeing him with his three-piece suit and jacket over his arm with his sleeves rolled up showing a full sleeve tattoo; holy hot. I still remember the way he demanded control last night. Just the way he spoke without touching me at all had me completely at his will.

"You better learn to walk better than that, sweetheart. I'm not sure I'm able to wait until we get to your place to show you everything I want to do to you."

If that's not bad enough, my mind decided now's as good a time as any to replay what he did to me once we finally made it back to my apartment.

"God damnit." He hisses as I bring my legs up to his shoulders. Grinning up at him, I reach down, take him into my hand and line him up to enter me.

Just Go   M. Dauphin

"Oh shit," I moan as he enters me. His rhythm damn near perfect, his moans in sync with mine. I feel him growing more and more tense as the seconds tick on, and all I can think is that I don't ever want this to stop.

Jesus my panties are soaked just thinking about it. I can't keep thinking like this. I have a test to take in an hour that determines if I'm good enough to become a teacher in the state of Illinois. I paid too much money to take this test, and I'm not about to fail it because I can't get my mind out of the gutter. Or away from this mystery man. Why can't I just remember his name? He did tell me, didn't he? How can I remember everything he did to me, but not his name?

The more I walk, the more I feel the reminder of what we did last night. I smile as I walk through the streets of Chicago towards DePaul University. Even when I lost my virginity, I wasn't this sore afterwards. I was sore, but it wasn't a good type of sore. Tyler Fatsini had absolutely no clue what he was doing, so needless to say I wasn't wet enough, he wasn't hard enough... it was all just a huge mistake. I cried for days after that, swearing off all men from the Bronx and anyone that lived within a fifty mile radius. Luckily for me, my father moved us to Chicago shortly after so I didn't have too hard of a time finding someone that fit my qualifications of not being a New Yorker.

No, this sore I'm currently experiencing is all the right kinds of sore from doing everything just right. A soreness that's a constant reminder of how attentive and amazing a lover mystery man was. Oh-so-hot memories from last night flood through my mind and I may be blushing a bright red thinking of the naughty but so nice things we did as I wait for traffic to slow enough to dart across the street.

He took me like he owned me. The words he used when he spoke to me were so dirty that my panties were going to need to be changed if I kept this up. His grin when he realized I meant what I said when I told him we would try to use all of Gabby's condoms. I'll never be able to look at our counter again without letting a sly, knowing grin escape my lips. Which reminds me, I really need to disinfect the countertop when I get home today as Gabby will freak out if she finds out about my hot night sexing up kitchen counter with Mr. Wonderful. Not that she'd be surprised, but I'm just not sure she wants her next sandwich to have a hint of Annaliese ass to it.

The light finally changes and I hurry across the street before the little light starts flashing orange again. Jesus, it's like they expect you to run across full speed just to make it to the other side before the light turns. I sigh when I see an old man trying to make it and lightly jog back to help him across before traffic buries him alive. Chicago traffic in the morning rush hour is brutal. We make it across the street just as traffic starts to buzz by us and he smiles at me, thanking me profusely.

"Very nice young lady. Very nice. Don't see that often enough around here," he carries on as he walks away from me, still smiling.

Just Go M. Dauphin

At least I can make someone feel good today. I still have a splitting headache, and if I don't hustle, I'm going to be late for the most important test I've ever had to take.

No pressure, Annaliese.

Rushing the last few blocks to campus, I nearly run like an Olympic sprinter about to cross the finish line, but I hold back and make it to my exam room with just minutes to spare. Grabbing my seat after signing in, I try to calm my mind from the thoughts that wouldn't stop running through it the entire walk here. Thoughts from last night.

The way he talked to me, so forceful, so domineering. No one has ever treated me like that before and I feel like a new woman. Maybe my recent break up from Rob was really the best thing that could've happened to me. Now I'm free to explore this new side of me. A side I wasn't sure I'd ever have.

"Alright, phones and notes away, pencils out," the test coordinator announces as she starts to go over the rules of the test.

I've never understood how a paper and pencil test could show whether someone's going to be a great educator or not, but it is what it is. I start the test, answering the questions I've been preparing for for months now. Getting half way through the test, I look at the clock. It's already been an hour and I only have one more before time is up and I have to turn it in, finished or not. My head is pounding and it's insanely hard to concentrate right now due to the hangover and incessant memories from last night running through my head.

What's wrong with me? I've had sex plenty of times. Why was last night so different? Why can't I get this mystery guy out of my head!?

With fifteen minutes left of the test, I finish up my final answer and skim for errors, then rush it to the proctor and get the hell out of there. I've never liked tests, never liked silent rooms. I just can't do it.

Walking outside, I'm met with a completely different day than I faced before my test. The clouds have rolled in, the wind's picked up, and it's starting to sprinkle. Shit! There's no way I'm walking home in weather like this. I'll either end up sick, or with my luck, it'll start to downpour halfway through my walk and I'll end up looking like a drowned rat. No thanks. A cab is way safer right now. I go to grab my wallet but remember I spent all my cash from last night and don't currently have a credit card since the asshole from the alley stole my clutch. No, this can't be happening. I was having such a fantastic day when I woke up. Up until I had to start moving around, my day was wonderful hanging out in bed and trying to memorize everything that happened last night.

Shit!

I hate to do this because I've made it clear to him that I can make my own way in this world, but obviously can't do that today. I pull out my phone to call my dad and he picks up on the first ring, all business.

"Vick," he snaps into his phone.

"Hey, Daddy," I smile as I speak, trying to hide the fact that I'm about to beg him for help.

"Oh. Oh my, Annie? God, baby girl, I'm sorry. Hey how'd your test go this morning?" His demeanor went from all business to all fatherly the minute he realized he was talking to his only daughter.

"Oh, uh.... It went good. Thanks," I say shuffling my feet as I sit on a bench under the awning of the school.

"Good, good. You're going to do great things in this world, Annie. I'm so proud of you," he beams and I cringe. I hate that nickname but he's been calling me that since I was five years old, so with him I let it slide.

"Thanks, daddy. Hey... I walked to school this morning for the test...." I trail off as he starts in on me.

"What do you mean you walked? If your car isn't working you should have called me, Annaliese. We Ryders don't need to be walking around the city alone," he growls at me and I shake my head in disgust. How can being the CEO and founder of the biggest chauffer company in Chicago make it dangerous for me to walk to school? He's always been too over-protective of me. I get it. Losing my sister when she was ten took a toll on the whole family, but I'm a grown woman now. I can defend myself.

Last night in the alley was just a fluke.

Oh God, now I'm thinking about mystery man again. He looked insanely familiar, but I was also pretty drunk. His hands were so perfect. His eyes... his cock. GAH! I wish I could just see him in the daylight. Maybe then I'd see him without my drunk goggles and not be obsessing over him.

"Annie, are you still there? Did you hear me?" my dad asks, breaking into my daydream.

"What? Yeah!? Sorry, Daddy." He's always been a sucker for the 'daddy' card and I've learned how to play it well. "It's gonna rain, Daddy. Can I use a car... please? Straight to the apartment, I swear."

Last time I asked him for a car, Gab and I ended up going out for about ten too many drinks and we coerced the driver to join us. He was a blast. I wonder what ever happened to him after my father fired him.

"Do you not have the money for a cab?" he asks worriedly.

"Uh," I can't tell him about what happened last night. He would assign me a personal bodyguard for sure. "No, I left it at home."

I hear my dad sigh, then hear the computer clicking away in the background. I smile because I know as much as he wants to tell me no, he's going to say yes. He always does.

"You're still on campus, right?"

"Yup!" I stand and start walking towards the door knowing he's going to have a car here for me any minute.

"Great. Joe will be right around to get you. He's just a block away right now." The phone disconnects and I smile to myself.

Score! I should be upset with myself that I had to call on my dad to help after making such a big stink about being independent, but I can't get down-poured on today. Tonight we're going out and the last thing I need is to have a cold from the rain.

Standing just inside the door, I wait until the black Cadillac pulls up and Joe gets out, smiling at me as he runs to open my door. I run towards the car, holding on to my purse tightly so it doesn't get rain-spotted, and duck into the open car. When Joe gets back into the driver seat he turns and smiles.

Oh this boy can melt my panties any day.

"Hey, Sweets. How'd the test go?" he smiles as he starts the car.

"How the hell did you know about that!?" It's like everyone around me knows everything I'm doing.

"Your father won't stop talking about you. It's annoying really. He's so proud of you, Annaliese."

"Ah, I should have known. Well thank you, it went terrible. I couldn't clear my mind of other... things. I'm just praying I passed so I don't have to take it again."

And so I don't have to face the wrath of my father, but I'd rather not think about that.

"I bet you did fine. So what're you up to today now that you're a free woman and all?" he asks as he pulls out into mid-day Chicago traffic.

I grin slyly, biting my bottom lip and look at him in the rearview mirror. I don't have to be anywhere for a few hours....

"No. Last guy of your dad's you messed around with was out of a job so fast he couldn't see straight. You're hot as hell though, don't get me wrong." He mumbles something else and I laugh.

"I know, Joe, I'm just giving you crap. I felt terrible after, oh... what's his face?" I hold back a laugh. Not only can I not remember his name, but he was probably the worst partner I've ever had. Well, second to worst.

"Ted. His name was Ted," Joe clips as he heads back to my apartment. He didn't need to ask. He was already instructed by my father where to take me.

Pulling up under the awning, Joe helps me out and kisses me on the cheek. I get goose bumps from the connection. I've always had a little thing for Joe, ever since he started working for my dad a few years back. He's only three years older than me, and as far as I know, he doesn't have a girlfriend or wife. He's been hands-off since Ted was fired, but before that we had our fun. The cheek kiss just reminds me that

I'm a free woman and can do whomever I want. Other than Joe, of course.

"It was nice seeing you, Annaliese," he whispers in my ear as his hand gently slides down my arm before walking back to the driver's side and slipping into the car.

I stand in the entryway of the apartment for a second longer, in shock that something that innocent could have me in such a needy state, but Joe's always been like that for me. If he didn't work for my father, if he wasn't such an honorable man, I would have tried much harder to have him by now. Especially since I know he'd be amazing in bed.

Not quite as amazing as last night, but pretty damn close.

I walk inside and head up to our apartment. Gabby has *Yuna* blaring through the apartment and incense is burning in the living room. I'm a country girl at heart, but I love her eclectic self. I grab a water bottle and head to my room noticing the door hanger on her bedroom door knob. I smile and look at the time. 2 pm.

Nice, Gab.

Shaking my head, I throw on my headphones so I don't have to listen to her sex noises and get to work on job applications.

Three hours later and I've submitted to everywhere that's accepting applications, but I have no clue if anyone is actually going to contact me. I stand and stretch, looking over at my bed and smiling. It's still unmade from last night. I'm sure his scent will still be on my sheets, on my pillow, if I walk over and sniff them. I'm not that girl, though. I don't need to obsess like this. I need to find someone else to wash the memory of last night out of my head.

Gab knocks at my door and I yell for her to open it. She comes in and plops down on my bed, already dressed to go out tonight.

"How was your afternoon?" I smile at her and walk into my closet, trying to decide what I'm wearing tonight.

"Meh. Rachel's good, but she just likes to receive. It gets tiring at times." Gabby sighs and lays back on my bed, rolling over to smell the pillows I was just staring at. "Good God, woman. Who was in here last night? He smells amazing!" She laughs and throws the pillow at me.

The whiff of air from the pillow hits my nose and I breathe in his scent. Immediately, heat rushes between my legs and I'm reminded of everything we did together last night. It was so hot. So uninhibited.

"No clue. He was gone this morning. Jesus, Gab. He was amazing," I shake my head to try and clear the memories and go back to picking out an outfit.

We're going to a hibachi restaurant tonight, then hitting up a club downtown, so my dress needs to be versatile. I pick out a white and blue polka-dot dress and smile, remembering when I used to wear it all the time because Rob thought it looked sexy on me.

Win.

I'm going for it. I need to look sexy tonight if I'm going to find someone to wash last night's memories out of my head.

"Damn, woman. You sure know how to rock the dresses lately, don't you?" Gab sits up on her elbows and raises an eyebrow at me. I laugh and look down, enjoying the dress a little more than I used to.

"Yeah, apparently." I smile and start messing with my hair, leaving it curled and straightening my side-swept bangs.

"Wear my red heels!" Gabby yells as she hops up and runs to her room.

Gabby is a free-love type of girl, or at least she likes to let people think that way about her. I feel like we've been friends forever, but it's only been a few years. Her first time being drunk about me, she propositioned me to have sex with her. I declined, but somehow that just made our friendship stronger. I don't swing that way, but she does, and then some. Men and women alike make it into her bed, sometimes at the same time. She's definitely the more adventurous between the two of us, but I'm working my way up there. Last night, one man; tonight, a different one.

That's the plan.

She runs back into the room and hands me her bright red heels.

"I'm gonna kill myself in these," I shake my head and push the heels away. They're beautiful, and I know they cost her a fortune, but I can't do it. I won't be the one to break her most expensive pair of shoes.

"You won't kill yourself. Just hang on to me all night," she grins devilishly and I laugh.

"If I have my way, Gab, I'll be hanging on to someone with a little less vag and a lot more dick."

"Ha! Oh, girl, that's fantastic. Then you definitely need these. Your legs rock and these will be the icing on the cake." She pushes them back in front of me and leaves to get her purse.

I shake my head and smile, slipping on the bright, shiny red heels that do, indeed, make my legs look fantastic. All those ballet lessons as a kid plus the hours a week at the gym helped perfect my legs, which I would say are my best asset. I pose in the mirror a few times and smile at what I see. Gab walks back into the room and whistles at me.

"Hot shit, you look great. Let's get moving before I change my mind and try to seduce you myself again." She winks and starts to leave the room.

"Funny. Now stop and help me with these bangs," I whine as I try to make them fall correctly. She grabs the straightener, a brush, and some spray, and within a few minutes they look perfect. How she always does it is beyond me. I can never get them to look that good.

Walking to the elevator, I pull my taxi app up on my replacement phone that Gab lent me and summon the closest taxi to take us to dinner. Sure I have a car, but drinking and driving is on my never-in-a-million-years list. As is asking my dad for a car unless it's incredibly necessary, like it was today. These heels are like walking on stilts; I'll be lucky if I make it through tonight in one piece.

We arrive about ten minutes early for our reservations and Gabby hits up the bar while I stand and wait. She's on her way back when I see her stop to talk to someone, holding my drink in one hand and sipping on hers in the other. I groan inwardly when I realize I'm going to have to walk over there if I want to start on my drink before the ice starts to water it down.

Moving slowly, I try to be as gentle with my steps as I can. Stepping to the side so an elderly woman can pass by, my heel hits a crack in the tile and my leg twists as I lose my balance.

Great, Annie. Perfect.

I go down, grasping for anything and everything possible to save me from hitting the floor. Everything is played out in slow motion in front of me as I fall to my embarrassing demise. I hear people around me gasp, a few chuckles, I swear I hear a camera shutter sound from someone's phone.

Fan-freaking-tastic.

Landing on my ass with a very ladylike 'oomph', I try and regain composure before standing back up on these death traps. My leg is a little sore but I'm more worried about walking away from this experience with the tiniest bit of pride that I have left. I can't look around me for fear that everyone will be staring at me, so I stand up and reach down to put my shoe back on correctly.

As soon as I finish fixing my shoes, I stand tall and start to walk away from this nightmare, but instead, end up slamming my body into a very hard male chest. A very good smelling, tall and well-built, male chest.

Awesome, Ann. Freaking great job bringing the sexy tonight.

I slowly and embarrassingly bring my eyes up to meet his, to apologize to the nice man that I just plowed into for being so clumsy, when I meet his face. His surprised face. He's not just any incredibly delicious smelling man. I know that smell. He's the man that sexed me up last night with earth shattering orgasms from the best sex of my life and has been invading my thoughts all day today.

It's the guy from last night and I've just run straight into his rock solid body. Holy shit.

I take a breath before apologizing and quickly walking away, noticing the black haired beauty on his arm and the intense stare I'm receiving from her. Oh my God.

Just Go   M. Dauphin

His smell is ten times better in person, those dark eyes are ten times more intense than in my memory, and his gaze doesn't leave mine as I walk away.

Chapter 2

Adam

"That's it, baby. All the way back," I moan as her mouth wraps around me and her blue eyes gaze up at me. My hand goes to the back of her head to guide her while I let my head fall back to my chair and close my eyes, picturing the one thing I haven't been able to get out of my mind all day.

Fucking Vick Ryder's daughter.

This girl's only been interning here for a week and I've already got her under my thumb so she's great for a quick stress reliever before a big meeting, but Jesus if I can't help picturing Vick's fucking daughter from last night every time I close my eyes. When I close my eyes while this Wendy girl is sucking me off, I see Annaliese.

Jesus, even her name. Annaliese. Those eyes. Those legs. Her ass. Fuck. I can't stop thinking about her. The more I imagine what she let me do to her last night, the harder I get. Wendy's hand cups my balls and all I can do is imagine Annaliese's hands doing the same.

"Jesus," I gasp as she starts sucking harder, and it's all I can do not to yell out Annaliese's name.

She moans as she takes me as deep as she can go, and I lose it.

Fuck!

"Mmm... yummy," she says as she smiles and smacks her lips from swallowing my orgasm. Wiping her mouth, she stands and smiles at me.

I try and smile at her but that comment and the bright orange fingernail polish really has me turned off to this girl. She's a decent lay and can suck dick like no other, but God she's annoying.

"I gotta get to my meeting. Thanks. You can see yourself out," I say impassively as I clean myself up and start to fix my suit.

I can see her pouting at me but the minute the door opens and Benton walks in, she scurries out like a lost and injured puppy. That's one more employee I'll need to be replacing. No doubt she'll be turning in her notice today.

"For real, man? What's that? Three this week already?" he asks as he relaxes on the couch in front of my desk while I adjust my shirt and throw on my suit jacket.

"Fuck off. You look like shit, man," I throw at him but he ignores me and rubs his jaw.

"For real, though. You're getting more now than ever before. Divorce looks good on you, A-Team."

"Funny. I'll say the same thing when Carly finally leaves your ass," I joke with him. Everyone knows if there's one couple that will never break up, its Benton and Carly. They just mesh and it's sickening how perfect they are for each other.

"Yeah, laugh now. One day you'll find your Carly."

"Not even looking, bro. Let's get moving. The meeting can't start without us there," I say and slap him on the back as we walk out of my office. He winces and I remember the bruise on his back he got last night.

Shit. This can't last. Carly won't go for it.

I see Wendy crying to my assistant, and I'm fairly certain she's shooting daggers at me right now, but I smile and nod as we walk by. I can't take drama. That's why I pay my assistant, Reese, the big bucks. She can handle anything for me. She filters out the bullshit and leaves me with the important stuff. Wendy is most definitely not 'important stuff'.

This meeting today. This meeting is important stuff.

It's not a business meeting per se, though on paper it looks just like any other company meeting. It's one that I've been looking forward to for a week now, and I don't typically look forward to meetings. I have more important shit to do with my time. That is, until last night. Last night I put my livelihood in danger by sleeping with the one girl in the city that is so painfully out of reach my balls hurt the entire way home this morning.

"You cool with sitting in on this?" I ask Benton as we approach the double door on the top floor of my building.

"Why wouldn't I be? Just another A-Team meeting." He sighs and grins. "How much you going in for this time?"

"He has me for one K already. I'm thinking about upping it. Double or nothing. I've heard the guy tomorrow night is on fire lately, but my guy's better." I slap his shoulder and he nods with a knowing smile.

"Let's do this shit. You know me, dude, I'm in."

"Alright," I sigh and let him enter me.

To everyone on the outside, this looks like a meeting between a chauffeur service and a high-profile businessman who needs our services.

Those of us on the inside know what it really is though.

"Mr. Callahan. I'd expected you to be on time this time," Vick grins slimly as he stands to shake my hand.

Vick Ryder is just about the most two-faced son of a bitch out there. On the outside, he's the typical family man. Poor guy lost his daughter in an accident when she was just a kid so the whole city rallied around him and his business. What they didn't know was that they were also rallying around him building up his second career. The real moneymaker. The reason we sit here in this room right now.

"Please, call me Adam, Vick. We've known each other for too long to use such formal names," I say keeping my formal tone to the meeting but trying to keep it as informal as possible.

I've got so much money I don't know what to do with it. I've always been a risk taker, a rule breaker. Even when I was a kid I was betting on games or throwing money away on stupid gambles. This is just another game that keeps my mind busy and my wallet constantly fluctuating. I'd never bet so much that losing would hurt me, but I like taking chances, definitely.

"Well, Adam. I'm sure you know why we are here today?"

"Absolutely. You have my fighter wrapped up so tight he can't perform properly. You really need to stop spreading these men out so thin, Vick."

"Ah, you've noticed. Well, he's had some... eyes... lately for my daughter. That dinner last week... he couldn't take his eyes off her. No one touches my daughter. He needs to learn that lesson, Adam."

"I can assure you, he's a happily married man. He only has eyes for his own wife." Fuck, I should've been the one going to that dinner. Then none of us would be in the mess we're in today.

"Ah, Adam. I've seen too many married men sway from their wives." His eyes pin Benton and I could beat the shit out of him right now. Benton knows better than to eye other women, especially Vicks daughter. Luckily, he also knows how to keep his mouth shut.

"No one touches my daughter, Adam," he growls, his eyes move to mine. "No one."

I try to calm my heart rate, try to form words, but I can't. I can't fucking believe I fucked his only daughter. His only child. I'm not normally one to get scared or nervous around people. Vick Ryder is the exception to that rule though. He's killed men for less than what I did, I'm sure of it. Especially when he's staring at me so menacingly. Like he knows where I was last night.

Shit. What in the hell am I going to do?

"Right, Mr. Ryder. I think what Adam means is that he just wants to make sure things are still going well with the deal." Benton clears his throat to try and get me out of my funk that has set in since Vick glared at me.

"Ah, the deal. Yes, so you're still in for a grand?" he smiles at me and I smile back carefully.

"I'd be in for two if you promise to stop fighting him every other night. He needs recoup time. I'm not one to throw my money away, Vick."

"No one ever said you were a stupid man, Adam." He's eyeing me like he knows more. Maybe it's just because I can't get his daughter and her perfect ass out of my mind, but I feel like he knows what we did last night. She definitely wouldn't have told him about it because I'm sure he'd be a lot more angry about things right now had she told him. Hell, I'm sure there's a lot of shit that girl hides from her daddy.

"You put two grand down and I'll move him to every four days. I can't promise it'll stick, but as long as he keeps his eyes and hands to himself, I'm golden." His eyes flick over to Benton then back to me.

I look over at him and his jaw is tight but he's positive about this. Benton isn't one to back out of a deal, and with the adoption process almost complete he's not about to stop this now. He needs all the money he can get.

"Fine. Deal."

Benton's nodding his head, his eyes squared in on Vick and the man sitting next to him.

The man he's fighting in just a few hours.

He's sizing him up. Looking for something that'll help him win tonight.

"Great. See you two tonight," he says and then nods before standing to leave. Turning back as he walks out the door, he smiles a genuine smile. "Oh! I forgot to tell you! My baby girl took her test today finally. One step closer to changing the world."

He's beaming proudly. I clam up the minute I hear him mention her, and Benton has to clear his throat to get me to function properly.

"Oh, that's right. I remember you mentioning that. Well, I hope it all goes well for her," I say and stand.

"Yes." His eyes narrow at me then he shakes his head and leaves the room, the other man following behind him.

"So...." Benton starts in but I don't wait to hear what he has to say.

I need to fuck someone else. Apparently the three days I went without fucking someone did a number on my emotions, since I can't get this chick, the only one in the city that I shouldn't have fucked, out of my mind.

Leaving the room, I hear Benton yell for me but I can't talk about it. If anyone knows I did Vick

Ryder's daughter, I'm a dead man. Or at least I'll wish I were dead. Vick isn't a very forgiving man when it comes to his little girl. He's a proud and overbearing asshole who has fired some of the best men he's ever had working for him over mere rumors. Granted, knowing his daughter like I now do, I would put money on those rumors being true.

"Hey, dude. What the hell was that all about?" Benton enters my office without announcing himself, as usual. I sigh and push the button on my intercom.

"Reese, hold all calls," I demand, then freeze all my lines and darken the glass around my office. Benton eyes me suspiciously and crosses his arms.

"You know as well as I do that man isn't the most trustworthy of men." I try and play off the fact that the majority of our meeting I was trying to hide the fact that I slept with the man's daughter a few hours ago, but Benton isn't fooled.

"Bullshit. We've met with him plenty of times in the past few years and you've never seemed so bothered during a meeting. Don't screw this up, A-Team," he grinds out and I shake my head.

"You need to leave, Benton," I say sternly, nodding at the door.

We've been business partners ever since he started fighting. There's only been a handful of times that we haven't seen eye to eye, and this is about to be one of them if he keeps this up. No way am I telling him about last night. No way.

"Have it your way, man. You're gonna explode one day from keeping all of that inside." He walks towards the door and turns before he leaves, "See ya tonight, A."

"Wouldn't miss it, B," I answer, then sigh and lean back in my chair as the door closes.

It's been almost 14 hours since my encounter with Annaliese, but it feels like I can still smell her on my skin. Like I can close my eyes and reach out and touch her firm skin, her rounded ass. And damn, those legs. It pisses me off that I can't get her out of my mind. I feel like I no longer have control over my thoughts, of my feelings. I need to find something to get my mind off her.

I need to find someone to screw.

Reese is informed, curtly, to hold everything for the rest of the day. I need some time out of this stuffy office. They can deal without me for the rest of the day.

Just as I close my car door, I cringe as my phone starts to ring.

"Shit," I curse as I pull it out from my jacket pocket and look at the screen. I don't notice the number so I answer with caution.

Being Adam Callahan can get a little tricky at times.

"This is Adam," I say into the phone then wait to hear nothing from the other end. "Hello?"

"You know he has to lose tonight, right?" the voice on the other end growls through the phone.

"I'm sorry, I think you have the wrong number," I say keeping my voice calm and collected. Who the fuck is this, and how do they know about tonight?

"Mr. Callahan. I most definitely do not have the wrong number. Remember what I said, for the good of all involved."

The phone line goes silent and the call ends.

What the fuck?

I sigh and turn off my phone, tossing it aside and starting my car. I love this car. An Aston Martin DB9. My first purchase once the Open-View deal went through. She's my baby. The only one I'll probably ever have. Pitch black paint, dark leather interior, the seat hugs me softly. She's perfect.

As I pull out of my parking spot, I make my way into midday Chicago traffic, cursing at the cabs cutting in and out of lanes. Public transportation is nice and all, but they don't have to be such terrible drivers. This is how I met Vick in the first place. Living in Chicago can get hectic, and at times it's easier not to have to drive places. His business was brought to my attention and I started using his driving services for all publicity events. Everywhere I'd rather not have to park my own car.

It wasn't until a month after I started using his services that the driver screwed up by dropping me off at the wrong location and I realized how Vick really makes his money. The driver was cute, and I might have been distracting her. So when I opened the door, she sped off embarrassed. I still remember the confusion and anger that was rolling through me when I realized I wasn't at the art gallery that she was supposed to be taking me to. Until I saw where I was actually. Once I saw the first blow, saw the blood fly, I was hooked. I needed the rush of watching someone get the shit beaten out of him. When I added in gambling on the fights, I was set. I could keep using his business on a day to day, as needed, basis, but once I started throwing more money into the fighting, my contract with him went down a few grand, making it easier to stay connected to him.

The same night my life changed from my newfound hobby was the first time I heard about Annaliese. Up until last night, that was the best night ever.

Parking the car at my condo, I sigh and close my eyes. Shit, this isn't how I wanted this afternoon to go. I should have called up one of the many nameless women in my phone to meet up for a quick fuck, but my mind wasn't in tune with my dick apparently. I ended up back at my condo where the only thing that's waiting for me is a full dishwasher and a very eager English Bulldog puppy that my sister just begged and begged me to get until I finally caved.

At least Thor will be happy to see me.

I hit the remote to lock my car and head to the elevators. The penthouse suite, my home sweet home, is a fifty second ride to the top, no interruptions, as soon as I put my key in its place. On the entire ride up to the top, I'm plagued with the vision of Annaliese perched on the counter, waiting for me to taste her, to fuck her.

Shit.

The elevator doors open and I walk into my lobby. My lobby. What twenty-nine-year-old man can say he has a lobby in his house? Me. That's who.

Adam *fucking* Callahan.

The man who's letting some brown haired, heaven sent, goddess... nope... she's not a goddess. She is just another lay. It's just been too long since my last one, and that's why my body doesn't want to forget her.

If I keep lying to myself, one day I'll believe it.

As soon as the door opens, Thor comes running towards me, full speed ahead. I laugh and scoop him up, laughing at his slobbery kisses.

"Oh... hey, buddy! Did Auntie not take you out yet today?" I ask him in the stupidest voice I can muster as I walk towards the leash.

"Of course I did, dimwit!" My sister's voice booms from the hallway. "He's just a puppy. So freaking full of cuteness and energy," she says as she smiles at me.

My sister and I are two totally different people but it's obvious we were raised in the same household. She's all kinds of professional on the outside, as am I, but we differ on the inside. She's a romantic woman at heart who wants to find 'the one' with the house in the 'burbs and kids. I shudder at the thought of all of that anymore. It's crazy how much a person can change in less than a year.

"Thanks for letting him out, Bug." I smile at her childhood nickname, knowing full well how much she hates it. When we were kids she used to scream anytime she saw a bug. Any bug, it didn't matter. She was so tiny though, that soon 'bug' became her only word. So it stuck, and she's hated it ever since.

"You know I'd do anything for you," she says in her playful, puppy dog voice.

"Aww thanks, little sis." I laugh at her as Thor licks her open mouth then runs away to grab a chew toy from his box of dog play things.

"You know I meant Thor, nutso. Hey, Mom and Dad are expecting you at dinner tonight."

She plops on my couch and I cringe at how backwoods she seems sometimes. We were raised with money, wealth, and status. This girl walks around naked half the time and eats while standing in front of the fridge. Sure she's sophisticated when she needs to be, but she's definitely not as upscale as she lets on to the public.

"I had dinner with them last night, Bug," I grind out. How many nights a week are they going to keep me under their thumb? I have a business to run.

That's why I'm sitting at home in the early afternoon. Because I'm such a busy motherfucker.

"Don't care. Just here to let my precious baby out to potty and inform you that you will be attending with me tonight," she cringes at the thought of dinner with my parents and I have to agree with her.

"Where?" I ask pulling out my phone, ready to text Benton that I might be late to the fight, but I'll definitely be there.

"One of those dumb cook-it-in-front-of-you places, and don't be late this time. Mom was all up in arms this morning on the phone that you were late to dinner last night," she complains as she stands to leave.

"That's bullshit. I would have made it if I didn't have to help that girl," I mumble to myself.

"What girl?" She stops and turns to look at me.

I never bring up the women I sleep with to my family. It would more than likely break my mother's heart if she knew all of the times I have sex with random women in a week. My sister wouldn't be heartbroken but I know I'd never hear the end of it. I'm not sure why I let the fact that I had to help Annaliese last night slip, but knowing my sister, she's not going to let it go until I tell her.

"I, ah.... I saw a girl getting manhandled in an alley on the way to dinner last night. She needed help and I stopped to help her. End of story. Don't you have somewhere to be?"

"I did, but this sounds more interesting. My brother, a knight in shining armor?" She grins and crosses her arms.

"Hardly. She was kind of a bitch," I spit out the lie and it tastes horrible. She was a vixen with a fucking hot body and smart as hell mouth.

"Hmm.... I seriously doubt that. I'll find out the real story. You can count on that." She winks at me and is out the door just like that.

"Shit." I rake my hands through my hair and try to breathe out the stress that's taken over me ever since I realized I screwed myself with Vick. Jesus, if he ever finds out he'll have my balls on a stick, and roast them for good measure.

Thor comes running down the hall full speed and tries his hardest to jump on my lap, yipping at me the whole time. I laugh and pick him up, helping him onto the couch. It bothered me when my sister sat on this and didn't show the Italian leather the respect it deserves, but Thor's my boy. I couldn't care less if he damaged this couch.

I've had Thor a few months now and ever since the first night when he snuggled up next to me on my pillow, I've been hooked. He's been jogging lightly with me or my sister every day since city dogs need the exercise due to being cooped up all day long. He sleeps in my bed at night. Sometimes he waits in the bathroom for me to get out of the shower. He's pretty much the longest running true companion I've ever had. I don't count my ex-wife.

It only takes me an hour or so to get ready, so before dinner I head out to my sister's apartment to pick her up. Now we have an excuse to leave early together. I'll just make up a work event that I forgot about. Then I leave and my sister will be without a ride so obviously she'll have to leave also. A win-win for both of us.

"Hey Bug, you ready?" I ask in her intercom.

"Be right down!" I hear her yell.

As soon as we're in the car it only takes us a few minutes to get to dinner and I shake my head in disgust at the hole in the wall restaurant I'm supposed to be eating at tonight.

"Are you sure this is right?" I ask reading the text my mom sent me.

"Absolutely. Yum-O," she says dripping with sarcasm.

"What's so special about this place?" I wonder out loud as we walk inside.

It's insanely busy, and it looks like there's a half hour wait for the poor patrons that don't have reservations. Luckily, the Callahan name comes with an automatic reservation everywhere in the city.

"Come on, let's grab a drink," I say as my sister, stunning in her black dress and straightened black hair, wraps her arm with mine.

"Why would Mom and Dad make us eat here?" she grumbles, obviously pissed that she's wasting a good dress on tonight's dinner.

"Hell if I know," I say.

As soon as I round the corner, I'm slammed into by a body. A body I'll never forget.

Annaliese.

Shit. She looks so hot tonight.

She looks at me, then at my sister, and after mumbling an apology, takes off like a scared cat.

What the hell? Maybe she didn't remember me?

I'm not one to easily forget; however, if she can't remember me, I'm just going to have to rectify that situation.

Chapter 3

Annaliese

I rush back to my group, trying my hardest not to look like I just saw a ghost. He's definitely not a ghost, and he's most definitely the man from last night. And I'm fairly certain that he's watching me walk away like a crazy woman.

"What the hell has you so spooked?" Gabby asks curiously as I walk up to her and take my now room temperature drink out of her hand. Not that the temperature registers much as I down it in two gulps. Her eyes narrow at me, but before she's able to ask any questions about my behavior, our group is called to be seated.

"Whoa there, Ann," Becker, an old roommate, warns as he takes the glass from me and guides me to our table.

"Don't. It's been a long day. Just let me not have any cares tonight, okay?" I'm not certain if he's still watching me, but if he is, I don't want him to see another man's arm around me.

Why, though? What good would it do for him to think I'm pining over him? I'm not pining over him. I just can't get his perfect body, and smell, and mannerisms, and voice out of my head. No biggie, right? It's nothing, and that just tells me I need to have sex more often with other men. That way the next time I do have a great lay, I won't be constantly thinking about how amazing it was. Right?

Sure, I'll tell myself that. Especially since he's obviously not stuck on it. Not with the arm candy that he's sporting tonight.

"Hey, chick, you sure you're okay?" Gabby leans in and whispers in my ear as the rest of our group sits around the long, rectangle table.

"Sure, fine. Why?" I smile sweetly at her, discreetly wiping my sweaty palms on my skirt.

"You look a little frazzled, girlfriend. Have anything to do with running into Mr. Chicago himself?" Her eyes are pinned on mine and my heart drops.

That's why he looked so familiar. Shit! How did I not recognize him last night!?

Adam Callahan.

Holy shit! I had sex with Adam Callahan. Not just sex either. Rough, dirty, hot, messy... the hottest sex I've ever had with the biggest man-whore of the entire city of Chicago. I almost feel dirty, in the way of 'hey, I've practically fucked half the population of Chicago just by fucking Adam', but the excitement of being one that he picked is enough to keep that feeling wrapped up tightly. Really, he didn't have much of a choice. I didn't give him one when I forced him to take me home. The memories of last night play through my head.

"Good Lord." He hums as he places small kisses everywhere near the one place I want most. My hand comes to rest on the top of his head and I start to thrust towards him. He growls and nips my leg, then pushes two fingers inside me smoothly and curls them up, finding that perfect fucking spot to set me into my first of many mind blowing orgasms.

"Ah FUCK!" I yell out as his fingers play me. He growls again, a sound I'm beginning to really enjoy, then leans in and starts sucking and licking in a rhythm that has me coming for the first time tonight in mere seconds.

So much has happened today that it feels like so long ago, when in all reality it was just twenty-four hours ago that he was throwing that man off me in the alley. Twenty-four hours ago. That's all.

Why does it seem like so much longer?

"You need a drink, Miss?" the waitress snaps me out of my daydream and I see my entire table of friends staring at me, waiting for me to answer so she can get to them.

"Oh, uh. Yes please. Martini. Dry," I smile at her as she writes down my order and moves on to Gabby.

Soon after drinks are delivered and orders are placed, our chef comes to the table and cooks our food right in front of us, making a show of cracking and frying the egg without using his hands, sautéing the onions in an 'onion volcano', and using his flippers to make different beats and songs. When it comes time for the shrimp, he makes everyone at the table attempt to catch a shrimp in their mouth, no hands involved. I'm laughing and enjoying myself so much, especially since I was one of two of us that actually caught the shrimp, that I don't notice *him* staring at me from the table next to us until I get up to use the bathroom. Our eyes meet and his immediately flash back to the stuffy group at his table, obviously annoyed with the loud, young crowd enjoying the dinner at the table next to them.

I walk by him, full of liquid courage, and run my hand lightly across his shoulders, slowly, then continue on my walk to the bathroom. I can't stop from smiling at myself at how brazen I've become in the last day. Sure I can party like the rest of the girls my age, but as far as men go, I really don't have too much experience outside of my ex and a few one-nighters in college. Something tells me that's all about to change though.

There isn't a line for the one room 'family' bathroom, so I look around to make sure there aren't any parents needing to use it, then attempt to slip in unnoticed.

"You're really going to do that?" I hear his voice behind me and smile.

Turning to face him, my hand still on the door handle holding the door wide open, I smile.

"I'm a family. I'm pregnant," I whisper, trying my hardest to laugh at my insane joke. The effects of the drink I downed a few moments ago is starting to make my body buzz and make me say things I normally wouldn't.

His face turns white and I realize what I just said. Stupid alcohol!

"You're not," he says quietly, all confidence from earlier gone.

"Ha! No. Not for me."

"Okay... so my question still stands. You plan on using that big old bathroom all by yourself?" His grin sets me off and I know exactly what he's doing.

"Looks like it," I say as I slowly bite my lip and glide my fingers down my neck.

His jaw clenches and he starts slowing shaking his head. When his eyes flick back to his table, more than likely to see if anyone is watching him, I turn and slip into the bathroom. I make it in, but the door doesn't close behind me. Not until he's standing inside with me, locking it, and turning to face me.

"What're you doing?" I ask feeling the effects of my drinks more and more as I stand in front of him. Or is that just the effect he has on me? I'm not sure, but either way I need to lean on something. I back up against the wall farthest from the door and smile, realizing there's a counter for me to sit on. Sweet! I hop up and sit, keeping eye contact with him the entire time. His eyes have darkened and his expression more menacing than it was out in the hallway, out in public.

"I could ask you the same thing," he grinds out as he slowly walks towards me and spreads my legs to stand in between them. Thank God I wore a loose skirt tonight or this would be incredibly awkward. Taking my right leg, he extends it to inspect the red heels Gabby let me borrow. "Very nice," he purrs as his hand slowly lets my leg drop and he brings his gaze back to mine.

"Thank you," I smile and sigh as his hands start rubbing my thighs. Gently, he massages my legs and his lips come close to my ear.

"I can't stop thinking about how you looked last night. How you felt and reacted to me with your ass on display for me. The only thing you had on were those damn heels. I can't get you out of my mind," his breath is warm on my ear, making every part of me light up with electricity and need. "Problem is, I see you here tonight with these sexy heels on and think,

'Damn, now I have to have her in those heels, too,' so here I am. And you know what I've decided?" his lips connect right behind my ear and waves of pleasure start rolling through me.

"What's that?" I manage to get out as he attacks my most sensual spots making me gasp.

"I want to fuck you in every pair of heels you own," he growls then bites down on my collarbone.

I gasp then smile when he plants kisses all around the fresh bite.

"Mmm... really?" I kid and he nips my earlobe making me squirm from the need for more friction between my legs. "These aren't my heels, though," I smile and he backs up to look at me, seriously.

"Then I'd very much like to buy you every pair of 'fuck me' heels in Chicago, then do you in them, and nothing more. Preferably up against the glass window in my top floor penthouse."

That kills every piece of desire I had for him. That one dumb, stuffy comment.

"Does that really work?!" I push him back, astounded that I almost fell for his lame ass line and him throwing his money in my face like that. "Is that all it takes to get one of your nameless bimbos back to your place? Throwing your money around like that?"

Why am I suddenly so mad?

"What?" he asks, his voice full of confusion, but I don't stop there.

"You know, I'm glad I fucked you when I was drunk. It was amazing but I'd never do someone as stuck up as you in my right mind. Either get some class or get some new lines. I'd hate to know the number of women you've actually fucked against that window." I shutter in disgust and grab my purse, prying myself away from the beautiful man currently staring at me like I'm nuts.

"You've got me wrong, Annaliese," he growls gripping gently onto my wrist before I make it to the door. "Give me a shot. Just me and you. Exclusive. What do you say?" His eyes are begging me and the heat radiating from our connection is making me so hot my panties are soaked, but I pull my arm back and force a laugh.

"Me and you... and half the population of Chicago," I whisper shaking my head, then leave the bathroom before realizing I completely forgot to pee.

"Crap," I say and sneak into the women's bathroom before he's able to walk out and back to his table.

I can't believe I let myself get wrapped up in him. My father has warned me to stay away from him. He told me that he's just a no good cheater. His poor wife was left with nothing after he apparently cheated on her multiple times with multiple people. Grade-A asshole. I almost let him seduce me for a second night in a row. I'll blame last night on being drunk and not really knowing who he was, other than some insanely good looking gentleman who helped walk me home.

Now that I know who he is, however, I'm going to be more careful. My body is still screaming for him, but my mind is currently winning.

Would I have liked to screw him in the bathroom just now? Sure! What girl would give up a chance to be with Mr. Chicago, especially two nights in a row? Apparently I would, and I did. Washing my hands, I smile at my reflection.

I've come a long way from the chubby, awkward teenager phase I went through. Now the dark hair, side-swept bangs, and perfectly applied makeup fits me perfectly. Heck, I surprise myself sometimes at how put together I actually look. There are plenty of men out there that are good enough for me, I just have to find them.

I sigh and wash my hands, taking a breath before leaving the bathroom. I keep my eyes down and walk back to our table without looking around. It takes everything I have not to see if he's in his chair at his table, but I don't.

Sitting back down, Gabby leans over to me and smiles.

"Have fun in there?" she grins and I see her eyes flick towards Adam's table.

"Stop. Please," I whine grabbing my water and downing it in a few gulps.

"I'm not sure, but it looks like you two went into the same bathroom and came out looking incredibly flustered," she says, her eyebrows raised and grin plastered on her face.

"Gab, drop it. Nothing happened." She doesn't know he's the man from last night, and I'd like it to stay that way.

"Fine, leave a girl hanging," she huffs and straightens herself in her seat, sipping her drink and looking my way every few seconds.

The rest of dinner is uneventful. What started out as such a great evening quickly became torture when I realized I couldn't look straight ahead without seeing him in my peripheral vision. The one time I glanced over at his table, his arm was draped over the back of that woman's chair. The woman who was so beautiful it was hard for me to look away. Why would he follow me to the bathroom, why would he pursue me like he did when he has someone like that wrapped around his pinky finger?

"Who's up for shots?" I hear one of the girls in our group yell and roll my eyes.

Some of us have grown up and grown out of the 'go out and get shitfaced every night of the week' part of college. Others in our group are still getting there. This girl, Magan, I think her name is, is dating Chad. So far tonight, she's been incredibly annoying. From whining about her new Audi that her parents bought her not having the right color leather, to complaining that her shoes don't match her dress perfectly. So freaking annoying. I'm not sure what Chad sees in her.

Just Go   M. Dauphin

"Maybe she has a golden pussy," Gabby leans over and whispers in my ear, reading my thoughts.

I laugh and shake my head. "Be nice," I warn.

"What? You had that look. I can't stand her either," she says, then groans and stands. "Alright you youngins'! I'm out. Let's go, Ann. This bitch needs her beauty sleep before her interviews tomorrow." She grabs my arm and helps me up as we walk out the front door.

Her mention of a job hunt makes me nervous of never finding something that I truly enjoy doing. The state of Illinois isn't the best place to go into education right now and if I don't end up in a classroom, I'm not sure what I'll do.

We sit in silence in the back of the car the whole ride home. Something's bothering her. She normally wouldn't have called it a night so early, especially when we already had plans of going out after dinner. Between the two of us, she's surprisingly the more socially active one. Sure, I have my fair share of nights out, but Gab used to go out every single night of the week. Leaving this early, before the party even starts, makes me think something's really wrong with her.

We get back to our apartment and she silently heads straight to her room to change. I follow her in and sit on her bed, waiting for her to finish changing to try and talk to her. I've been best friends with Gab for years. Ever since we started college together. She's always been the free love type of woman, never showing a care in the world of what people think of her exploits. I know she has a past she doesn't like to talk about, so I've never pushed. She has her bad days, but mostly she's a great person just trying to find herself. The fact that her mood tonight's been all over the place kind of worries me, though.

"Hey, doll. You wanna talk?" I say gently as she moves towards her bed to lay down. Just a few hours ago she was ready to go out and party the night away. Now all she wants to do is go to sleep.

She sighs and rolls over in her bed to face me.

"I think it just hit me tonight, you know? We're not in school anymore. We have all these responsibilities and shit. You're gonna find a great job somewhere, and I'll end up working at some firm I hate, making way too much money than I know is good for me. And for what?"

"What are you talking about, Gab?"

"I mean.... Everything just came on so fast. Everything's changing, and I'm scared you'll leave me. Now with you pulling away tonight and not telling me everything about this man from last night, it's starting. I can see it."

I sigh and roll to my back staring up at the earth toned drapes she has hanging above her bed. She's right. We share everything.

"I'm sorry, Gabby," I whisper. I don't want to tell her, but I feel like I have to.

"What's wrong with you today, Annie? You don't have one night stands, you don't take random people home, and you always talk to me."

"Don't start sounding like the jealous best friend, Gab. I just can't. I...."

"Was it him?"

"Who?"

"Mr. Chicago. That's why you let him in the bathroom so easily tonight, isn't it?" Her eyes light up waiting for my reaction.

"Uh...." I sit up, giving away too much shock from her question.

"I knew it! I knew it was him! Shit, Annie, you fucked Mr. Chicago!?!" She jolts up in bed, suddenly wide awake and ready to talk.

"Gabby, stop, you have to—"

"You have to tell me everything!"

"Gab, are you sure you're okay? You just went from super sad to super animated in no time flat." Her weird behavior is worrying me. I know her mom has a history of mood swings. I think she said at one time she was bi-polar, but I can't remember now. All I know is that I've now seen three different sides of Gabby in the last hour and that's a lot of dramatic swings.

"I'm fine, bitch. Now spill." Her eyes are pleading with mine and I sigh.

"You can't tell anyone, Gab. If word got back to my dad, I'd be dead. Jesus, I was so drunk. He was so amazing. But then tonight, when he followed me into the bathroom? Total ass. Completely self-absorbed, only worried about throwing his money around," I sigh and roll to my side to face her. "It kind of sucks. He was so freaking good in bed. But then he had to open his mouth."

She laughs and shakes her head at me.

"My Annie. A notch on Mr. Chicago's beaten and battered headboard," she says grinning, as she slaps my leg. "I can't believe you weren't going to tell me!"

"I couldn't! I didn't even know who the guy from last night was until it all clicked at the restaurant tonight. And no, we didn't do it in the bathroom. He fed me some line about his penthouse and the mood was immediately killed."

She starts to laugh, then continues on her mad questioning skills. We spend all night dishing about the most eligible bachelor in the city of Chicago. It's great just getting to spend time with her. This last semester has been so busy for both of us that we haven't had bonding time like this in months.

"I'm glad we came home tonight instead of going out," I tell her honestly.

"Me too. I missed you, bitch." She then continues to push me completely out of her bed, leaving me laughing on the floor at her insane antics.

"Now get out. I meant what I said about my beauty sleep. Some of us don't get it as naturally as you do."

"Funny. Night, ho. Love ya," I smile and laugh as I start to walk out of her room.

"Love ya, bitch." She smiles and closes her eyes.

Heading back to my room, I grab my phone on my way seeing a few missed calls and texts from the couple of hours I was away in Gabby's room. Jesus, who needs me this badly? And why didn't they just call Gabby? Everyone who knows us knows we live together.

The first one I open is from my mom, asking about dinner this weekend. I text her back that I'll be there and make a mental note to freshen up the color of my hair and nails before meeting with her. She's always been so judgmental. I don't want to give her any more reasons to pick at me.

The next messages are all from the same number, and it's one I don't have saved in my phone.

-It was wonderful seeing you tonight, Annaliese.

-I meant what I said about you.

-Are you ignoring me?

-Come to me. Tonight. 555 E. Bellmont. –AC

What the hell? AC.... Adam Callahan? No... he couldn't have my number. I never exchanged it with him. Even if he did, he isn't crazy enough to chase down someone like me when he has plenty of other women falling at his feet. Especially when someone like me made it very clear she doesn't play games with someone like him.

There's a missed call from his number, too. Looks like it came through in the middle of his texts, right before he sends me the one asking if I was ignoring him. I'm smiling, not because he's paying attention to me, but because he honestly thinks he can throw his money in my face and it'll make me fall to his feet.

Sorry, think again buddy.

I turn my phone on silent and plug it in, setting it on my nightstand and lay down in bed. As soon as I hit the sheets, I curse to myself, remembering I completely forgot to change into my pajamas and now I'm way too lazy to get up and do so. Instead I lay there and awkwardly strip off every layer—panties and all. I toss my clothes on the floor, spent, and decide it probably would have been easier had I just gotten up. Hindsight's twenty/twenty, right?

I slide under my satin sheets and roll into my pillows. I momentarily forget that Adam was here last night, sleeping on my pillow, until I take a breath in and his scent fills my nose and assaults my senses. How can one scent get me so horny? One scent from a man I've only met a little over a day ago. One scent, and I'm a goner.

Just Go   M. Dauphin

Lying in bed, completely naked, my thoughts drift back to the night before. The night I spent screwing Adam Callahan in this bed. On our counter in the kitchen. It was just a day ago but it feels like forever since he had me. My hand slides down between my legs and I let out a sigh as my fingers find my already wet slit. Pushing a finger inside, I pull it out and wet my clit, rubbing and pressing slowly in small circles. My other hand moves to my nipples and pinches softly and I groan as I feel my orgasm building. I close my eyes picturing Adam on top of me last night, pushing into me with all of his hard length. My fingers abandon my nipples and I reach into my nightstand to grab my vibrator. Pushing it inside me and turning it on, I thrust it slowly until my orgasm is close enough to reach, then pull it out and press it onto my clit, immediately sending me into one of the best vibrator-induced orgasms I've ever had. My fingers and toes go numb and my legs are still tingling when I let the vibrator fall to the bed and close my eyes. I tried my hardest, but I still can't get last night's memories out of my mind.

I fall asleep, still utterly unsatisfied, breathing in his scent with every breath. Before I fall asleep, I hear my phone buzzing on my nightstand, but I'm so tired I choose to ignore it until tomorrow. I know it has to be him. And he can wait.

      ***

It's nine in the morning before I finally roll out of bed, but I've already been awake for hours. The daunting task of more applications to be filled out for a teaching positions is ahead of me today, and I'm really not looking forward to it. So far I've filled out about twenty and have yet to hear back from anyone. I realize many schools don't hire until a week or two before school starts, but I'm holding hope still that I'll be one of the lucky ones chosen before crunch time. I'm also still waiting to hear back from my certification test I took, since finding a position means nothing if I didn't pass the test. The nerves running through me are normal for any person in my position.

What's not normal is the added pressure of responding to Adam. Mr. Chicago. I hate that nickname but the first time a local news-anchor called him that in an interview, the name stuck and now it's used everywhere. I don't even know what's so important about him. Sure, he has a ton of money, but so do my parents, so do many people, and they don't get the publicity he does. Maybe it's because he has such a scandalous life. Whatever it is, it's added a pressure to my nerves that I can't stand. So much so, I've been lying awake for hours, unable to sleep with his scent on my pillow.

Frustrated, I finally get up and first thing I do is rip the pillow cases and sheets off the bed. I'm not doing this song and dance every night with my feelings. I don't need someone like him in my life. I need to stop thinking about him and obsessing over him.

I need to, but I can't.

So I do everything else I can around the apartment to keep my mind off of him—dusting our bookshelves and the fireplace mantle, vacuuming, mopping, laundry, and dishes. By noon the entire place is spotless and smells amazing. And I've not turned in a single application.

"Shit." I sigh and throw my cleaning supplies back in the closet.

I'm starving, and I need to go to the grocery store. It's never good to shop for food when hungry though so I grab my purse and head down the street to the deli. While riding the elevator, my phone buzzes in my pocket and I remember it's been on silent all day. Pulling it out, I see his number calling me again and let it go to voicemail. He's relentless in this pursuit of me. The trouble is, the more he pushes, the more he wears me down. Turning off my phone, I waltz out into the Chicago sun to grab some lunch before an afternoon full of interview questionnaires and applications.

I won't let myself get distracted with delicious thoughts of Adam Callahan.

Or so I'm going to tell myself.

I grab lunch and walk home the long way, going about three blocks out of the way before landing back in front of my apartment. I really do love Chicago. Sure, it's not as glamorous as New York or as hip as California, but it's a taste all its own. The skyscrapers, the busy streets. I love it all, I just wish it loved me back sometimes. I'd really love it if it loved me enough to get me a local job. Moving isn't something I'm looking to do, but I might not have an option.

"Gabby, you home?" I call out as I walk into our apartment and close the door, hanging my purse on the hook by the door.

I kick my shoes off and walk to her room to see if she's home yet from her interviews. Normally when she's home there's some sort of noise; music or moaning most of the time, and both at the same time. Today the apartment is eerily silent. She probably isn't home yet, but she only had a couple morning interviews. Nothing should have kept her this long.

Her door is open and I let myself in to see her sitting at her desk with her phone to her ear. One leg tucked under her, the other bobbing gently up and down. She's excited about something and trying to hold it in. I throw myself on the bed to get her attention and she jumps spinning to glare at me while addressing the person on the other line.

"Sure. Yes, that's great. Thank you," she smiles at me and raises her eyebrows. "Sounds good. See you then. Thanks again."

Hanging up the phone and setting it gently on the desk, she closes her eyes and takes a huge breath before opening them. Any time she's so excited she can't function without screaming she does this. There's been a few times when she didn't do it and went into a screaming fit of how excited she was. That was the first time we had security called on us, so ever since then she's been really good about reigning in her excitement before talking. I sit and wait for her to look at me, and when she does, her eyes are glowing with excitement and I can't help but smile at her. She did it. She nailed a job.

"So do I even need to ask how today went?" I ask smiling, waiting for her to tell me everything like she always does. I can't help but feel a ping of jealousy at her finding her career a day after finishing school, but she's been at this for about three years longer than I have, so it's about time she gets started with her life.

"I just got one of the best jobs in the city, Ann! Clayton and Moll!! Me! Working at Clayton and Moll!" she squeals and pulls me into a bear hug on the bed, tackling me and ending in a ball of laughter. "Holy shit, Annie!" She's still laughing, and smiling, and so happy I just want to keep hugging her, and at the same time go hide in the corner and cry because my life isn't anywhere near being as put together as hers is.

"I'm so happy for you, Gab. You deserve this," I smile taking her face in my hands and kiss her forehead. A quick peck that I'll give her sometimes when she's down or really needs one.

It's the truth, too. I am happy for her. She's found something she wants to do and is actually excited about it. Last night she seemed like she was completely unhappy with her life, which bummed me out. Gab worked so hard to get to where she is now. All she has to do is pass the BAR and she's a full-blown lawyer. She can do it. She's the smartest person I've ever known.

"We should celebrate!" she yells, then hops off the bed and runs for her phone.

"Oooh... three nights in a row, Gab? You sure our wallets can take that?" I groan inwardly, dreading the thought of having to go out again for the third night in a row. I feel like an old lady, but tonight all I want to do it sit at home in my pajamas.

She looks at me, holding her phone in her hand, about to text the group to meet up somewhere. Her eyes go to her phone then back to me. I smile sweetly, hoping that maybe she's considering staying in. I hope so. She's my best friend so I'll have to go out with her if she decides she wants to.

"Will you buy me Chinese food?" she asks skeptically. Sneaky little bastard. She knows I hate Chinese food.

"If I do, are you gonna bitch all night about not going out?" Because she would.

"As long as you promise not to bitch that you're bored once we start *The Notebook* for the thousandth time." She's grinning at me. The dork picked two things I'm very open about disliking.

If it means I can put my PJs on though, I'm game.

"Deal, whore," I say as I smile, holding my hand out to shake hers in agreement.

Just Go   M. Dauphin

And now the daunting task of finding something that I'm going to enjoy for dinner.

She's lucky I love her.

Chapter 4

Adam

She actually walked out. Like she wasn't impressed at all by the fact that I have a penthouse.

Honestly, I don't think she was. I'm not certain I've ever seen such a look of disgust from a woman that I was about to fuck. Well shit. She might have actually been offended by that.

She's fucking nuts if so.

Every woman—married, single, moms, grandmas, babysitters—is looking for a chance with me. With Mr. Chicago. The man behind the biggest start-up in Chicago. The man whose law firm helped get that one chick out of her murder charge, even though it was painfully obvious she was guilty.

I take a moment to collect myself, knowing fully that if I walk back out there right now I'll be sporting more than just a scowl on my face. Who does she think she is? Other than the first woman ever to turn me down, she's just a teacher. Really, she's not even that yet. She just finished school. A Goddamn student, and I fucked her. Not only that, I was more than willing to fuck her again in the public bathroom of this hole in the wall place my parents call a restaurant. I look around the small room, cringing when I see the discoloration of paint on the wall behind the toilet, the dirt collected around the sink handles. Is this really what people call clean and healthy? There's probably shit all over this room, and I almost fucked her in it.

Well... good thing she turned me down I guess.

After a few minutes, my dick finally decides to stand down and I can make my way back to my table. I approach slowly and take in the company. My sister Cara, beautiful in her own right, smiling at me through her dark bangs and gorgeous (yet fake) eye color. Next to her is my aunt Grace, my Uncle Tom, their two children Jen and Jane, and on the other side of the long table sits my parents. Everyone's conversations stop as I return to the table, all eyes on me. Mr. Fucking Chicago.

"Adam, dear, are you feeling okay? You were in there an awful long time," my mother croons as she brings her wine glass to her bright pink lips and takes a sip, leaving a lipstick ring on the side of her glass.

"I'm fine, Mother. I had to step out and take a call while I was up. I do have a business to run, you know," I say sweetly, adding in that I will need to be heading out soon.

"Great, you can take me with you. I need to meet some of my girlfriends at Marties," my sister says as she smiles a knowing smile at me.

"Leaving so soon after dinner, both of my children. You'd think they were raised with no manners whatsoever," my mother bitches and my aunt gasps.

"Don't talk about your kids that way. They're busy adults," she glares at my parents then turns to me. "It was wonderful seeing both of you. You two have a lovely evening."

"You do the same, Aunt Grace." I kiss her on the cheek, shake my uncle's hand, and nod a goodbye at my cousins.

My father stands and pats me on the back while saying his goodbye. My mother stands stiffly while I hug her goodbye, my sister following my lead. She's not one to push limits with my parents like I am. I know how controlling my mother can be, though, so I'm constantly trying to push back to keep her in place.

Once we finally make it to my car, Cara slides into the leather seat and sighs.

"So—" she starts but I stop her.

"Home. You're going home. What you do after that is up to you, but I have things I need to take care of tonight."

I look over and she's transformed into a pouting child. Arms crossed, bottom lip jutting out, everything she used to do as a kid when she didn't get her way.

"Bug, you have to go home. I can't take you with me tonight," I warn.

"You know I'll just find my own way," she chides, sitting up straighter in her seat than she was. She buckles her seatbelt and stares out her window.

"Tonight's not a good night, Bug. You know I'd take you with me if I could, but... I can't tonight."

My sister knows about the fighting ring, as her ex-boyfriend used to be a fighter for Vick before he made it big into the MMA and moved to Vegas. I don't worry about her going to the fights with me, but I do worry about her going to the fight tonight. Whatever that phone call I received earlier was, I have a strange feeling it's trouble. I couldn't live with myself if she were hurt because of something I was involved in. It's useless telling her about the threat. She'd do everything in her power to keep me from going tonight; I wouldn't put it past her to get my parents involved if it meant keeping me safe. She's that type of little sister.

"Fine. Have it your way."

We're stopped at a red light in the middle of the city when she turns to me and smiles.

"The chick with the legs. The one you followed into the bathroom. Who was that? She looked familiar," she says as she cocks her head at me and grins. Her mention of Annaliese makes my palms clam up immediately and my heart rate rise.

"I don't know what you're talking about," I grind out.

She laughs hard, shaking her head. My sister's always had a way of reading my mind, sometimes before I even know what I was thinking.

"You can't keep your dick in your pants long enough to sit through a family dinner."

"Knock it off, Bug. You don't know what you're talking about." I feel my anger rising the longer she laughs at me.

"Jesus, women like her disgust me. One look from 'Mr. Chicago' and they lose all morals. Whore—"

"I said knock it off!" I yell at her, my voice booms through the car.

The light has turned green but I'm not moving the car like I should be. I hear the horns and people yelling at me, but I can't stop my hands from shaking. She's not a whore. She's not a bitch. She has morals.

Why am I defending her? I don't defend the women I fuck.

"Well okay," my sister says dejectedly. Looking out her window she adds, "You were never that passionate about your wife while married." Then she turns back to look at me, "Are you hiding something from me, A?"

I sigh and shake my head, blinking my eyes a few times to regain composure.

"No. I'm not hiding anything. Tonight's fight isn't the place for you to be. There are things in place tonight that could get ugly."

"Did you finish the deal with Vick?"

"Yes, but there were things he requested on his end. I need to be there to keep an eye on my fighter. I won't be able to keep an eye on you, so you need to stay away."

"Fine. Done. Just stop being an uptight ass. You're no fun when you're moody."

I smile at her. The only girl that can make me smile when I'm on the edge of exploding from all of these damn feelings running through me. My little sister and I grew up best friends, and after we connected again after college we were right back at it. Always talking, telling each other everything. She's got a great big brother in me, but I'm the lucky one. She tries her hardest to keep me grounded, and sometimes it actually sticks.

I drop her off at her apartment, hugging her goodbye, and wait to pull away until she's safely inside with the doors locked. Sure she's probably going back out again tonight, but at least I did my job of getting her home safe.

Moving my car back into traffic, I turn on Bluetooth and dial Benton. It goes straight to voicemail, but since it's an hour to fight time I'm assuming he's already warming up. I try his work cell but it's turned off. Great.

Finding my way through the city to the North side, I park my car and pray that my baby stays safe while I'm in this basement. These fights have to be in warehouses or basements in the bad part of the city due to crowd control and not as many eyes watching out for illegal things, since there's a lot more than illegal fighting happening here. People up here mind their own business and don't try to ruin others' days for the hell of it. Not like the rich part of the city, where one bad look can cause you to get sued.

Walking to the address a few blocks away from where I parked, I notice a few other people milling about, but don't make eye contact. If they're here for the fight, they are just nervous to get inside before they are seen. If they're not here for the fight, they're probably going to hit me up for money, something I definitely don't do.

"Maynard Bastille," I say the password quietly to the man standing by the door. He looks around then nods and opens the door, letting me quietly slip inside before quickly shutting it behind me.

It's pitch-dark in here, but I've been to this location before so I know where I'm going. Heading down the hallways I make my way to the stairs and start my descent. A few seconds later, I round the corner in the basement to lanterns lighting the hallway to the fight room. The doors swing open and I'm greeted by the familiar rush of violence and money. Smiling at the doormen, I make my way to my seat ringside and wait for the fight to start. I have no need to get involved with the betting since mine is all done through the man himself; all I have to worry about is my fighter winning.

When the fighters are introduced, Benton comes out second and looks scared shitless. I perk up in my seat seeing him have this look. He's not a scared man. He's built. He's strong. He doesn't lose. Why would he look like he's afraid for his life?

Oh shit.

He probably got the phone call too. Dammit! Why didn't I tell him about it? I was so wrapped up thinking about Annaliese that I had completely forgotten about warning him until it was too late.

Shit!

There's nothing I can do about it now but pray that he makes eye contact with me and I can somehow relay to him that throwing the fight is a bad idea. Once the round starts, my fears are confirmed as he takes double the amounts of hits that he's throwing out. Typically I sit back and watch silently at these fights; watch the money flow in. Losing two grand isn't going to kill me, hell that's pocket change; it's the fact that whoever needs him to lose tonight didn't sound like the type of person to stop after one threat. We can't back down and let this person win.

As soon as the first round's up I run to the cage behind Benton. He's sweating, bleeding from multiple points on his face, and the bruises on his ribs are starting to darken.

"Sorry, man, he's too good," he gasps.

"Fuck that. You got the same call I did, I see it in your eyes. Don't let him fucking do that. You're better than this, B. We can't let this person think they're in charge," I growl at him, pissed that he gave in that easily. He pushes his aid helpers back and leans closer to the fence, closer to me.

"He threatened my adoption, A. I have to." His eyes are so sad, so pitiful, that rage fills me.

"Fuck no you don't! Don't forget who I am! I can get you whatever you want, B. Don't let them run you!"

His eyes focus in on mine and something clicks. Like he hadn't yet thought that I'd be able to help him if he asked.

"Money talks, B. Take this asshole down."

He nods quickly and the bell rings. Not four seconds into the second round he's on his opponent like he has a score to settle. Within the first minute, he has him pinned and the ref is calling it. My jaw is tight and I nod slightly at him as I walk to the bar to grab us a drink.

"What'll it be, Mr. Chicago?" Bart, the regular bartender asks as he wipes a glass and puts it away.

"Scotch on the rocks. Two of 'em," I say, then throw a twenty in the tip jar. He smiles and thanks me, handing me our drinks.

I pass by a few of Vick's men and notice them staring me down. That's interesting. Taking mental note of their faces, I keep on my way to Benton, sitting on the side of the raised fighting platform getting his wounds tended to.

"You look like shit, man," I say handing him his drink.

"You should see the other guy."

I shake my head and wait for them to finish up with him. We sit in silence as the bandages are placed and cream applied. He really does look like shit. Jesus.

"Carly's gonna be pissed.

"Dude, she's always pissed lately. I don't know, this whole baby thing has been terror for our relationship," he admits dejectedly.

"Stop. She loves you. What she's not gonna love is your face looking like that."

"I know. I'm hoping it goes down before our next adoption meeting."

I nod and we sit for a few minutes, watching the crowd disperse. I notice the men from earlier still staring at me, but no one makes a move towards us.

"So, what'd they say to you?" he asks as he moves the ice to another spot on his face.

"Just that it'd be best for everyone if you lost."

"Yeah, man. They told me that too. They also told me they knew about the adoption and winning would throw a huge wrench in my plans to ever have a family."

"Dude, don't. You guys will get your family," I stand and pat his shoulder. "I'm making sure of it. I'll have your winnings tomorrow in the office."

He nods at me and I walk away.

Passing by the men from earlier, none of them speak, but all of them keep their eyes on me until I'm out of the building. As soon as my face hits the outside air my phone buzzes.

"What," I growl, not having the patience to play these games.

"That was a silly move," the voice says.

"No, what was silly was threatening me. You better pray I don't find out who this is." I hang up and turn my phone off, just to turn it back on immediately. I can't afford not to have my phone on and next to me. I'm Adam Callahan, someone's always in need of me.

Getting in my car I head back to my place. The one drink doesn't have me drunk, but from everything that happened today, it's made me want more. After the ride up the lonely elevator, I walk into a quiet lobby and unlock my door, just to be met by an overactive puppy ready to play. Laughing, I scoop him up and walk to the kitchen, grabbing a beer from the fridge and the leash to take this little man out.

"Just me and you tonight, dude," I say to him. Jesus, I'm going nuts, talking to a dog like he can understand what I'm saying.

After about two hours of drinking alone, talking to an animal that only wants to chew on my shoes... my expensive designer shoes... I grab my phone to check my messages when she pops back into my memory.

Annaliese.

I just want to hear her voice. Hell, that's a great idea. Maybe she can finally explain to me what's wrong with her, and why she doesn't want me. That has to be the only option, as there's absolutely nothing wrong with me. It only takes a few phone calls to get her number. When you're rich like I am, money talks. And when you have the right connections, that money talks at all hours of the day.

I shoot her a quick text, opening up lines of communication.

Adam- It was wonderful seeing you tonight, Annaliese.

Five minutes go by and no response. Maybe she didn't hear the first one, so I try again.

Adam- I meant what I said about you.

After I finish off the bottle of Patron and am staring at an empty glass, there's still no response. Little she-devil thinks she can ignore me, huh? Time to tempt her with Mr. Chicago.

Adam- Are you ignoring me?

Adam- Come to me. Tonight. 555 E. Bellmont. –AC

A beer or three later and there's still no response. I did read her right, didn't I? She does want me, right?

If she's going to ignore her texts, I'll up my game and call her. No woman ignores Adam Fuckin' Callahan.

So I call her.

She doesn't answer. What. The. Fuck. I may be losing my mind, but I text her again and tell her to come here... now. I plan to explore her body more thorough than I did last night. The curves, the legs, those heels. Shit. And now I'm way more horny than I was before, but I'm so tired and fairly certain I'm drunk. Doing anything but sleeping on this counter isn't happening unless Annaliese decides to give me a chance. And she still hasn't responded. I am getting so worried over her not responding like a woman waiting for a man to call her that my man card may be in serious jeopardy. Fuck. I need to go to bed and dream about puppies and rainbows or some shit. Anything except Annaliese.

****

Just Go   M. Dauphin

The sun glares in my wall of windows, waking me from my drunken slumber.

What the hell?

I look around, trying to remember how I landed to sleep on the couch, but last thing I remember was taking Thor out when I got home, and the rest of the night is a blur. How much did I drink last night?

I squint my eyes at the brightness and curse. Why does Chicago always feel like having blaring bright sunshine on the days when I'm so hung-over even a small flashlight would feel like fire burning a hole in my head? Why can't it be cloudy and grey today?

"Shit," I curse and get up and off the couch, looking at the bottles littering the counter. I shake my head. Since when do I drink alone? At the very least I would have called over a piece of ass to fuck last night, but from the looks of my surroundings, there's nothing here that suggests anyone else but Thor and I were in this apartment last night.

Speaking of Thor, he's currently curled up on the foot of the sofa that I just got off of. Jesus, I wish I could still be sleeping. Unfortunately, I'm supposed to be the first into the building today. I've always run meetings, and have never called in due to a hangover. Normally I'm more careful about drinking on weeknights.

Just Go M. Dauphin

I shower quickly and grab an English muffin on my way out the door. Stopping by Starbucks, I grab my coffee and walk the block to work. I wish I could enjoy the sunshine but right now I want to curl into a ball in a dark room and take a very long nap. God, I feel like I'm in college again, trying to get over a hangover before having to sit through an hour-long class. Unfortunately for me, that hour-long class has turned into an hour-long meeting that I am in charge of.

Once I'm in the office, I open the doors and close the blinds, blocking the sunlight from killing my mood any more than it's already been killed. I pull out my phone to check the time and something tugs at my memory. Weird.

Ten minutes until staff shows up. Today's meeting is nothing new, but I always like to have them prepared for the week to come before Monday. Monday meetings are pointless, because everyone hates Mondays and meetings. Putting both of them together on one day makes everyone hate their boss. I don't want my employees to hate me.

My company is one of the biggest start-up companies in Chicago. When I was eighteen, I took the advance trust fund money my father gave me for college and invested in a small accounting firm in downtown Chicago. When they made money, I made money. When they lost money, I lost money. I love the thrill of making things grow and grow, and never losing. It soon became an addiction. My ex-wife was there with me the entire time, helping me build the business. Carson and Lewis is approaching its tenth birthday, and each year it's grown exponentially. We now have offices in twelve major cities in the US, as well as France, Japan, and Australia. My team here, a team of about thirty employees, helps keep an eye on the branch investments, as well as keep an eye out for new possible investments. We have our fingers dipped in about every pool you can think of. From accounting, to lawyers, to daycares, to head shops. Our money is spread everywhere, and we're currently at the top of the charts for start-up companies you want behind you.

It's like *Shark Tank*, but way more profitable for both parties.

The meeting starts on time and I notice Benton in the back, trying to hide his wounds from the nosey employees. I dare anyone to approach him about it. They'll be looking for another job faster than they can blink.

Luckily, my crew senses my mood and disperses quickly and quietly after the meeting, leaving me and Benton in the conference room staring at each other.

"The Nova deal gonna go through?" he asks looking at me through one swollen eye.

"Yeah, it looks that way," I say wanting to apologize to him but not finding the words. Instead I find something else to fill the awkward silence, "How are you doing?" I nod to his wounds and he chuckles and shakes his head.

"Been better. Glad I've got a few days to recoup. Carly was pissed, but once she sees the money, she'll be fine," he says, then stands and nods at me.

"It'll be in your desk by two," I promise, then nod at him as he walks out of the conference room.

By noon, I'm starving, angry, and so sexually frustrated that I consider calling in one of the interns for a little release, but I can't. Something is stopping me from it. I send an email out, informing everyone that I'll be out of the office for an hour or so, then head outside to grab some lunch. On the elevator ride down, I pull out my phone to check my messages.

That's when my stomach drops.

Shit, what did I do last night?

From the looks of it, I called her and texted her four times. I either grew a fucking vagina or I was incredibly shitfaced last night to not remember that. How could I be so stupid?!? And how the hell did I even get her number?!?

For my entire lunch, I sit alone at a table outside, watching people pass by, and for the first time in a very long time, I can't get a girl off my mind. Maybe it's because she has a fight in her that most women don't have when they get around me. Maybe it's that she pushed me away, which makes the game of cat and mouse even more thrilling. Either way, she's embedded herself into my memory and doesn't even know it.

Making it back to the office, I see my winnings envelope on my desk, discreetly tucked inside an inner office delivery envelope and smile. At least they still know what they're doing. I open it, expecting the bills to spill out, but instead I get a pile of pictures and a note. What the hell?

Opening the note first, I look around to make sure there's no one watching me. The handwriting is sketchy, but it's not hard to make out:

You should have listened to us.

That's it. And there's no Goddamned money! Shit!

The pictures are of me outside walking Thor last night after the fight. Most of them are from afar, which means they didn't have access to a long-range zoom, or they want me to think that. The last few are of Benton and Carly.

What. The. Fuck.

I shake my head and look at the clock. It's only one, I can get his cash to him in time still. Sending Reese an email to forward B a note to get to my office, then to transfer a thousand into his account, I sit back and sigh. I know she's good for it, and I know she's not going to tell anyone. That's why she's the best secretary in the city of Chicago. Because she keeps to herself and does what she's told, no questions asked. If only all women were like that. I bet Annaliese is.

I get a text as Benton walks in the room, and as much as I'm itching to see if it's her responding, I don't. I can't seem too eager with her, and I've already proven myself to be a pussy when it comes to waiting for her.

"What's up, man?" he asks as he shuts the door behind him. I darken the glass and put my phone on hold, locking the door with my remote.

He looks around then whistles, "Damn, what'd I do?"

"Here," I say shoving the envelope at him.

He's confused, but he takes it and opens it. His eyebrows pull together at each image, and when he gets to the bottom of the pile to the pictures of him and Carly, he's red-faced and furious.

"What the fuck, Adam?" he growls

"Listen, I don't know who sent these, but I have my suspicions. Vick doesn't spread word about fights openly, so it has to be coming from the inside. From the way he seems to hate you, I wouldn't be surprised if it were him sending these threats, just to throw you off your game and get you beaten down enough to lose so bad you don't come back."

"Right…. But I don't see him doing that."

"He's fucking nuts, B. You didn't really let him see you ogling his daughter, did you?"

"No, man! I'm married! I just—"

"Couldn't take your eyes off those damn legs?" I mumble out loud and he laughs sharply.

"So you've noticed, too, huh? Damnit, she's—"

"Fucking beautiful." Damnit, I said that out loud too, didn't I?

"You need to tell me something, A?"

He's watching me curiously, and I could tell him. Hell, he probably already knows, but I feel like telling him would make him an accessory if Vick ever found out about what I did. That's just too risky; I'd hate to put him in more danger than he already is.

"Nah," I shake my head and pin my gaze back on him. "They didn't send the money, which pisses me off, but I'm still transferring money to you so Carly doesn't leave your ass." I laugh, knowing she wouldn't leave him, but hoping I at least spared him a fight or two with her.

"Adam man... you don't need to do that."

"I know. But it's being done as we speak so don't try and talk me out of it. You'll still get your cut a soon as the money comes in. Just think of this money as 'I'm sorry' money."

"You didn't—"

"Shut up and take the damn money. And go home. You seriously do look like shit."

"Will do. As soon as I follow up with this firm about a new hire they want to bring in. Some new chick, who knows. They seem to be hiring a lot of new people lately, which is great news for our pockets, right?"

"Absolutely," I answer.

He leaves me to my empty office, closing the door behind him.

I contemplate for the hundredth time today, just getting a girl in here as a stress reliever, but nothing will compare to her, and it pisses me off that my mind even goes there. Hell, my mind hasn't left there since our encounter a few days ago. Add with the sassy attitude she shot off in the bathroom, she has me completely hooked.

Shit, I'm screwed with this one.

Chapter 5

Annaliese

It's Friday morning, and by ten a.m. I've hit the gym, had coffee and breakfast, and even showered and gotten ready for the day. I'd gotten so used to getting up for my practicum that I've grown used to early rising, and even prefer it. Even when the night before is spent watching sappy movies, crying to your best friend that you're never going to find that type of love, then falling asleep on the couch with her before the movie's even over.

The phone rings and I run to the kitchen to where it's plugged in to answer it before it goes to voicemail. It's not Adam's number, and it's not any other number I know, so I answer as professionally as I can, hoping that this is a call for an interview.

"Hello, this is Annaliese Ryder," I say trying not to laugh at myself for being so nervous. The person on the other end of this line is human, just like me. I shouldn't be so nervous.

"Ms. Ryder. This is Deborah Cullings from the Academy of Science and Math. I want to personally thank you for applying for our current open position," she starts, and I can feel my heartbeat quicken as she goes on. "Unfortunately we have filled the spot this morning. We thank you very much, and wish you well in all of your endeavors."

"Oh, thanks. You too," I manage to squeak before the phone call is disconnected.

Well that sucks.

I stare at the phone screen for what feels like hours. My stomach is upset and my head is starting to hurt from trying to hold back the tears. The only good thing about this week so far is that I had amazing sex. I try not to think about whom it was with, or our encounter in the bathroom, because then I'd just get even more depressed that I just happened to screw the most un-eligible person in the state of Illinois. Then my mind would go into a spiral about everything else sucky that has happened this week. From probably blowing my test, to my credit card and ID getting stolen, to me having absolutely no leads on a job; it would all go downhill. So I choose not to think about him.

Mr. Chicago.

Adam.

"Hey, bitch, who was that?" Gab yawns and reaches for the coffee pot.

"A school where I applied. They already found someone to fill the spot."

"Oh, baby, I'm sorry." She hugs me and holds on tight. "You'll find something. I have faith."

Easy for her to say as she starts her new job soon.

"Yeah. Thanks," I manage, not wanting to talk about my situation.

I'm currently pissed at myself for making such a big stink about not needing my dad's money and doing things on my own. In about a month I'm not going to have enough money to cover rent and my portion of the bills, which scares me. And I don't like to be scared.

I've been that enough in my life.

"So I'm gonna head out and get some new clothes today. You wanna come with me?"

"Yeah, I'd love it. But I need to watch my money if you want me to keep living with you. This jobless wonder needs to save everything she can."

Just Go M. Dauphin

"Oh, come on! You know you could have a job if you really needed one." She raises her eyebrows at me and I know exactly what she's talking about.

Could I really work for my dad? I mean, it'd be money coming in, it couldn't be that difficult, and it wouldn't be me going back on my word since technically I'd be making my own money still and not just accepting his handouts. Still, I'd feel like it was a pity job if I took it. Would I be able to live with myself? I spent so much time in school to become an administrator. I love working with kids. Would working in an office make me as happy?

No, the answer is no. However, it will let me stay living here with Gabby.

"I know, Gab. If nothing comes up soon I'll call him."

She smiles and hugs me before heading out the door, leaving me all alone and pretty depressed about the route that my life is taking. I could have went for an easier degree to find a job in, but I'm passionate about helping kids, especially in the city of Chicago. There are so many schools that need good educators and great leaders that I felt it was my only option: do something I'm passionate about and help people at the same time.

I walk out to our small balcony and sit at our table, watching the cars move below and start to really think about my life. What if I can't do what I'm passionate about? What if I have to settle just to have money to survive? Money. It always comes down to money.

Just the thought of money brings me back to my night with Adam. Maybe because he has all the money he'll ever need. That's what I tell myself since it's obvious that I haven't really stopped thinking about him, especially after our little scene in the bathroom. I did text him back yesterday, but only to tell him to stop harassing me. So far it seems like the text worked since he hasn't tried contacting me anymore and I'm not really sure how I feel about that. As much as I don't want to admit to myself, there was a small part of me that enjoyed being sought out by him. By the man that most women claw and catfight over just to have drinks together. He was actually seeking me, fighting for me. And I was a total bitch.

Suddenly my phone rings, breaking the dangerous path my thoughts were taking.

"Hey Daddy," I say smiling into my phone.

"Hey, Baby Girl. How are things going?"

"Fine, I guess." I sigh, really wishing he hadn't called.

"What's wrong, Annie?"

"I got a call from a place I put an application in to today. They already found someone to fill the job. I'm just worried, that's all."

"No reason for my little girl to be worried about anything. Tell you what, I've got a management position open that you'd be perfect for—"

"Stop, Dad. I don't want your handout," I say cutting him off.

"Listen to my offer, Annie," he grinds out pissed I cut him off. "You have all the requirements for this position. Hell, you're probably more ready for it than some of the other managers. All you'll be doing is keeping track of the books on a few drivers, riding along every now and then as checkups on them. Pretty simple stuff. It's a salaried job, starting at sixty a year and going up from that."

"Daddy, that's insane! I can't do that!"

"You can too, Annaliese. Ryders don't say they 'can't' do something."

I sigh and think about his offer. The money would be great. It's not teaching or working with kids, but it's a job that's stable and pays well.

"What if I get an offer for a position at a school while I'm working for you?"

"Then you take it. Hands down. I'm not wanting to lock you into the company if you don't want it, Annie. I just don't like my baby girl to worry about money issues."

What've I got to lose?

"Alright. I'll do it." I feel so defeated right now.

"Great. I'll have Lisa e-mail some details to you tonight. And tomorrow night keep open. I know you technically don't start until Monday, but I want you to ride a route of a Saturday night to get the feel of things."

"Sounds good, Dad. Thanks."

"Anything for my baby girl."

He hangs up and I stare at my phone. Technically, I'm not his baby girl. I'm the older girl. The one that lived.

Feeling completely overwhelmed, I spend the rest of the day cleaning our already spotless apartment. It's clean, bright, and stupidly quiet. Why the quiet's making me so mad today I'm not sure, but it really is. There's too much of nothing happening here. The thought that maybe we need a dog crosses my mind more than once, but I laugh it off. I'm not sure Gab would love a furry creature biting her on the toes all night long.

By the end of the day I'm exhausted from doing absolutely nothing all day. It's really depressing sitting in a house all alone, all day, with nothing to do but watch TV. I really should find a hobby. Now that school's over and I'm waiting on my 'grown up' life to start, I'm starting to see how much time school work really took up.

The next morning I'm up before the sun again. Throwing on my gym clothes, I opt for an early morning run through the streets of our neighborhood.

Just Go M. Dauphin

I love this city. The crisp morning air, the historic buildings mixed with newer construction on one city block. It's truly a great city to live in, full of all different walks of life.

I grab a coffee and head to the park to sit on a bench and watch the sunrise. I'm glad I stayed with the early rise routine these last few weeks since my practicum ended. It'll make it so much easier having to get up and be at work by eight when my body's already used to rising early and leaving the apartment right away. There are people jogging and milling about on the lawn,. The constant traffic of Chicago is starting to pick up. Horns, sirens, train noises. I take it all in, smiling at how lucky I really am.

I spend the rest of my day wandering around the city. I window shop, find a new outfit for tonight, something professional but fun, and grab lunch from a hotdog stand near my apartment. By the time I get back to the apartment, Gabby is already in the middle of... something... with the door hanger on her door knob and music blaring from inside. Just walking by, I hear moans coming from her room. Manly moans. She's got a man in there. Good for her. Maybe he'll pay more attention to what she needs than the last girl she was with.

Once I'm back in my bedroom, I can still hear them going at it. Part of me is actually jealous that in the middle of the afternoon she can be as sexually active as she is. The other part is annoyed that I have to hear it.

Just Go   M. Dauphin

    I grab a change of clothes and head for the shower, turning on the vent and the shower radio to drown out the moans and other noises coming from the room down the hall. Only a few hours now until my orientation at my new job. I'm not as depressed about it as I was when first took the job. I know it's summer vacation, and schools aren't necessarily hiring right now. I know my dad told me I can get out whenever I need to, if something else were to come around. I'm just going to think of this as a filler job to keep me busy until the time comes for me to start my career.

    At six I tell Gab my plans for the night and she hugs me, telling me she's happy that I won't become a hobo living in a van down by the river. I laugh and we joke for a few minutes before it's time for me to head out. My stomach is full of nerves and I'm not really sure why. I've met all of my dad's drivers. We all get along. Maybe it's the fact that I'll now be considered a boss to some of them. What if they hate me because of this? What if they don't like that I'm just waltzing into the company at such a high level? Why am I so nervous?!

    The black car is out front waiting for me and I smile when I see Joe step out of the driver's side door and grin at me. My stomach flops and a genuine grin comes across my face. Tonight's going to be fun.

    "Hey, you," he drawls as he hugs me lightly then holds me at arm's length and looks me up and down, whistling. "You're not technically my boss 'til Monday, right?"

"Right." I grin at him, waiting for the inappropriate comment to fly from his beautiful lips.

"Great. Then I don't feel bad for telling you that you look so fucking delicious tonight."

"Why thank you, Joe," I say and give a joking curtsy towards him as he shakes his head at me. His eyes lock with mine and for a second I feel like he's going to kiss me, but he looks down just before I go in for the kill.

"Right. So we need to get movin'. A lot of important people are waiting on us to be on time tonight."

I nod and he helps me into the passenger seat, then leans over to help me buckle in, getting so close I can feel his breath on my shoulder as he slowly stretches the belt and clicks it in place.

"There. Safe," he murmurs and his lips part when his eyes quickly flash to my light pink, glossy lips.

"Thanks," I whisper enjoying this game we're playing. I already feel the heat pooling between my legs. This man knows how sexy he is, and he knows what he does to me.

Not quite as good as my night with Adam, but I'm starting to believe nothing will ever come close to that again.

Joe backs away slowly and shuts the door, only breaking eye contact when the door closes tight. He moves swiftly into the driver's seat and turns to full on business mode. For the next four hours we drive around the city, picking up the rich, some famous, and some incredibly drunk patrons. I've always wondered how my dad makes so much money on just a chauffeur business, but seeing the clientele tonight I'm a little more at ease that it's just because they have the money to throw away.

Growing up, my friends always made cruel jokes that my dad was involved in more than just driving people around. There were always whispers about him being someone that the law didn't even want to mess with, but I never saw that side of him. I always saw the family man who loved his daughters... daughter. The man who loved his wife and worked his ass off to provide for them. Seeing the people he pretty much works for, my mind is put at ease that he isn't some mobster thug that steals money from people.

We drop off the last client for the night and Joe sighs as he shuts his car door.

"This shit isn't easy." I smile at him as his head falls back on the headrest and his eyes close. As soon as he opens his mouth to reply, his phone rings.

"Shit," he curses pulling it out of his pocket. "This is Joe." His curt tone tells me it's not a welcome call. "Yeah. Got it." He hangs up and puts his phone in the cup holder.

"Listen, I gotta make a run. I get it if you don't want to hang around, but I was really hoping to hang out with you tonight. If you hang around...."

"I'll stay. I'm in this. I have to see how the job works before they throw me in the office."

I want to tell him I'm looking forward to hanging out with him, but that would suggest that I'm expecting more than just friendship. As much as I would like to, I don't want to be the reason he's fired.

"Great, buckle up." He smiles and looks a little nervous as he pulls out of our spot and towards the Northern part of the city.

"So, what's up here? I can't imagine the clientele coming from this part of the city."

He doesn't answer right away and when I look over at him, his hands are tight around the steering wheel and his jaw is set tight.

"Joe?"

"What?" he snaps, his mood suddenly changed.

"Where are we going?"

"Annaliese, sometimes you just need to go with the flow. Don't ask so many questions. God, maybe I should have brought you home first...." he trails off, mumbling to himself that this was a mistake.

"What the hell are you talking about?"

"Just… listen, we're almost there. Don't get out of the car this time, okay? This isn't a run your dad approved."

"He's not the boss of me, Joe. Not yet," I grind out, pissed that someone is hiding something from me.

Joe sighs and goes silent for the remainder of the drive. The neighborhood we're driving through is anything but upper class. Not that I'm judging, but most people in this part of the city don't have the money to spend on the services that my dad's business offers. We slow in front of an empty warehouse. No lights are on inside and there's no other living being in sight.

"What's going on, Joe?" I ask, my heartbeat speeding up.

"Wait here," he grinds out and gets out of the car. I watch him speed to the door and knock a few times before it opens up and a figure slips outside quickly.

"What the hell?" I say to myself. I watch the familiar figure walk towards the car and when his eyes flick to mine, my heart drops.

He freezes then looks at Joe before storming to my door and throwing it open.

"Nice to see you again, Annaliese," he purrs, his smile melting any sort of wall I had built up against him.

"Mr. Callahan," I say in a sexy voice and smile seductively while Joe cocks his head at us then nervously looks around. "It'd be even nicer if you could get in the car."

He turns to look at Joe and nods, then his eyes flick between the two of us before he speaks again.

"Not until you get back there with me."

"What?" I gasp. The balls on this man!

"Sir, that's not auth—"

"And I could have your job title taken away in two seconds flat, Joe. I don't think you really want the boss man to know you've been ogling his little girl, do you?" He smiles a winning smile and Joe's frame goes tense, as if he's preparing for a fight.

"What the fuck is going on! Get outta here!" A voice booms from the building we're parked in front of. My nerves are on high alert since this isn't the best part of the city to be sitting in a nice ass car in the middle of the night. My whole body is screaming at me for not throwing it at Adam, and my mind is telling me to shut it off and stop thinking about him and his body. God, his body.

"Get in the car, Adam," I growl back at him.

"Okay." I sigh when he gives in. "After you." He reaches in, takes my arm and pulls me out of the car, throwing me over his shoulder like a caveman and I take a breath to scream when I end up inhaling the best scent I've ever smelled. God, he smells so good.

"Adam, put her down!" I hear Joe yell but as soon as I take a whiff of Adam, I'm a goner.

"Joe, it's fine. He's just being an asshole." As much as that's true, I'm also incredibly turned on by this caveman act. The heat that Joe brought earlier is nothing compared to how I feel around Adam.

"I'm just getting her to the backseat. We have business that's left undone, and I'm ready to finish it." I hear the low growl in his voice when he opens the back door of the car and slowly lets me slide down his body. Jesus, his body is rock hard and smells so freaking delicious. I want to lick him and taste every part of him. His eyes meet mine and lock into that emotion I've been toying with all week: infatuation. Good Lord. Every worry from the week melts away when he looks at me like that. I'm his lifeline. I'm in a trance and don't notice Joe talking to me until he snaps his fingers in my ear.

"I'll call your father, Annie," Joe whispers as his gaze flicks to Adam then back to me.

"I'm fine, Joe. Adam and I go back. He just needs to put me down before I kick him in the balls," I smile sweetly as Adam's hands drop from my hips and my feet hit the ground.

"Then get in. Both of our asses are gonna be on a platter for this stint," he growls then walks to the driver's seat.

I slowly and seductively slide into the car, grinning to myself when I hear Adam sigh and curse under his breath. When my ass hits the seat, I smile as I remember I'm not wearing any panties tonight. I hate them. So restricting, and really not needed when wearing pants. The only time I wear them is when it's that time of the month, or when I have on a short skirt and don't feel like giving others a show. Tonight it's neither of those. These pants are so tightly fitted around my ass that panty lines of any sort would have ruined the effect.

"Jesus," he sighs again and finally clears his throat and slides into the car.

The minute the door shuts, his hand finds my leg and starts slowly caressing it. I feel the jolt of electricity and jump.

"Shh...." he whispers so Joe doesn't hear. "Hey, Joe?"

"Yes, sir?" Joe clips.

"Does this car have one of those sight/sound partitions?"

"I'm not sure I know what you're talking about, Mr. Callahan," he says in the most professional tone.

"Oh, sure you do, Joe. You've used it plenty of times with me. It's that button right there next to the heater control."

"Ah, yes." Joe keeps driving, not making a move towards the button and I smile to myself, knowing what these two are doing. It's essentially a test to see which male is going to win the girl. A power play between two overly sexualized males, and I'm the pawn.

Sorry, buddies, this girl only belongs to herself.

"Mind pushing it, Joe? All the way up please," Adam growls and waits for the entire partition to be closed before locking it shut from our end. When it's locked, he turns in his seat and smiles at me.

"Now, Mr. Callahan. Why'd you go and do something like that? Are you aware who my father is?"

"I am very aware of your father and his status. He won't find out, believe me." His hands make their way up my leg and he cups my sex over my pants. "I can't stop thinking about this," he whispers as his lips hit my neck and he sucks. Hard.

I gasp and pull back, not wanting any proof that he was here. Though the wetness in my pants and my rapid heartbeat are proof enough, I'm not ready to admit how hot I am for this man. I can't be attracted to someone like him. He's such an asshole, but Jesus Christ, he's the hottest asshole ever.

"I'm also aware of how much I turn you on, Annaliese," my name rolls off his tongue like he's been saying it all his life. Most people have a problem with it, but not Adam.

"Are you, now?" I moan as his teeth find my ear lobe and nip gently, his hand still massaging me between my legs. The pressure from his fingers on my sweet spot is almost enough to set me off. Almost.

"Feel what you do to me." He takes my hand and moves it to his crotch and I feel his hard length under his dress pants. "Just one more time, Annaliese. Jesus, I need you one more time. Give that to me, please." He pulls back and his eyes hit mine. My heart speeds up as I realize what I'm about to do.

One answer will change everything

Chapter 6

Adam

She hasn't answered yet and I'm actually nervous she's going to tell me no. Me! Adam fucking Callahan is worried a woman might tell him no. What the hell is wrong with me? Did I suddenly grow a damn vagina?

Shit.

I shouldn't have to go through all of these hoops and barbaric shows just to get a woman. Hell, I'd have an easier time finding someone on the side of the road to fuck right now, but that's not what's going to satisfy me.

I need this woman. The one that has captured my every damn thought since I had her less than a week ago.

Her eyes are begging me to be nice, to not be an asshole, but that's who I am. I haven't been able to fuck anyone since her. Hell, I can't even get hard anymore without thinking of how perfect she felt when I was buried deep inside her. Her ass on display for me. Those damn sexy legs still ending with her fucking heels. Jesus.

Just answer me already!

"Just one night?" she whispers and my stomach drops at those words. What the hell was that all about? That's what I said, right? One night. One more time just to get another taste of her, preferably more than one time. But one night is what I asked her, so one night I have to stick to.

Why did I say that?

"Uh... yeah. One night." She threw me off my game and now I feel like a bumbling idiot.

Her gaze hits the partition and I know what she's thinking.

"He can't see any of this, and it's soundproof so he can't hear us either," I whisper in her ear and feel her body loosen up under me. My hands, having a mind of their own, find their way up her flat stomach and over the swell of her breasts. "One night, Annaliese." Her nipples harden at my touch. She's so damn responsive, and I'm so damn hard right now I don't think I'd last long. Shit, three days is too long.

"Okay," she gasps as I squeeze her breast and nip her neck.

Shit yes!

Why do I feel like jumping for joy? I'm not getting worked up over this girl. I just need a fuck and she seems to be the only one my dick wants to respond to at this point. That's all this is.

I moan as she pushes her body to me, giving me her all. Her hands find my shoulders and she pushes me back on the seat, then straddles me and grins.

"Your place or mine?" she whispers as her lips find mine. I break the kiss quick enough to manage to tell her my house, then she knocks on the partition, still straddling me. My hands, resting on her thighs, are itching to explore more parts of her, but with the glass divider lowering, I know that's a bad idea. I let them rest there, squeezing harder than I probably should, but it's taking a lot not to let them roam with Joe watching.

"Joe, please head back to Mr. Callahan's place first," she says, never breaking eye contact with me.

"Ms.—"

"No. Just do it. That's all, Joe," she says and waves at him to close the glass once again.

She's smiling so brilliantly right now it's contagious and soon I'm smiling just as brightly. Shit. Why do I feel like the awkward teenager who just asked out his crush? I've already had hot fucking sex with this woman. The second time shouldn't make me feel so nervous.

"So, Mr. Callahan—"

"Please call me Adam, Annaliese."

"Okay... Adam. Do you mind telling me what that was all about tonight, with the creepy ass dark building we just picked you up from?"

Jesus, she doesn't know or else she wouldn't be saying anything. That's the rule: don't fucking talk about it.

"I was at a meeting for a job and needed a ride. Joe was free so he picked me up. Nothing to worry about."

The lie felt terrible coming off my tongue. I've lied so many times before. Why all of a sudden does it feel so... wrong?

"Mmmm... okay," she moans as my lips meet hers again and I part her lips slowly with my tongue. Jesus, she tastes so good, so sweet.

My hands roam under the hem of her shirt, following her smooth skin up and over her ribs. I feel her tense as I run my fingers down her ribs, then laugh as she tries to get away from the slight tickle. Her fighting me is making me even harder, which I didn't even think was possible. I move higher, enjoying the feel of her cool skin through the lace of her bra. Everything in me wants to rip this top off her and enjoy the sight of lace over her plump breasts, but I know we'll have company soon and don't want her to be embarrassed. She's not like the other girls I fuck.

She moans when I caress her nipple over her bra, moving my lips to her neck, right behind her ear. Her nipples tighten under the thin fabric and she gasps when I pinch her gently. I move my hands behind her, hoping to unhook her bra for better access to her beautiful tits, but she stops me and shakes her head, looking at me with those striking eyes.

"Not here," she whispers, then continues to kiss me. The sweetest, best tasting kiss I've ever experienced.

We stay like this for the remainder of the drive back to my place. When the car stops, I suck at her lower lip, leaving her pouting for more when I break away.

"Care to come up?"

"Oh, I'll be coming, alright," she whispers in my ear, making me curse the growing bulge in my pants, then as quickly as she can, she gets off my lap before the back door opens and Joe is waiting impatiently for us to get out.

I laugh at her, at the situation, then get out of the car and face the one man that I hate more than my ex-wife: Joe. I've always been good with him, never really had any problems. Once I realized he had eyes for Annaliese, though, it all went downhill. The second I saw her in the car, in the front seat, I knew he was working on getting her back to his place tonight. Joe's not dumb. He knows when the boss man is looking and when he isn't. With Vick being out of town tonight, most of his men are working on filling in the gaps, so no one would notice her going home with the help.

No one but me.

He's glaring at me and all I can do is smile that I won. Feeling like one lucky bastard, I slap him on the back and smile.

"Thanks, man."

"It's my job, Mr. Callahan." He reaches his hand out and helps Annaliese out of the car. When he pulls her in close enough to kiss her, I feel like I'm about to go into Hulk mode. I'm not about to get sloppy seconds tonight. She's my girl.

Tonight. She's my girl *tonight.*

Shit, Adam, where's your brain?!?

"You sure about this, Annie?" I hear him whisper, then see his eyes flick to me. I don't back down, though, and glare right back at him as my breathing threatens to turn into a low growl.

"I'll be fine, Joe. I know he's not gonna pull anything stupid. Mr. Chicago over here wouldn't do anything to tarnish his reputation. You're a good friend." She grins at him and he leans in to kiss her cheek.

"Let's go, Annaliese," I take her arm and pull her away from him, practically plowing over the asshole who's trying to take my girl.

"I'll call you in the morning, Annie. You better answer." His eyes connect with mine and I see the threat. The menacing tone doesn't get past me, but I'm too worked up to care. I'm currently sporting a serious hard on for this chick and I just need to be inside her. I just need to blow my load and go to bed.

That's all she is to me. A means to an end.

Nothing else.

At least that's the shit I keep telling myself.

Joe waits until I have her inside to move back to his door and get in, but I barely notice. Everything in my body is screaming at me that this is a bad idea. That this girl is going to ruin me worse than I thought I was ruined by my divorce, but I can't stop. I need her. I need her body. I need her moaning my name. I need her eyes on mine when I make her explode around my cock.

We make it to the elevator and I put my key in, signaling us to the top without any stops. I'm shaking from nerves and it pisses me off. So I grab her the minute the doors close and kiss her like she's my last breath, like after tonight, nothing will remain. She pushes her body against mine and I feel her lips turn to a smile when she feels my hard length pushing against her.

"Mmm, very nice," I whisper as she pushes the swell of her breasts into me. She groans as I reach down between her legs and rub gently. "Jesus, so hot."

The door dings and opens to my lobby, breaking the spell she has on me when I hear Thor yipping from the other side of the door. Shit, I can't believe I forgot about the puppy. Normally I have someone take him on nights I bring girls back here, but this was unplanned so I have to roll with it.

"Oh my gosh! Do you have a dog!?" she practically yells at me, smiling brightly and walking towards my door. Her eyes are lit up at the thought of me having a dog. Not the fact that she's currently walking into the penthouse in the tallest, most expensive condo in the city of Chicago. Not the fact that the floors are pure marble, nor the fact that the crystal chandelier is real. No, she's excited about the tiny, wrinkly, slobbering animal on the other side of the door.

Maybe she really is crazy.

"Oh yeah. Sorry about him, I can put him away for the night." I smile when I see I hit a nerve.

"No you won't! Open up, I wanna see!" She's so excited I can't help but smile. I need to make her smile like this again. A lot.

Just Go   M. Dauphin

I unlock the door and slowly open it. Thor's pudgy nose peeks in first, then his paw comes through the gap, trying to paw the door open. She giggles and pushes the door open, letting him run out and attack her with slobbery kisses. I stand in awe, watching her interact with my dog, and realize this girl isn't someone that deserves to be fucked and left. She deserves to be loved. She deserves so much more than I typically give girls, but I think I'm up for the challenge. When she smiles up at me, holding a very excited and wiggly puppy in her arms, I no longer think I'm up for it. I know I am.

"What's his name?" she asks, still smiling and laughing as he licks her cheek.

"Thor."

"For real? You named your dog Thor?" She giggles as he attacks her with slobbery kisses.

"Absolutely. I don't joke about my superheroes."

"I love it," she says, then turns her attention back to the dog. Hell, now I'm jealous of the damn dog. "You need to go outside, Thor?"

And there it is. *Zero* women that I have brought back here would have enjoyed being licked by this wrinkly mess. None of them would sit on the floor to hold him and never would they be caught dead taking a dog out to use the bathroom in the middle of the night. Annaliese isn't like those girls though.

She's the real deal.

"Can I take him out?" She's still smiling. How are her cheeks not hurting yet? Do normal people smile this much when they aren't post-orgasmic?

"Uh.... Yeah. Let me grab his leash. I'll walk out with you."

We take him down together, making small talk about life with a dog in the city. Apparently she's always wanted one but her roommate wouldn't do so well with one. I try and think of Vick having a dog for her when she was growing up, but the only dog I can see him with is a trained to be mean Doberman.

After we get back up, I take her inside. Finally she's in, the door is shut, and I don't have to share her with the world anymore. Not for the rest of the night.

"Welcome to my penthouse," I say grinning, but when she scrunches her nose I realize I said something wrong. "What? What's wrong?"

"You sound like an asshole when you talk like that," she says flatly. Shit. She's not joking.

"Talk like... what?"

"Do you have to point out every time we talk that you live in a penthouse? It's annoying."

"Sorry," I say, confused at her reaction to my money. She grew up wealthy. Hell, she probably lives off of daddy's money to this day.

"It's okay. Just don't talk." She smiles and walks slowly towards me.

"Oh yeah? What do you suggest I do instead of talking?" I can feel my body reacting to her already and she isn't even touching me yet. This could be very bad, but so very good.

"I can find other very useful things for you to do with your mouth."

She tugs at my tie, bringing me to her and her lips crush into mine. She's gone from sweet girl who's in love with my dog, to sexy as hell vixen within a matter of seconds. Her hands start pulling at my tie, ripping it off and dropping it to the floor. She's at my shirt next, and after one button, she's lost all patience and pulls hard enough to pop off the remaining ones.

"Shit." I look down at her and she's grinning. "That was a nice shirt," I say as the final button hits the hardwood and stops spinning.

"You've got money. I have faith you can replace it without any problems." The snarky comment makes me chuckle and pull her in for another hard, lust filled kiss. Her lips are so perfect, and her moans make me harder than I've ever been. She nips my bottom lip and smiles when I pull back and glare at her.

Jesus, she's feisty as fuck and no other woman turns me on like she does.

When her hands go to my waistband, I grab her wrists. She's taking this way too fucking fast for me. I need her for longer than tonight. Hell, I'd be happy doing her every night, but she made me promise tonight only, and I keep my promises. As much as they suck.

"Slow down, Annaliese."

"You say that, but I think just the opposite. Do you know how many times I've gotten off to the memory of you, Adam?" She pushes me back and my back hits the wall. The way she's one-upping me so far should have me pissed.

No woman takes over. I fuck and leave. I did, at least before Annaliese.

In all reality, what she's doing is turning me on and making me so damn hard I'm not sure I'll be able to get myself out of these pants if I don't get free soon.

"Tell me," I whisper, my eyes locked on hers.

"Seven."

Jesus Christ. Seven times?!? She's gotten off to me seven times? It hasn't even been that many days!

"Impressive."

"It was hard to sleep with your scent on my pillow."

"I bet. I'm an easy man to miss."

"See, there you go talking again and ruining everything." She backs up and shakes her head, like she's second-guessing even being here.

No, she can't do that. She can't think about leaving. I've worked too damn hard to get her here tonight. I was pissed walking out of the fight and losing two grand, but the minute I saw her, I forgot all thoughts of getting back at whatever asshole is doing this to me and my bets. Once I saw her, my only thoughts were of being with her and being inside her.

"I need you to stop thinking. If I promise to try my hardest not to be an asshole, can you promise to stop overthinking things?" I ask, my hands cupping her face.

Her expression changes to a lighter one, and her eyes are wide.

"Just one night," she states.

It's not a question. She's truly just here for the sex. I try my hardest not to furrow my brows at her and ask her what's so wrong with me that she won't give me a chance at more than one night. If one night's all she's giving me, I'm making sure it's the best damn night she's ever experienced. And ever will experience. I'll make sure she'll never want another man but me again.

Chapter 7

Annaliese

My heart is hammering in my chest as his eyes pin me to my spot. I should have known coming here would bring more than I bargained for and his promise was bullshit. He makes me so damn hot that it's hard to think about anything else other than fucking him senseless when he's around. I should've told him no and that I had to get home, then forced Joe to bring me back to my apartment. I should have, but I didn't because the man standing in front of me is a man that infuriates me so much, I actually get turned on by his smartass comments and smug self. I should hate men like this. The rich and entitled. No one wants to be with someone who's constantly rubbing in others' faces how much money they have, so why do I want to be around him? He's a prick.

What's wrong with me?

"Annaliese?" my name rolls off his tongue so naturally and with an added growl to it that makes it all the more sexier.

"Yes?" I whisper, completely afraid that my emotions will get the better of me and my nerves will make me bolt out his door.

"There's no need to be scared. We've done this before, you know." The smirk on his face makes me want to slap it off. Jeez he's so smug, it's... gah!

"I do know and I'm not scared," I whip back at him, gaining nerve and moving towards him again.

His back is still against the wall, so I move as close as I can, pressing my body against his bare, chiseled chest, and slide my hands down to gently squeeze the bulge in his pants. He groans and his eyes leave mine, closing as his head falls against the wall. His reaction to me makes me more daring than I typically am.

"I'm not the one who should be afraid, Mr. Chicago," I whisper in his ear, cursing my nerves for making my body start to shake.

"I beg to differ, Ms. Ryder." His hands go around me and grab my ass, pushing me against his hardening length. "There's plenty you should be afraid of. None of those things are here tonight though.

Tonight, it's just you and me. You're giving me one night, and that's exactly what I'm taking."

He growls as he lifts me up to kiss him. My legs instinctively wrap around him and the slightest pressure between my legs from his hard member is making me want to grind against him. Just the smallest movement will set me off. I've been so wound up since our night together that even a vibrator doesn't seem to give me the release I've been searching for.

But he will.

He starts walking through the living room, then another massive room until we reach a dim hallway. The entire time, his lips are moving from my neck, to my shoulder, back up to my lips. My body is buzzing from the thrill of being wrapped around him. When he reaches his room, he walks in and clicks the door shut, grinning.

"Don't want any ankle biting tonight," he growls setting me on my feet and cursing under his breath. "You're completely unaware of how beautiful you are, aren't you?" he shakes his head and I'm frozen. His words cut through a wall I would have much rather kept fully intact.

"So, your bed?" I ask turning to walk towards the bed, trying to break the connection. He reaches out and stops me, his thumb gently rubbing my arm as he turns me back to him.

"Not yet," he whispers as he comes to me and kisses me.

He starts unbuttoning my shirt, taking his time, kissing my skin behind each opened button. By the time he's done, I'm shaking with need for the man kneeling in front of me. I need him to fuck me, I need to leave, and I don't need to get emotionally wrapped up in this man. When his eyes look up and connect with mine, his fingers go for the waistband of my dress pants and slowly undo them, slipping my pants down my legs slowly, kissing his way down.

By the time he stands back up, I'm only wearing my bra. The second my pants hit the floor, he growls, noticing that I'm not wearing panties. Now seeing the whole package, his eyes light up with lust.

"Dammit, so beautiful," he breathes, his eyes admiring my toned body.

I grin at him, and raise my eyebrows when he meets my eyes again. Without words, I reach out and grab him by the waistband of his pants, quickly removing them from him a lot less patiently than he removed mine. I'm feeling a lot more need filled right now and a lot less emotionally filled. When he springs free from his pants, I nearly lick my lips and have to fight the urge to drop to my knees and taste him. He looks bigger than I remember, but I was also really drunk the last time.

"There, now we're even." I smile and start to tug him towards the bed so we can get this moving a little faster. I feel myself falling for him in ways that I don't want to. The longer I'm here, the better he treats me, the more I'm apt to want to stay.

I can't stay. I shouldn't stay. Right?

When the back of my legs hit the bed I sit and scoot towards the headboard, waiting for Adam to follow. I'm smiling nervously, and I'm not sure why. Like he said, we've done this before. There's no need for me to be nervous tonight.

"Aren't you gonna join me?" I manage to whisper as I let my fingers start playing with the lace on the edge of my bra.

"Shit," he huffs then moves his hands down his face.

"What?" He suddenly looks wary, like he isn't sure about this anymore.

About me.

"You're so damn sexy, Annaliese. So... so fucking sexy." He crawls up the bed and kneels between my legs, slowly caressing them.

"But...?" I raise my eyebrows at him and cross my arms in a pout.

"Shit, don't do that," he says as he sighs and shakes his head. "You don't know how badly I just want to fuck you."

I reach out and grab onto his firm length, grinning as he hisses.

"What's the problem then, Adam?" My voice is low and husky.

"You're...." he gasps as my other hand starts gently massaging his balls as I stroke his cock. Closing his eyes, he throws his head back as I start pumping him harder. He growls and leans down to me, kissing me harder and needier than he has all night.

When I kiss him back, my hands move to his head, pulling him all the way down to me. I press my core up to him and my breath hitches when he rubs against my clit. I'm so hot for him I feel like I'm going to come before he even enters me.

I need him to enter me.

"Condom," I manage to pant between kisses. He moves to my neck, then my shoulder, biting his way down towards my nipples.

"Top drawer," he growls as he starts moving down my body with his kisses, trailing from my nipples down between my legs.

I'm able to reach over and open the drawer just as his lips come in contact with my clit. I grab a condom and lay back on the pillow, trying to regulate my breathing as he licks and sucks all around the one spot I need him most.

"Shit!" I yell as he pushes his fingers into me suddenly and continues licking. Every nerve in my body is screaming for release, but it's not happening. I need more. I need him in me.

"Fuck me, Adam. Please," I beg, practically throwing the condom packet at him.

He chuckles and sits up, smiling at me and wiping my juices off from around his mouth. I've never been so wet for another human being, especially not before coming. This man is doing all sorts of things to me that I've never thought I'd experience, and I'm starting to love all of it.

He takes the packet and opens it, sliding it on with ease, then hovers over me. As slowly as he can, with his eyes locked on mine, he enters me. I can feel every glorious inch. This is what I've been craving since our night together. We fit so perfectly together. My body is so attuned to his, so responsive. Each inch he slowly enters me is lighting another fire inside me. Every movement, every slight push puts me closer to release. His eyes are still locked on mine; neither of us can break this connection. As much as I don't want a connection with him, it happened. When he's fully inside me, I start to grind up to him, getting the perfect amount of friction on my clit. His eyes show me a side of him I haven't seen yet. A vulnerable man. One that I could shatter. Needing to break the emotional connection, not wanting to get wrapped up in him, I close my eyes and moan as he pumps into me, feeling every movement.

"Shit, Annaliese," he groans.

His head drops to my shoulder and my arms go around him. He starts moving slowly, cursing under his breath. Our connection is so perfect that I'm already feeling the buildup of my release. Moaning and pushing into his thrusts, he notices my walls starting to tighten and speeds up his movements. Sitting up to his knees, he snakes his hand down to play with my clit just enough to send me into a mind blowing orgasm.

"Aaaah!!!" I scream as I come around him. Feeling him harden inside me, it's not long after my world changing orgasm that he follows suit.

"Fuuck!" he bellows as his orgasm rips through him. Bending down, he pushes his lips to mine and kisses me as he rides out his own release.

Panting, he moves his mouth to my neck and sucks so hard I'm sure he's going to leave a mark. I can't bring myself to care though. Part of me, a dark part that I don't want to accept, likes the fact that he's marking me. Just his lips being there are making me tingle all over again, and the fact that he's showing to everyone that can see that he was here makes me hot for him. Hotter than I would like.

He sighs and looks me in the eyes.

"Wow," he huffs and smiles. That smile. He's definitely the most gorgeous person I've ever laid eyes on.

"Yes, wow," I say while trying to catch my breath and smile back at him.

He pulls out gently and kisses me again before heading into his bathroom to deposit the condom in the trash. As he walks out of the room, I get up with a speed I never knew I had and start dressing. The feelings that came over me tonight were simply feelings of hormones going crazy during sex. Nothing more. I can't feel emotions for a player who hops from one chick to another in the span of twenty-four hours, someone who cheated on his wife. I can't feel for someone, can't learn to love someone, that rubs their wealth in others faces so willingly. He's everything I should stay away from, but the longer I'm around him, the more I want him.

"Hey, what're doing?" he asks, confused. Jesus, even standing in the middle of his room with nothing on, hands on his hips and no shame whatsoever. Not like he should have any, the man's beautiful. I feel a pull towards him that I'm not sure I want to feel and look away.

"Uh...." I trail off and look down at my half-dressed body. "Dressing?"

"Why?" his eyes go wide, but as soon as they do, he refocuses in on my eyes as if he's trying to hide something.

I cock my head and laugh, smiling at him.

"Because."

"Because why?" His tone is getting more demanding sounding, almost with a hint of frantic.

"I guess I didn't figure you as the type of guy that wants his fucks to stay the night," I say sweetly, hoping that my nerves aren't showing in my shaky hands. To busy them I start to button my pants when he speaks up.

"Stop, will you? Can you please... stop?" He walks over to me, his tone pleading, and takes ahold of my shoulders. "You gave me one night. That's all I get, and I'm taking it all. The night isn't over yet, Annaliese."

My heavy breathing matches his and I can't take my eyes off him. There's a look in his eyes I've never seen before. Something there that wasn't there at the restaurant the other night. Begging. His eyes are begging me. What for, I'm not sure. He's not the type of man to beg, so I slowly nod my head, afraid if I attempt to speak he would hear the emotion running through me. An emotion I never thought I wanted to feel for him.

"Will you come back to bed, please?" he asks quietly, unsure of how to do this part. Obviously he's never had a girl stay over after sex, as he seems incredibly out of his element. So why did he ask me?

I smile and nod and start taking off my pants when his hand stops me gently.

"Let me," he whispers as he strips off the layers I had just put back on.

He kisses my shoulder when he's done and takes a breath before making a move. His head comes up and his eyes lock onto mine before he speaks again.

"Beautiful, Annaliese," he whispers, then walks towards the bed.

Following suit, I walk slowly to him and crawl under the covers. I'm not sure what he meant when he said the night wasn't over. When his arm comes around me and pulls me into him, he kisses the side of my face and I get an immediate sense of comfort, and insanely wet for him all over again. Pressed up against his hard body makes me want to turn around and take over for a change, but when his soft snores grace my ears, I sigh. That's the fastest I've ever known someone to fall asleep. I can't imagine he falls asleep that easily on a normal night, and I can't help but wonder if it has anything to do with me being here.

Maybe I make him feel just as comfortable as he makes me feel.

Or maybe I should stop hoping and dreaming about the future as it will probably just end up biting me in the ass.

****

The next morning, before the sun comes up, I wake up to a warm body wrapped around me. Man, I must have fallen asleep fast. Normally I lay there and worry about so much it keeps me up, but last night I was so comfortable in Adam's arms that I didn't have any worries, and my dreams were happy. Strange, really.

He's sleeping on his stomach, the dark grey sheets tangled up between the two of us, and his arm and leg are wrapped around me. I take a moment to admire his chiseled body in a relaxed state. He always seems so on edge. It's nice to be able to see him completely relaxed. The defined muscles on his back form as he takes a deep breath and adjusts himself in his sleep. His ass is half covered by the blanket, and the part that isn't is so glorious that I want to pull the rest of the blanket off of him. I let my thoughts drift to the things I could do to him to wake him up, but then I hear Thor scratching at the door.

"Shit," I whisper as the tiny puppy scratches and whines.

How could we have forgotten about him? All night we left him locked out there, and though this place is probably huge, that's lonesome for a tiny dog! He keeps whining and scratching and I see him trying to slide his tiny paw under the door and feel so guilty. He's not my dog, but he's so freaking cute.

Trying my hardest, moving as carefully as I can, I slide out from under Adam's strength and almost fall to the floor in the process. I stand up and move to grab my clothes but really don't want to have to get fully dressed, as I plan on returning to bed after Thor has done his business. I opt for doing a quick search through Adam's drawers to find a t-shirt and a pair of his boxers. Throwing them on, I quietly slip out of the room to an overly eager puppy who's having a hard time deciding whether he wants to run in circles, run to the door, or lick my face all morning. Laughing, I take the little man to the door and grab his leash. I'm not about to put on my heels again, so I opt for barefoot and head out, grabbing the elevator key that Adam set on the table by the door for my way back up.

On the way down, Thor is so excited I'm afraid he's going to wet the elevator. Thankfully he's old enough to hold it until we hit the grassy area outside, but he doesn't waste time getting to doing his business.

"Hey, Thor buddy." I hear a voice behind me and freeze. It's not even six in the morning. Who would be out here at this time of the day that knows this puppy? And why am I so nervous to show my face? Thor recognizes the man and runs towards him, jumping and yipping. Now the leash is tangled and I have no other choice than to turn and make my identity known. I turn and smile at the older doorman holding Thor and letting him lick all over his bearded face.

"Hi. Sorry about that," I say as I take Thor and set him on the ground.

The man smiles then looks at me curiously.

"Interesting," is all he says then walks back into his station, leaving me out in the Chicago air wondering what the hell just happened.

I walk back inside and get in the elevator with Thor, entering the key that takes us up to the penthouse with no stops. This lifestyle is definitely luxurious, but I've been here for less than twelve hours and already am ready to get back to my apartment on the other end of town. At least there I have character, and nice doormen, and more grass than a tiny spot in front of the building for my dog to play in if I ever have a dog.

The sun's starting to rise by the time we make it back inside Adam's apartment and I'm welcomed with the comforting aroma of coffee floating throughout the apartment. He probably has it scheduled to start at a certain time every day. My thoughts are cut short when I round the corner to the kitchen and stop dead in my tracks at the sight in front of me. Adam's standing in the kitchen with his back to me, which tells me he hasn't heard me walk in the kitchen yet. His pajama pants hang low on his hips, and he's not wearing a shirt. It looks like he's deep in thought about something the way he's leaning on the counter with his head down. I slowly and quietly walk over to him and wrap my arms around him. He straightens and turns, wrapping me in his warm hug.

I keep telling myself that this is a bad idea, that one of his bimbo sluts is going to show up and ruin what my mind is playing out as happily ever after, but I can't get myself to leave. Especially since it's Sunday and I have absolutely nothing on my agenda today.

"Morning," his says in a voice still rough with sleep and I immediately feel the effects of it between my legs. Jesus, does he have to be so sexy all the time? I wake up with a rat's nest on my head and makeup smeared across my face. He wakes up with perfectly sleep-tousled hair and sexy as sin morning voice. And the muscles. Jesus, the muscles.

"Hey. I hope you don't mind I took Thor out. He was begging and it pretty much broke my heart," I say into his chest.

He chuckles and says, "Yeah, he's pretty good at that."

"His tiny paw was sliding under the door. It was so sad!"

"You just wait, you haven't seen anything yet." He sighs and I'm brought back to reality.

He's acting like this is going to last. This isn't going to last. We're from two totally different worlds, and there's no way I can compete with the bombshells he has throwing themselves at him daily.

"Sorry I stayed so long," I say pulling away from him.

"What?" His eyebrows push together and he cocks his head at me.

"I said one night. Now it's turning into one night and the next day. I'll get out of your hair now."

As strongly as I can, I muster up the strength to walk back to the bedroom and start dressing, leaving him in shock in the kitchen. As much as I want to stand there with him all morning, take him back to bed, and do all kinds of things to him, I can't. It wouldn't be good for either of us, and my heart can't take being broken right now. Not when I start a new job tomorrow, and hopefully find my passion in a Chicago public school soon.

Chapter 8

Adam

She's moving like something scared her and all I can do is sit here and watch in shock. Why does she want to get away from me so much? I had to stop her last night, but I can't do it this morning. It's not fair. As much as I want to ask her to spend the day with me, I promised one night and one night is what I got, even if the majority of it was spent just... sleeping.

I haven't been able to sleep that well in a very long time, so the fact that I fell asleep that fast in bed with her after our incredible night of hot sex, when I had full intentions of taking her multiple times before finally passing out from sheer exhaustion, is huge. I'm so comfortable with her being here. I'll admit when I woke up after she slipped out the bedroom door, my heartbeat spiked. I honestly thought she left me like I skipped out on her last week. It would have been my fault had it happened, but the relief that washed over me when I saw her clothes still on the floor was enough to put a smile on my face.

She stayed for me. And she's still here.

I didn't hear Thor when I opened my door either, which shocked me until I saw his leash was gone. That's when I really smiled. She took my dog out for me.

Now I stand here while she dresses like she's late to work, when I know for a fact she doesn't have a job. And it's Sunday.

"Why—" I try to form a coherent sentence but when her eyes hit mine as she's slipping on her shoes I know she's gone.

Shit.

"Listen, last night was fun. Awesome. That's just what it was, though, right? Just one night?" I can't read the look in her eyes, and I suddenly wish I had more practice caring about women's feelings. Usually I just brush this shit off, but I don't want to do that with

Annaliese. The second I decided to do her last night, I threw caution to the wind. I almost didn't. I couldn't stop worrying about Vick, and what he'd do to me if he found out. Then she touched me and all other thoughts evaporated. All I was left with was the intense pleasure I felt just from her touch.

"Okay," is all I'm able to spit out. My brain isn't working this morning, and my awkward comment is like one from a teenager after his first time.

"Can I take some coffee for the taxi ride?" Shit. She doesn't have a way to get home.

"I can take you. Make yourself at home. I'm gonna get dressed then we can head out if you want."

She looks at me with a sheer look of panic and I'm almost afraid to leave her alone for fear that she'll bolt. When she smiles and nods, I nod and tell her I'll be right out. She walks towards the kitchen, which is opposite the house from my bedroom and I hightail my ass into gear, throwing on the first thing that I see to get out to her before she leaves. Sweats and a button up shirt won't cut it, however. I still have a look to uphold, so I grab a pair of khakis and a polo, throwing them on as I walk down the hall, trying to regulate my erratic behavior before she sees me and knows something's up.

I don't want her to leave, but if she's going to leave I will be the one to take her. At least that's more time I get to spend around her to try and make her see I'm really not the bad guy she's made me out to be. Rounding the corner to the kitchen, my stomach drops at the sight of her. She's leaning on the counter, flicking through her phone, her ass right in front of me and her long brown hair pulled up into something messy and hot on the top of her head. It takes all I have not to walk up behind her and touch her the way my hands are itching to touch her. Instead, I clear my throat so she knows I'm in the room.

"Hey." She turns and smiles at me, holding a to-go mug in one hand. I glance down at my favorite mug and cringe inwardly. "I hope this one's okay?" she asks holding up the mug.

"Perfect." I smile. I have throwaway coffee cups in the cabinet next to my travel ones, but I'm not telling her that. Now I'll have a reason to get to see her again, all I have to do is get her back to her place before she finishes the coffee.

"Great. Then I'm ready when you are." She walks by me and I catch a whiff of her scent as she leaves the kitchen. She smells like freshly cleaned clothes, even though she's wearing her clothes from last night so I know for a fact they aren't freshly cleaned. Hell, she shouldn't smell that good, and I shouldn't be so attracted to it, but I am. And I really don't want to have to take her home, but I do. I can't exactly keep her here with me all day when she obviously wants to leave, even though that's exactly what I'd like to do. I'd like to fuck her more, I'd like to see her smile more, and I'd like to get to know her.

Just Go   M. Dauphin

Annaliese is the first girl in a long time I've wanted more with and she wants nothing more than one night with me. Fucking irony.

I sigh and rub my face, wondering how I got so wrapped up in her. At first, I thought it was the image of her that I kept playing in my mind. I thought it was the fact that she was insanely hot, and insanely drunk, and insanely willing. Part of me figured that I dreamed her up to be so much better than she really was, but spending the best night I've spent with anyone, ever, I learned last night that I didn't give her enough credit. She's way better, way cooler, way hotter than I built her up to be.

Because she's real.

"You coming?" Her hand is on the doorknob, she's staring at me with a slight grin on her lips, and something pulls in my gut, almost forcing me to ask her to stay, but I don't. I just smile and nod, grabbing my keys as I walk toward her, escorting her out the door and to the elevator. I know I'm going slower than I usually would, but I have this feeling that this is the last time I'm going to see her privately like this, so I'm really trying to milk this for all it's worth. As we wait for the elevator I glance over at her and she's sipping her coffee, deep in thought about something. Her face is relaxed, but there's a bit of stress in her expression, like she's worried about something.

"You okay?" I'm not one to really care much about the emotions running through the women I fuck, mostly because they range from crazy serial killer to roses and rainbows coming out of their ass in a matter of hours, but Annaliese isn't like that. She shows true emotions that pull at my heartstrings when I'm least expecting it. I don't want her to be worried. I don't want her to hurt.

"Fine." She smiles a fake smile at me and goes back to sipping her coffee absentmindedly.

When the elevator doors open, she walks in and I wait a second before moving inside the small metal room. All of these feelings I'm feeling and I'm afraid to say anything to ruin this time I have with her. She's made it perfectly clear she doesn't want to keep someone like me around. The entire ride down to the parking garage is silent. I keep trying to think of things to talk about with her, but she's off in her own little world. It's giving me time to catalogue all of her features though. The legs that don't stop, the dark brown, messy hair. Her sunglasses are hiding her eyes, but I know the beauty that lies behind them. My sunshine in an otherwise dark world. She's radiant and she doesn't even know it. We make it to the garage and she waits to follow me to my car. I have three. I don't take her to the AUDI, since I know how she feels about me rubbing my money in her face. Instead, I head to the Corvette, hoping that's low-key enough for her. Approaching it, I click the locks and she laughs from next to me.

"Seriously? An AUDI and a Vette?" Her laughter is like a drug and I'm suddenly laughing with her.

"What's so wrong with that? Can't a boy have his toys?" I smile and ask as I walk to her side and open the door for her. She smiles and thanks me, and before she leans down to get in she stops and my breath hitches when she places her sunglasses on top of her head and those eyes land on mine.

Shit. She's beautiful.

"Thanks for everything."

"My pleasure," I whisper and lean in to gently kiss her cheek before she tucks her head down and sits in the passenger seat.

She's in the car. I have her in my car. The first woman that isn't my sister to grace the seat of this car. Why am I so nervous to be in a car with her right now? I take my time walking to the driver's seat so by the time I get the door open and slide into the cool leather seat, my heart has stopped racing and my hands are no longer shaking. She's doing all kinds of things to my emotions, and it's scaring the shit out of me. I swore off things like this after the divorce and became the man I wanted to be, not caring about women's feelings. This woman has me rattled, to say the least, but I like this feeling. The feeling of wanting to make someone else happy with no benefit to yourself. I want to make her happy, even if it tears me down in the process.

I start the engine and I hear her hum and giggle as the engine revs up. Her reaction to the force of this car is enough to get me hard, and when she leans forward and runs her hand over the dash I moan inwardly, weirdly jealous that her hands aren't doing that to me right now.

"You a fan of Vettes?" I ask smiling.

"My dad deals with different types of cars for a living. If I didn't have a thing for hot muscle cars, there'd be something wrong with me." She's looking around like she's never seen any of the details this car has. I know she has, since her dad owns one identical to this. Maybe she's just being nice.

"You wanna take her for a spin?" I ask. Typically I don't let anyone else drive my cars, but letting her drive will give me more time to convince her I'm not such a bad guy after all. I need her to realize that spending time with me isn't the worst thing that could happen to her. And then, I need her to realize that she wants me just as badly as I want her.

"Really?" she asks timidly, which is cute as hell. Even thinking about her behind the wheel of this car is making my dick jump eagerly.

Down boy.

"Sure. As long as you don't have anything pressing. We can head out of the city so we might be gone a while. There are some back roads I used to play on when I was younger we can hit up."

She's eyeing me suspiciously, but she doesn't ask for clarification of my statement. Not that I wouldn't tell her, but I really don't want to go into that part of my life today. I just want some time with her, without the stress of the city, the business, or the stress that I'm fucking Vick's daughter, weighing down on me.

"I'm good. Let me text my roommate and let her know I won't be home 'til later." She pulls out her phone and sends a few texts, laughing as she reads the responses. I want to ask what they're talking about, I want to be involved, but I don't want to seem pushy. Too soon to seem pushy.

We drive for a little over an hour and by the time we're outside the city, she noticeably relaxes. This area always calms me. A little west of the city limits of Chicago, fields, no skyscrapers. There are a few towns nearby, but nothing near as busy as downtown Chicago. I haven't been out here since my grandma passed away years ago, but coming back with Annaliese by my side is calming.

"How do you know this place?" she asks quietly, finally breaking the silence between us.

"My grandparents owned a family farm out this way. It's how I got my start in the business world and where all of my family wealth came from." I look over at her as I continue driving down a two-lane road, one I've driven down plenty of times in a past life. One that didn't involve my millions spread out over multiple banks and high-class underground fights where I could lose two grand in one night. A life that involved first loves, first times, and first heartbreak. Everything good and bad happened here, at this small family farm.

"It's beautiful out here. I've never had the chance to come out this way, but it's really nice." She looks out her window, then back at me and grins. "When do I get to drive?" The smile that breaks across her face as her eyes flick to the steering wheel and back to me is enough to make me want to give her anything and everything she wants.

"Right over here." I nod at the barn that sits at the back of my grandparents' property. We keep it in the family, but pay someone else to upkeep it.

"Aren't you afraid the owners are gonna be mad?" she whispers like they can hear us.

I let out a chuckle and shake my head at her innocence. "Nah. Being that they're living in my family home, being paid by my family, I don't think they're gonna mind. Just don't screw up the fields." I point to the fields in the distance and she laughs. Her phone dings and as she's checking it, a strand of hair falls out of her bun and I instinctively reach over to push it behind her ear. When my fingers graze her cheek, I feel the warmth on my fingertips from our connection. She looks up at me, stunned that I would do something as sensual as that, but I don't move my hand. Slowly, I continue tucking the stray strand behind her ear as our eyes stay locked on each other's.

"Didn't want to hide that beautiful face," I whisper, my voice filled with lust. Her eyes are wide and she's not saying anything. When her eyes flick to my lips I know she's thinking the same thing I am, so I take the opportunity and move my hand to the back of her head, slowly connecting my lips to hers. Her lips are perfect for kissing, so plush, and they still taste of the vanilla lip-gloss she applied before we left. It doesn't take her long to relax into my kiss and start kissing back, trailing my lips with her tongue, asking to taste me. I groan and open my mouth more, letting her in, and tasting her fully for the first time. Every time we've been together, I've been so focused on the rest of her body that I haven't paid her lips much attention. Being here now, I think I could kiss these lips all day. Her hands come around my face and she pulls back slightly.

"I know they may not mind us driving around here, but public sex isn't something I feel like getting arrested for," she breathes, her eyes drilling into mine, showing me every emotion she's hiding from me. My dick is so hard just from this little encounter I need to start thinking about puppies or some shit just to be able to get out of the car without sporting major wood.

"Right," is all I'm able to get out. What is she doing to me? Adam Callahan doesn't do girls in public. My publicist would have a hay day with me if he found out about this little excursion today. He's already going to be pissed that I left my phone at home today, not wanting to be bothered by anyone.

"So... is it my turn yet?" Her smile breaks through and she takes a deep breath.

"Oh, yeah. Absolutely!" I say with a little more energy than I had before. She feels more, just like I do. She feels it, but she doesn't want to because she still thinks I'm a bad guy. I'm not a bad guy. I just need her to get to know the real me and not the one the magazines make me out to be.

She hops out of the car and practically runs to the driver side as I turn off the car and move the seat back before getting out. I smile as she glides into the seat like she was built for it, then lean in to show her where some of the controls are.

"Cruise control, wipers, blinker—"

"Um, Adam. I'm not stupid. I can handle a car." Her eyes lock on mine and the heat between us is insane. If she isn't feeling this, there's something wrong with her. "Question is, can you handle my driving?" She bats her eyes at me and caresses the steering wheel and I stand and groan.

"Jesus," I bitch to no one after she shuts the door and smiles at me, her massive sunglasses taking up the majority of her face when she smiles. She looks so damn cute and sexy all at the same time, if that's even possible. Sitting behind the steering wheel of my car, I can't help but smile at the energy radiating off of her. I slide in the car and click my seatbelt, praying she's not a terrible driver, and trying to find some type of emotion other than incredibly happy. I'm happy with her. Small things like this make me happy, and it's all because of her.

Just Go   M. Dauphin

"Good to go, driver." I smile as she looks over at me and grins, lifting her sunglasses and winking at me before she reapplies her focus to the car. She pulls out of the small gravel parking area and starts off like any normal person would do in a car.

Then she hits the road.

The moment all four tires are on the pavement, she's a totally different driver. These roads out here aren't straight, and they aren't flat. I've never went over 50 on these roads for fear of killing myself, but when I look over and see we're already pushing 60 I can't help but grip on to my 'oh shit' handle. I look over at her, maneuvering the car like it's second nature, hands placed on the steering wheel, not gripping it too tight, not nervous at all. She's grinning and flicks her gaze over to me before chuckling and returning it to the road. I wouldn't be worried if we were somewhere else, but she doesn't know these roads like I do. There are curves coming up that killed a kid when I was in school.

We approach a turn in the road, surrounded by corn fields now on both sides, and before I'm able to warn her about the turn, she anticipates it and slows just enough, maneuvering her way around it with ease, like she's done it hundreds of times before.

I sit in disbelief, eyes wide, heart slamming in my chest.

She looks over and grins at me before returning her gaze to the road. She's still smiling and I can't take my eyes off of her. The most beautiful woman to ever grace me with her presence. I decide right then and there that I'm keeping this woman.

She's mine and I'll do everything to ensure that she knows it—inside and out.

We drive along at a faster speed I've ever tried on these roads, and almost a half hour after taking off, she slows the car to a normal rate and at the next driveway, one that belongs to a house sitting empty, she pulls in and stops the car.

"Woo!" She laughs hard, her head falling back on the headrest. She turns it slightly and lifts her glasses, smiling at me. "Glad I didn't kill you." She keeps laughing and it makes me crack a grin through my utter shock.

I look at her and I'm sure I look stupid with my eyes wide, my breathing erratic, and my mouth hanging open.

"What was that?" I ask, so utterly confused at how she knows how to drive like that.

"What?" she asks in a sweet tone, laced with sarcasm.

I narrow my eyes at her, "You played me. I figured you'd never driven something like this before."

"Ha! I didn't play you, first off. Secondly, have you met my father? Sure, he has a luxury car business, but all cars are his business and his little girl was determined to be a shining star in his eyes, even if it meant years of racing lessons. Finally, I'm almost offended you thought that little of me."

I'm speechless for the first time in my life. Even when I walked in on my wife with her boyfriend in my bed, I wasn't this speechless. This girl has completely blown me away today. She's like no one I've ever met.

"Right." I can't get my mind to stop racing, nor can I get my heartbeat from racing out of my chest. Fairly certain I'm still in shock, I stare at her as she smiles so freely I feel like my heart is going to beat out of my chest for other reasons.

"That was great," she says as she looks over at me. Her sunglasses are hiding her beautiful eyes and all I want to do it look into them. Without another thought about it, I reach over and slowly take her sunglasses off her face to reveal the deep, glowing beauties underneath. Her makeup is all washed off from last night, but dammit if she isn't even more beautiful without all of that stuff caked on.

"Hi," I say quietly, mentally kicking myself for not being able to form a full sentence yet.

"Hi to you, too. Thanks for letting me—"

Before she can finish I'm slamming my lips to hers, taking her head in my hands and kissing her harder than I planned on. She melts into my kiss and moans when my tongue slips past her lips. The noises coming out of her are making my dick start to get incredibly uncomfortable in my pants, but I can't stop. I've never seen such true emotion, true joy, coming out of one person. She's so beautiful, so carefree, and I want to make her feel like that every day of her life if she'll let me. I want to be the reason she is that carefree and happy. I want her to know that I can be a good guy. I want more time with her.

My hand slips down to her back to pull her closer to me, and she takes the invitation to swing her leg over the middle console and climb into my lap. I'm already sporting wood, and having her straddle my lap like this isn't helping it go down. She notices the hardening in my pants and groans while pushing down the tiniest bit, still kissing me fervently. Her hands wrap around my neck while mine find her bra and unclasp it, lifting her shirt enough to give me access to her nipples. Leaning down I kiss each gently and feel her moan as my lips come around them. She pushes down on me harder, grinding on my raging hard cock, and for the first time ever, I feel like I could come from the friction of grinding alone. This woman has me all kinds of wrapped up, and just thinking of her makes my dick start to stir. Having her grinding on me like this, playing with her breasts, fully aware that we are in a car in broad daylight, and any point someone could walk up and see us, is incredibly sexy.

"Jesus, Adam," she moans as my mouth comes around one of her nipples and bites gently.

I need to fuck her, but there are way too many barriers between us.

"Let's go back to my place," I gasp as she grinds down on me again and her lips suck on my ear lobe.

"Way too far away," she whispers, her warm breath in my ear, then sits up and looks around. "Come on." She smiles and opens the door, pulling her shirt down and climbing out, not waiting for me to take off towards a dilapidated barn.

"Son of a—" I start but she turns around and pulls her shirt off completely, bra and all, before grinning at me and slipping inside the bar. That shuts me up, and makes me move faster than I've ever moved to get to her.

I slip inside the barn, the door creaking loudly, and cringe, hoping no one is here to hear us. It's one thing to be caught making out in a car; it's a whole larger thing to be caught screwing in a barn on someone else's property. Not that I would care if we were caught, however. I couldn't hold back if I tried. This woman has a spell on me, and makes all logical thinking go out the window.

"Annaliese?" I whisper into the barn, letting my eyes adjust to the darkness, a huge contrast to the bright sunlight outside.

"Over here," I hear her, her voice laced with desire, and I follow it across the barn, noting her articles of clothing laying in a path. I follow the clothes and round a corner to see her laying in a massive pile of bailed hay, completely naked, and playing with herself already.

"What're you doing?" I ask letting the twang I worked so hard on getting rid of slip back into my voice. Her eyebrows raise and her hands stop playing with herself long enough to crack a smile at me. "I thought you weren't into getting arrested for sex in public?"

"Did I just hear you right, country boy?" she smiles. "Was that a country twang that just came out of your mouth?"

"Depends."

"On?"

"If you like men with country twangs," I growl as I strip off my top and toss it across the room. She eyes my bare chest and stands to walk over to me. Her hands find the button on my pants and she undoes them, slipping them down and freeing my raging hard on. On her knees, her eyes flick up to mine before her mouth goes around me, taking me all the way back, and then some.

"Shit, Annaliese," I growl as I instinctively pump into her. Her hand comes around the base of my shaft and my hand goes to her head to guide her. She's pumping so perfectly I'm about to blow my load in her mouth, when she pops me out of her mouth and stands to kiss me. "Turn around" I growl. She does as I say and I gently push her shoulder down, groaning when she bends her body in half and grabs her ankles, her ass perfectly on display for me.

Just Go M. Dauphin

I slip a finger inside her, then two, and feel how wet I've made her already, without even touching her in this barn. She's so sexy, poised here, waiting for me.

"Fuck me, please," she gasps as I push two fingers back inside her, then slowly remove them and apply the slightest amount of pressure on her puckered hole. I'd love to keep up this torture but my balls are starting to ache and my dick is screaming at me to be inside her, so I align myself and slowly enter her, not wanting her to lose her balance from her stance. "Harder, please," she moans as I wet my thumb and gently push it into her ass, adding the perfect combination of pain and pleasure to the sensual assault. With my free hand, I grab her hips and start pumping harder, feeling every glorious muscle contraction of hers as her orgasm threatens to rip through her. As soon as hers begins, I feel the starts of my release and quicken my pace, wanting to come with her at the same time.

"Ahhh!" she screams and bucks back to me as her orgasm peaks and everything inside her tightens, milking me of my own release.

"Shiiit—" I moan as I pump into her, emptying my load inside her.

"Fuck!" she yells as the realization we didn't use a condom rushes over both of us.

She stands quickly and looks at me with betrayal and fear in her eyes.

"Shit, Annaliese—" I start but she interrupts me.

"No.... It's fine. I'm on the pill." She looks around for her clothes then starts silently dressing. I see her hands shaking and move to console her, to tell her that she's covered, but she pulls away and glares at me. My heart sinks; that's a look of hatred. I've seen it plenty of times before and it's never bothered me. Coming from Annaliese, though, it really fucking hurts.

"I'm sorry," I whisper, reaching out to touch her shoulder. I need some sort of connection, because from the looks of it, she's pulling away. She's made her decision about me and it isn't good.

"I'd like to go home now," she says, then slips her sunglasses back over her eyes and walks out to the car.

Chapter 9

Annaliese

The entire drive home I'm silent. I can tell he wants to talk about something from the way he keeps looking over at me, but I can't do it. I've *never* had unprotected sex, and the first time I stupidly do, it's with Mr. Fucking Chicago or more like *Mr. Fuck All of Chicago*. The man who fucks multiple women in one day. Jesus, I pray he doesn't have any diseases. How did that thought not cross my mind? How did I end up screwing him an hour away from home in a random barn?

I know how. Those dark and dangerous eyes. I couldn't get those eyes out of my mind the first time I saw them, and now that I've seen how they look in the middle of mind-blowing sex, how they look when he thinks I'm not watching him, I can't get them out of my head again. Hell, I'll probably never be able to forget them. He's scared me, making me believe that he can be just as carefree and easygoing as any other guy, and then pulls something like that. Sure, I'm not fully innocent, as I could have told him to wrap it, but he's the one that needs to carry that shit with him. He should have thought of it before he slid into me and made me lose all brain functionality.

Shit.

My ears are still ringing from what was close to the best orgasm I've ever experienced, and my hands are shaking, though I'm not sure if that's from the sex or from the nerves that I could now have an STD, be pregnant, or both. Why did I have to get mixed up with him?

"You alright?" he asks, breaking the silence as we near closer to the city. I almost feel guilty for giving him the silent treatment on the way home, but I've been reminding myself that it's for the best.

"Fine, thanks," I weakly smile at him, then turn back to the window. I can see the skyscrapers in the distance and my heart physically hurts knowing that once we get back, I'll be gone from his life and probably his memory.

He's a player who has way too many women at his beck and call. I can't be one of his bevy of bimbos who will drop her pants for a manwhore. I want more from the person I give my heart to—the white picket fence, dog, and kids. He doesn't seem to want the same thing, and that's his choice. I can tell he has feelings for me, but I'm not certain how much those feelings reach out from the bedroom. Sure, we have amazing chemistry between the sheets, but when it comes to day-to-day functioning, does he really have what it takes to be committed? He cheated on his beautiful wife with lord knows how many women. If he can cheat on her, he's going to cheat on anyone. Once a cheater, always a cheater, right?

"Are you hungry?" he asks, trying his hardest to make a connection with me. I am, but I'm not telling him that. The more time I spend with him the less resistant I have to his advances. I just need to get back to the apartment and have some alone time.

"Nope, I'm good."

"You haven't eaten all day. You've got to be hungry."

"I really have to get home." The lie feels terrible.

His lips press together and he nods, looking back at the road. After a few moments of silence, he speaks up again.

"I had a good time with you. It's nice to let loose every now and then."

I feel bad that he's trying so hard and I'm just being a raging bitch at this point, so I grab on to the topic, hoping he'll just talk the time away and I won't have to say much.

"Why'd you choose to take me out there as opposed to staying on some of the less traveled city streets?"

"Wasn't really a choice... it just felt right." He shrugs and glances over at me with a slight, almost shy, grin on his face. "This... it feels natural with you... like nothing else I've ever felt." His voice is so raw and emotional that it almost makes me think it's someone else talking. Adam is typically the self-assured man that has all the answers. He's confident and knows what he wants. This almost nervous Adam is throwing me for a loop, and I'm not sure how to read him right now.

"Uh... thanks." I'm not sure how else to respond to that. I'd love to say that it all felt natural to me too, but I'd rather not delve that far into my feelings for him. I'm scared of what I'd find.

We stop at a red light, the city now even closer than before. I know my time with him is coming to a close, and I'll probably never have another night with him. It was, and will always be, the most intense sex I'll ever experience, but I'm starting to come to terms with the fact that he isn't ready for something like me. The city approaches fast, and before I know it we're in my neighborhood. I can feel my nerves revving up for the goodbye. If someone would've asked me a week ago if I'd be a nervous wreck just over getting out of someone's car and going home after a night of hot sex, I'd probably have laughed in their face. Today, though, if asked that same question I'd just show them my shaking hands. I don't want this to be as hard as it's about to be. Why did I have to go and see his nice side?

He clears his throat and I notice we're sitting at the light still and he's looking at me expectantly. I narrow my eyes and cock my head at him in a silent question.

"Your place?" he asks. "I asked where your apartment is."

Oh crap. He was talking to me while my mind was daydreaming about him.

"Oh, sorry. Uh... take the next left. It's just a few blocks down that road on the right," I say, only half hearing the words coming out of my mouth. My suddenly dry mouth makes talking incredibly hard to do.

We spend the next couple of minutes in the car in silence. A heavy mood settles over the car as I tell him which building is mine. It gets worse when the car stops and I take a breath before grabbing for the handle. His hand reaches over and takes ahold of mine, his face so close to mine I could kiss him. His smell so intoxicating I almost do.

"Wait," he says quickly. I turn and look into his eyes then he slips out of the car and runs to open my door for me. Why does he have to be so kind, so gentlemanly?

"Thank you," I say timidly.

Time for the awkward goodbye.

"Adam, I had a re—"

"Go out with me again," he blurts over my goodbye speech. The one I had been attempting to form the majority of the ride home. His words cut into me and I stand there, wide eyed, staring at him.

"I, uh...."

"I can be a good guy, Annaliese. You're the best, most real thing that's happened to me in a while. Please. One date, a real date. Give me one more chance to show you I'm not the prick you think I am." He takes my face in his hands and lays a gentle goodbye kiss on my lips. I kiss him back, not nearly as hard as I'd like to because my elderly neighbors don't want that show. I can do one more date with him. He's being so nice about it. What's one more date going to hurt?

"Okay." I smile and his smile breaks through his face, radiating his features.

"Really?" His smile is huge, he looks like a boy on Christmas morning and it warms my heart to see him so happy. Is this what being in a relationship with him would be like?

No, Ann. Don't think that way. He's not ready for that. He can't be. Dinner would be nice, however. What could having dinner with him hurt? I'm sure it'd be an adventure.

"Sure. You're paying though. I'm broke and jobless." I only half joke.

He looks at me, a worried look crosses his face and he shakes his head and smiles.

"Don't worry about it. I'll be expecting a call from you, Mr. Chicago," I whisper and lean in to kiss his cheek, then turn and walk towards the door of my apartment building.

"My name's Adam, Annaliese," he yells after me and I have to wipe the stupid smile off my face before turning back to him.

"I'm glad you remember it," I strike back, winking at him, then turn and open my building doors. When he's out of my sight, I feel like I'm finally able to breathe normally again.

The elevator ride up to my floor is quiet and slow. Not near as fast as the high class one that Adam has in his building to take him to the top floor of the skyscraper he lives in. Nope, this one stops on all floors, since some douche pressed all the buttons before I got on. On the second floor an elderly couple that lives below us gets on and smiles sweetly at me. They're holding hands, whispering to each other, and I try to picture them as a younger couple. Maybe they were high school sweethearts, or each other's second chance at love. Whatever their story, they look madly in love, even at such an old age. Makes me worry I'll never find the one I'll turn old with. The door dings and I smile and nod at them as I get off on my floor, sluggishly walking towards my door. I hear Gabby's music before even opening the door, and sigh. Home sweet home.

Just Go   M. Dauphin

"Gab, I'm back!" I yell over the music blaring from her bedroom. The incense smell is intense today, but it relaxes me so I don't mind it so much.

Her door is open and she's focused on the computer screen in front of her, legs curled under her and hair in the same mess of a bun that I'm currently sporting.

"Hey," I say as I walk into her room and sit on the bed. She glances over at me and weakly smiles, then goes back to the screen. "What's goin' on?"

She sighs and slips her glasses off, rubbing her eyes.

"I start this new job tomorrow and there's a ton of stuff I have to read and learn before then. I feel like I'm on overload, Annie."

"Already the adult world is wearing you down," I joke, then stand and head out of her room. "I'll leave you alone to pack your brain full of useless knowledge."

She throws her pen at me and I dodge it, heading down the hall to the bathroom for a shower. I need to wash his smell off of me, then I need to go to sleep for the rest of the day. Not before eating my weight in whatever food we have in the kitchen, since I'm actually starving from not eating all day. Tomorrow I start a job I don't want, in a company I never wanted to work for, earning the money I tried to stay away from my whole life.

***

Just Go   M. Dauphin

The morning comes quickly, as I fell asleep right after my shower and slept all night. I wake up and frown at the night sky that's laughing at me. The sun isn't even up yet, I feel as if I'm going to have to get up this early, I should be getting up to go to a job that I really love. Not something that I'm settling for. Not that I'm ungrateful for my father's help in keeping my income rolling in, but I can't get over the fear that I'm not going to ever find a job that my degree supports.

I get to the office about a half hour before the rest of my employees are scheduled to show up, making sure that my office is all set up and I can look through the emails that were forwarded to me over the weekend. It's all boring scheduling conflicts, driver requests, and even more conflicts of interest between drivers. Boring. This is what my life has become.

"Knock, knock."

Joe's standing in the doorway with coffee and a bag of something that smells amazing. I didn't realize until right now that I totally forgot to eat breakfast due to my nerves, but now that I see the coffee and smell the food, I realize I'm starving.

"Hey you," I smile at him, happy to see a familiar face. I'm sure today I'll be surrounded with all kinds of people that are jealous and mad that someone from outside the company waltzed into this position, so I'm truly happy to see Joe.

"Glad to see you're here today."

"Why wouldn't I be? It's my first day, lots to do."

"After the way things were left Saturday night, I wasn't sure if you'd want to stay with the business."

"What does Saturday night have to do with this business? It was an after hour call from a friend. Right?"

My eyes lock on his and I think I see a hint of regret there, but it's quickly masked with a passive look.

"Right. And then you went home with him." He walks towards me and sets the coffee and bag on my desk. "Just glad to see he didn't eat you alive. He's... just be careful with him, Ann."

"I'm not 'with' him, Joe. Very far from it. We had our fun, but he's not tied to me nor am I to him. I'd appreciate it if you kept this all under wraps."

He smiles at me and his posture changes to a straighter, more confident stance.

"Sure, sure, anything for you, Annie." He walks towards the door, but before he leaves he turns to me. "Be tough today. Some of your drivers are known to be assholes. Word's already going around the grapevine that you don't deserve this job. Make them realize you do." He winks at me then leaves.

If I wasn't rattled already by the kind gesture and the sexy as sin grin he gave me when he realized I wasn't with Adam, I am now due to the wink he just gave me. He winked at me! Who does that? I smile at myself and the situation I'm in. This Joe thing is going to get me nowhere good, and fast.

By the time I finish my breakfast and coffee, the majority of the office has already settled in to their morning routine. Drivers can start moving any time after six am, special calls happen before then for certain clients, but this week we have nothing scheduled out of the seemingly ordinary routines. No one has stopped in to say hello yet, but maybe that's because they're all busy getting their week started. I send out a group-wide email, calling for a short meeting at ten am, and prepare myself for my well-planned welcome speech. I don't want to be their best friend, but I need them to respect me. I also want them to like me. That shouldn't be on my list of things I want out of this job, but it'll make my life a lot easier if I work with people I like and that like me.

When the meeting comes around, I've already sent out a few emails to clients introducing myself, and handled some HR paperwork that needed to be finished today. I head into the conference room that will hold all of my drivers, and wait for them to start trickling in. By quarter after they are all finally here and I'm already pissed that they have no sense of time management. What part of ten am meeting did they not understand?

"Thank you all for coming, I just want to introduce myself."

"We know who you are," a voice from the back of the group says. I can't make out who said it, but it was a female voice, and I only have two female drivers.

"Right, I'm sure you all do. It's no secret that—
"

"You're the boss's daughter, handed this job on a silver platter," the voice says again. Everyone else around me seems to be getting more and more uncomfortable.

"The only person I have to run my qualifications by is my boss, who happens to be my father, yes, but he wouldn't put someone who isn't qualified in this position. I'm sure he went through all of his employees before coming to me." She doesn't have a comeback, and I'm able to finish up my speech. "I know we're all busy. I just wanted to say 'hi', and that I hope we have a good working environment. Come to me for anything you need."

I had some smiles and nods, a few scheduling questions to take notes on, but all in all my employees seem to be on the same page as I am. It shouldn't matter that I'm the boss's daughter. What matters is that I can do this job. Everyone gets up to leave and I'm finally able to see the girl that was making all of the comments earlier. Skinny, fake boobs, bleach blonde hair, and smacking gum like a cheap whore. Great.

"Annaliese Ryder." I put my hand out to shake hers, hoping for a more personal introduction, but she stares at me in disgust.

"I know." She fakes a smile.

"And you are?"

"You're the boss. Shouldn't you already have that figured out?" She's right. My mind scans through the notes I spent the morning reading, trying to put a face to a name, or match a profile picture to the woman standing in front of me when it clicks.

"Kayla Harris. Your hair is a different color than in your profile." And she looks like a completely different person, but the scar on her cheek doesn't lie.

"Ah, there's a brain behind the beauty. That or it was a lucky guess. Either way, boss, I have things to do this morning before my route starts." She stands and slides past me.

"Great. Nice meeting you, Kayla," I say, trying to make my voice as happy as can be, when all I want to do is fire the bitch. I figured there'd be some people upset with the big change, but I didn't think I'd have someone so openly hateful right at the start.

She doesn't return the sentiment as she leaves me to an empty conference room, contemplating my next move with her. I'm not one to whine about things, so telling my dad about her behavior is not going to happen. I'd rather not be the boss that has it out for one of her employees so transferring her right off the bat isn't happening either. It looks like I'm in need of a third option, but short of throwing her bitchy ass off a roof, I'm not thinking of anything else worthwhile.

The rest of the day is spent about like the first part of it. I'm bombarded with a whopping zero lunch invites as I sit in my office and watch groups of people leaving to grab lunch. The groups are small as we have a few drivers out and about on runs, but not one of them offered a smile or a goodbye as they leave me to an empty office.

What am I doing here? It's not like this has anything to do with my degree. Sure, this is a means to be able to stay in the apartment with Gabby, but I'm sure there are jobs out there that I could have gotten that would pay enough for me to live there. Right? I hope this was the right choice, but each time I see Ms. Kayla glaring at me, my decision starts to make less and less sense in my head. I probably stole someone's raise and promotion just because I am the boss's daughter.

"What's got you looking so down?" Joe's voice comes from the doorway. I look up from my computer and smile. He always knows when to show up and make my day a little brighter. "Thought I'd take you out to lunch. First day lunch on me." His smile warms parts of me that I'd rather it not. He works for my father so nothing between us can happen.

"Oh. Um...." If I tell him yes, he could get the wrong impression and think it's a date. If I say no, word could get around the office that I'm a cold bitch, and I'd rather not have that happen. "Yes. A business lunch with a friend sounds great." I smile at him and he holds his hand out for me to take it. Awkwardly, I hold on to his hand as he leads me out of the office.

When we reach the hallway, I pull my hand away from his warm embrace. He glances over and me but I look down and tuck my hair behind my ear. Being around Joe is starting to make me uncomfortable, simply for the fact that I'm insanely attracted to him. Now we work together at a company that my father owns. Even if I really wanted to see what develops with Joe, which the more time I spend with him the more I want to, I can't act on it.

By the time we get to the sandwich shop across the street it's a little after the lunch rush and we're able to get a table right away. I sit down while he orders for us, that way we can hold a table while our food is being prepared. In Chicago, even if it isn't rush time, places like this are always busy.

"So, how's your first day going?" Joe asks taking a bite of his sandwich. I pick at my salad for moment and take a bite, contemplating my answer. I don't want to be whiny, but I should have someone to vent to, right? That person shouldn't be Joe, though. That person should be Gabby or someone else that doesn't work in the company.

"Oh great. Really good, I'm learning a lot."

"You just turned on your professional voice, Annie. What's really going on?" His eyes are full of concern but I can't tell him. I'm already disliked

because of my father. I'd hate to add in that I'm
chumming it up with the top driver, making him angry
at everyone else.

"No, things are great."

"I'm your friend, Annie. Not just another
coworker."

"I know, Joe. And I promise that if problems
arise, I'll come to you for your opinion."

He looks at me and sighs, then takes another
bite of his sandwich before changing the subject. We
talk about our lives outside of work, his life inside of
work and how he came to be the top driver in the
entire company. Apparently, it all has to do with
punctuality and professionalism. Two things that my
entire crew lacks. I'll be fixing that.

By the time lunch is over, it's almost two in the
afternoon and I really need to get back to the office. I
thank Joe and we go our separate ways at the front
door of the building. As good of a friend as he's being
today, I have the feeling he has something up his
sleeve. And I can't say that it worries me. He's hot,
smells amazing, and has a rock hard body. Any girl
would be lucky to be with him Hell, part of me wishes
I could be that girl. I can't though, so I'll take what I
can get with him. If close friendship is all we can have,
then close friendship it is. Anyway, I have a date with
Mr. Chicago coming up. If he ever calls me that is.
Considering my luck lately, I'm going to be sitting
around for a long time waiting for him to call.

.

Chapter 10

Adam

It's been a week since I've seen or spoken with her... a week of picking up the phone to call or text, just to put it back down again. Annaliese was dead set on leaving me the last time I saw her and couldn't wait to get inside and away from me. Sure, she agreed to a dinner date, but what if that was just to shut me up so she could get inside? I'm sure she got a good laugh out of it, that, or she hates me now since I haven't called for an entire week. What's the rule nowadays anyway? Three days? Four? If I knew how she was feeling about this whole thing between her and me, I'd feel much better about calling her and asking her out on a real date. Why am I being such a vagina about this?

There's a knock on my office door, bringing me out of my now hourly daydreaming about the girl that I can't seem to stop thinking about.

"Come in!" I yell not looking up from my paperwork, trying to make myself look busy as opposed to a lust-struck fool.

"Hey, man, what's up?" Benton asks strolling into the office. He sits on the sofa and reclines back, stretching his legs out and crossing his ankles. He hasn't fought in two days and I can tell his muscles are starting to feel better than they did when he was fighting multiple nights in a row. Finally, he's getting back to normal and I'm able to come through with my promise to him.

"I looked into the adoption thing for you," I say, not able to look him in the eyes for fear of the emotion that will be radiating out of them soon. I love this man like he's my own brother. I'd do anything for him. "I talked to a few people and they're willing to help get your application pushed forward."

"What?" he leans forward and puts his elbows on his knees. "How?"

"Money talks, B. Even people in the highest places will do things that aren't exactly by the books for the right price."

He smiles at me and nods, his jaw tight with emotion.

"Now, get the hell outta here before you turn into a pussy. Go tell Carly you guys should be expecting a call this week."

"Shit, man, that...." he clears his throat, obviously full of emotions that he's trying to hide from me. Good. I don't want to see any of that shit. "Thank you." That's all he's able to say before speeding out of my office, unable to keep his emotions in control.

I know how hard they've worked for a baby. It's taken him years to come to terms with the fact that Carly's body simply cannot carry a child. Once they accepted that, adoption was the very next best thing. Unfortunately, they've been at the bottom of the list for about a year now, seemingly not moving anywhere. All it took was a phone call to the woman they had been working with, a slight change in a little bit of funds, and their name was bumped to the top of the list for newborns. I try to be a good man to the people that I care about, but all the media only wants to portray me as is a ruthless businessman. There's so much more to me than you see on the news channels, and only a few people in my life that know the real me.

These thoughts bring me back to Annaliese, and how I want her to be one of those people. She started seeing the real me the last time we were together. The me that practically grew up on a farm, helping his grandparents out because his own parents were too busy for him. The me that lost his virginity at the young age of sixteen to his first love in the back of his pickup truck. The me that no one knows, and I'm only willing to share with a few. I want her to know me, and the only way she's going to do that is by spending time with me. Getting up the nerve, I pick up my phone and shoot her a text. This is easier. I'm able to control what I say and not put my foot in my mouth as easily as I do when speaking to her. I'm not sure why I do it, or that I even know I'm doing it until it's too late, but I always seem to say something that knocks her off balance and sets us back a step or three.

> **Me**: Hey you

I hit send before I'm able to chicken out, then laugh to myself that the thought of chickening out just crossed my mind. It's happened multiple times in the last week, not that anyone knows. If word got out that I've gone soft over this girl, all hell would break loose. It's ten minutes before I realize I'm staring at my phone, waiting for her to text back. I need to get my mind off of this girl. If she doesn't want me, I'm okay with that. Right?

There's a knock on my door and I yell for it to open, not even trying to put on the show that I was working. Whoever it is that's barging in unannounced can go screw themself.

"Boss man." One of Vick's men walks in and shuts the door tightly behind him. He stalks to the desk and glares at me. "Where's your money for the fight tomorrow?" he grinds out, obviously pissed that he had to make the trip down here.

"I'm holding off on the next few fights," I say calmly. No need to bother him with the details of why. "I'll be returning to betting as soon as I get some shit figured out."

"Ryder's not gonna be happy."

"I don't care."

"You should," he growls. He actually growls at me. This man is about a foot shorter than me and a dirty grease-ball. The pudge sticking out from the bottom of his shirt tells me I could take his out of shape ass in no time.

"I don't. Vick and I have no ties. That's the way I see it. We owe each other nothing." I'm trying to keep myself calm, but it's not working.

"We'll see what he has to say about that," he says then storms out of my office, slamming the door behind him.

Shit.

All I need to do is figure out who keeps having the fights that I bet on rigged against me, take care of them, then I can get back to betting. Sure, I've always loved adventure and the thrill of gambling, but throwing money away isn't something I enjoy doing.

I text Benton to meet me at the office later today to talk things over when I notice that I have a new text waiting for me. My heart beat speeds up and my stomach drops when I see her name with the number one in parentheses next to it on my message screen. She texted me back. She texted me back and I'm so nervous about what it says that my hands start to shake. Shit, Adam, get ahold of yourself! I touch her name and see the message load, smiling to myself absentmindedly when her words are displayed on my screen.

Annaliese: Hey you ;)

She winky-faced me. What the hell does that mean? Is she flirting with me? Should I flirt back? If I do and she wasn't flirting with me, it's going to make me seem like a creep. If I don't and she was flirting with me, then I'll seem like an asshole. Why are women so damn complicated? I need a cheat sheet for this shit.

There's a knock on my door interrupting my minor meltdown.

"Mr. Callahan, there's a woman on the phone that says she needs to speak with you. About the Meltourne account." Reese is standing at my doorway waiting for an answer. "Sorry for interrupting but you weren't answering the phone." She was trying to call? I didn't even hear the phone buzzing.

"What's it mean when a girl sends a guy a winky face in a text message?" I ask, and add, "For a friend. He's curious."

"What?"

"When a girl texts a new guy friend and it has winky face in it. What's that mean?"

"What was the message in the text?"

"It just said 'hey you'."

"She's flirting."

"For real?"

"Of course. The message has no happy message in it, or anything else that would make her have to send it, so obviously she's trying to convey other feelings by it. She must like your *friend*." She stresses the word *friend* and smiles.

"Oh," is all I'm able to say. She's flirting with me. I like this, and can work with this.

"So, what would you like me to tell your client?"

"Just take a number. I'll call them back."

She smiles and nods, then retreats to her desk, leaving my door wide open. Typically, I like leaving it open, but I would rather people didn't walk by and see the stupid smile on my face today. However, closing it will give the office a sense that I'm in a bad mood, and things start happening when people think I'm in a bad mood. They all get weird, and clingy, and way too nice, and some even a little scared. I'd rather not put everyone on edge, so I guess I'll just have to hold in my excitement that Annaliese Ryder is text flirting with me. I type out another message and click send before I'm able to think things through.

Me: Dinner tonight?

She sends one back before I'm able to set my phone down on my desk.

Annaliese: Thought you'd never ask. Pick me up at 7. What should I wear?

I really want to tell her nothing and that I'll be feasting on her body all night, but I told her this would be a real date. I haven't been on a real date in a while, but I do know they don't involve naked bodies exploring each other the entire time. More like half the time. Shit. My dick's getting hard just thinking about her. Annaliese in bed. Her in those damn heels. Damn. She needs to wear those 'fuck me' heels again tonight. It's been a week since I've fucked anyone, simply because thinking about Annaliese makes my dick limp for any other woman that isn't her. I'll take her to an Italian restaurant downtown. It's a small place, but the owner and I go way back.

Me: Casual. Italian okay?

Annaliese: Perfect. See you tonight ;)

She did it again!

Me: ;)

Annaliese: Did u just winky face me?

Me: Yes. Problem?

It takes a moment for the next to come through and now I'm worried that I shouldn't have done it. When I met my ex-wife, we didn't so stuff like this. The playful texts, the teasing. None of this happened, so this is all new to me, but I really enjoy it. Finally my phone dings.

Annaliese: None at all. Just wanted to know what I was getting into tonight. See you later…. Mr. Chicago.

This woman will be the end of my streak as a playboy bachelor. If I didn't know it before, I know it right now. I will make her see the real me, and she will love me.

The rest of the day I spend locked in my office, never actually meeting with Benton. I texted him telling him I'm not going to the fight tonight. Usually, I'd still go even if I weren't betting just to watch the competition, but I have more pressing things to do tonight. I sort through papers, eat a light lunch, but honestly don't get much else done other than thinking about Annaliese. I considered rubbing one out at my desk to my mental image of her, but I don't trust my brain. Without her here, I'm not sure it'd be that good anyway. Hell, even if I called in one of the interns, I'm not sure I'd even be able to get off. Tonight I'll get a picture of Annaliese. Tonight I'll make sure she knows how I feel about her. Then there won't have to be mental images because I'll be able to have her every day.

Hopefully tonight isn't as catastrophic as the back of my mind keeps warning me. Adam Callahan dating a down to earth beauty, who happens to be the daughter of Vick Ryder. Shit. I didn't think about publicity. We'll need a back entrance to the restaurant in a private booth, and no walks on the street. Don't let any eyes hit us together or I can kiss my chances with her goodbye.

By the time five p.m. rolls around I'm ready to go. Practically running out of the office, I lock up and head home to get changed into something a little more casual. Not too casual, but the man should never out dress the lady, right? My nerves are a wreck and I'm more worried now that someone is going to see us and realize who she is. If word gets back to Vick, I'm a dead man.

Driving over to her place, I catch her neighborhood in a completely different light than I did last week. There's a homeless man who looks to have set up camp on the corner a block down from her, and a couple cars on her block sitting on cinderblocks, tires completely removed. Why does she live in an area like this when daddy has all that money?

I park my car and beep it three times, just to make sure it's locked, then rush to her door, trying to calm my nerves before pushing the Ryder/Gab buzzer. Interesting. Who's Gab?

"Come on up, Chicago," the voice says through the speaker, then the door buzzes open.

I open it slowly, looking back at my precious car, praying that no one touches her while I'm not around, then slip inside the dark apartment building. The girl over the intercom, who was most definitely not Annaliese, told me to come 'up', so I head up the elevator and stop at the top when the doors open.

Just Go   M. Dauphin

There are four apartments up here and I wasn't smart
enough to look at the numbers, so now I have four
rooms to choose from. Just great. I'm fairly certain the
night we came back here a couple of weeks ago, the
first night I met Annaliese, we went into a door on the
left, but I can't remember for the life of me. My brain
was too foggy with the sexy, drunk woman that was
trying to rip my clothes off.

A door swings open from a room on the right
and a wrinkly old lady shuffles out into the hall, her
cat twisting between her feet, then she grabs a paper
and goes back inside, slamming the door behind her.
Well, that's one apartment I know she's not in. I look
around, wishing I would've looked harder at the
apartment numbers downstairs when a door at the
end of the hall opens and a girl steps out into the
hallway.

"You coming or not? Wait, don't answer that.
I'd rather not know." She rolls her eyes and sighs.
"She's in here." She holds her arm out in a grand
gesture, way too overdramatic, and I walk down the
hall and enter their apartment.

Small doesn't even cut it. The floors, all
hardwood, have seen better days. The living room,
dining room, and kitchen are all one room, no walls
separating them. I'm certain the windows haven't
been replaced since the building was built, and the
exposed brick wall looks like it could crumble any day.
The girls have done a good job at decorating and
keeping it clean, but what I don't understand is why
Annaliese would live in a place like this when her dad

has so much money. I wonder if Vick knows what this place looks like.

The entire time I'm scrutinizing their apartment, the girl that answered the door is staring at me. Arms crossed, scowl on her face, not happy at all. When she clears her throat, I turn around and see Annaliese. My dick jumps to instant attention like it's fucking saluting her, my mouth goes dry, and I'm at a loss for words.

She's perfect.

"Hey," she says as she stands in the opening to the small hallway that leads to their bedrooms. "You're early."

"I know. I couldn't wait. Sorry," I say, embarrassed that she called me out on being fifteen minutes early.

"It's fine. Let me grab some shoes and I'll be ready to head out." She smiles at me and turns and walks back into her room, only gone for a few minutes before returning with a huge smile on her face and the bright red heels from the restaurant on her beautiful feet.

"You look... ravishing," I grind out as I lessen the space between us and pull her in for a quick kiss. "So beautiful."

"Well thank you, Adam." She leans in to my ear and her warm breath spreads across my neck as she whispers, "You look pretty damn delicious, too."

Just Go   M. Dauphin

I close my eyes and steady my breath, mentally preparing myself for a night of torture from being around her and not being able to fuck her. The girl that opened the door clears her throat and claps her hands together once, getting our attention.

"Oh sorry. Adam, this is my roommate and best friend Gabby. Gabby, this is Adam Callahan," she says sweetly, then raises her eyebrows at Gabby expectantly. Gabby reaches out and shakes my hand curtly.

"As much as this is so sweet, I'm about to barf. You two need to leave. Now." She opens the door and starts to scoot us out the door. When Annaliese is in the hallway, she pulls me back in and slams the door. My eyes go wide as she pins me with her death rays.

"You hurt her, mentally or physically, and I will find you. I'll cut your balls off with an exacto knife, I'll filet your dick, and I'll feed it to you. Raw."

Shit, she's fucking nuts!

"I don't plan on hurting her." Why do these girls think I'm such an asshole?

"I bet you didn't plan on cheating on your ex-wife either." She grinds out, then opens the door and looks at Annaliese. "Sorry, babe, he had toilet paper stuck on his shoe and I didn't want to embarrass him. Whoops... guess I just did." And with that, she walks through their tiny apartment and into her bedroom, slamming the door.

Just Go   M. Dauphin

I'm stunned by her words, but everything is starting to make more sense now.

Chapter 11

Annaliese

We ride the elevator in silence. Something she said to him has him in a totally different mood than he was in before. I'll kill her if she ruined tonight for me. I can't keep up the charade that Mr. Chicago really wants to be with me and only me, and I'm not the type of girl to be okay with sharing him. Tonight's just for fun because I can't stop thinking about him and I have no self-control. After tonight, though, I'm not sure I'll be able to see him again. The more we hang out, the more I want the happily ever after with him, and that's not a good thing when it comes to Adam Callahan. Manwhore of Chicago.

Just Go M. Dauphin

He lets me into his Audi and I sigh as I mold into the leather seats. Jesus, this man has good taste in cars. My father taught me to appreciate cars growing up and it seems that Adam has that same sense of appreciation.

When his door shuts I think he's going to start the car right away, but instead he turns and looks at me with a worried and confused look on his face.

"Why do you think so low of me?" The hurt in his voice breaks my heart. I never said I thought low of him. Where is he getting this from?

"What're you talking about, Adam?"

"You don't think I can do this. That I'm capable of a relationship. I see it in your eyes and it hurts. Why do you think like that?"

My eyes are wide and I'm afraid he's going to make me get out of the car. He's not angry, but he looks hurt that I feel that way. The scary part of all of this is that he's actually right. I don't think he can do it. I don't think he's capable of a monogamous relationship. Once a cheater, always a cheater.

"Tell me," his voice, barely a whisper, urges me.

"I don't know what you want me to say."

"I want you to tell me why you're so certain that I'm not able to do this. What did you hear?"

This is not the way I thought tonight would start. He was supposed to sweep me off my feet with his romance, but instead he's breaking my heart. The only thing I can do is tell him the truth. If there's one thing about life that I always had drilled into my brain, it was that the truth, no matter how hard, is always the right choice.

"Adam, I just... once a cheater, always a cheater, right?" I whisper it, hoping that he doesn't heat the hurt in my voice. It hurts just saying the words, but it's the truth. He's a cheater.

His eyes widen and he sets his jaw so tightly I feel like I can hear his teeth grinding. Without saying anything, he nods his head, shifts in his seat, and turns on the car. I reach and buckle my seatbelt, not asking what that was all about or inquiring whether or not he accepts my answer. He has to accept it. It's the truth.

The drive to dinner is awkward and silent. There are a few times I feel like I could have started a conversation about something, but he doesn't seem like he's in a talking mood. I'm just happy my honesty didn't cost me my night with him. He's a great person to just be with—especially when he lets his walls down. I see it in his eyes. I saw it when he was talking about his grandparents, and I feel bad for him that the media has taken a liking to portraying him as an asshole. I want to tell him I don't think he's a shithead, but I don't. I want to tell him that it's okay he cheated, but I can't because it isn't. I want to tell him that I'll be with him, that I'll give him a chance to prove to me that he can do the relationship thing, but I'm not sure that my heart could take it when he fails at it.

Just Go   M. Dauphin

By the time we get to the restaurant, we've made small talk, but nothing too consequential. I notice him glance my way, worriedly, as we pull into the back alley of the small Italian restaurant, but I don't say anything. I just smile warmly, reassuring him that I'm still here with him. I'm going to kill Gabby for whatever she said to him to make him feel the need to ask me that in the car. She can be intimidating when she wants to be, and I wouldn't put it past her to threaten him in one way or another. I just need to ask him what she said to him. If any type of friendship is going to come out of this thing we have, anything at all, it needs to be built on trust and the truth.

"Adam, so nice to see you! It's been too long." A very thick Italian accent booms through the open window of the Audi and Adam laughs and opens his door.

"Paolo," Adam says as he hugs the man, then glances at me as I shut my car door.

"Adam, you made this beautiful woman open her own door? Shame, my young friend. You have much to learn," he chides as he walks towards me and pulls me into an embrace, kissing me on each cheek.

"Um, hi," I smile and say as he lets go of me. "I'm Annaliese."

"Beautiful name for a beautiful woman. Adam is very lucky to have you."

"We're just friends," I say. I'm not sure what made me feel the need to clear that up, but I regret it when I look at Adam's face. His face that was relaxed, transformed into a tight jaw, stern eyes, directed right at me.

"Well then, *friends*," Paolo stresses and looks over at Adam, "Let's get you two to your table."

We walk through the kitchen to get to our table, not caring who sees us as I believe the man who met us at the door is the owner, and come out into the restaurant from the back. He lets us sit in a small booth in a back corner, probably so Adam isn't recognized, then leaves us to get a waiter. Adam lets me sit first then takes his seat like a true gentleman. The waiter quickly arrives at the table and takes our drink orders, then retreats as quickly as he came.

"He couldn't take his eyes off you," Adam says in a low voice, his eyes slowly moving from the back of our waiter to me. When they hit me, I feel the warmth start to grow. Just a look from him and I'm lost for words. He does that to me every time those dark and expressive eyes hit mine.

"He was being polite," I say as I try and shrug off the comment though he does have a point. That waiter was definitely looking at parts of me I'd rather he didn't.

"He was checking you out," he states flatly.

"I'm sorry," I whisper, not knowing why, but I really want him to lighten up.

"Don't. You have nothing to apologize for. I'm sorry for being so moody tonight. It was a long day today," he says, then sighs and adjusts his tie. "So, tell me, Annaliese. I'm very curious what you think you know about me."

"What do you mean?"

"I mean that you seem to have me all figured out, without ever actually having a conversation with me about my life. So tell me... what do you think you know about me?"

His eyes are drilling into mine, his hand gently and absentmindedly wiping the condensation off his glass, and a smirk has started playing on his lips. This is the cocky Adam that I'm getting used to, but still don't enjoy. He has so many different sides, and the more time I spend around him, the more sides I'm learning about. He's staring at me, waiting for an answer. How does someone answer a question like that? Isn't he supposed to be woo-ing me? Do men even woo anymore? Why the hell am I talking like I'm eighty?

"Well... umm...." I stutter a bit. "I know you have all kinds of money, you own your own company that is the biggest start-up company in Chicago, and you like women. A lot of them."

He nods his head and takes a drink, never taking his eyes off mine. Swallowing his drink, he sets it back down and cocks his head.

"Go on."

"What else should I say?"

"I want to know everything you think you know. Everything."

"I'm not sure what you're searching for, Adam." This night is not going anywhere nearly as planned. By now, I was hoping for the night to be full of dirty talk and the promises of a long night of hot sex. Right now, though still fully aware of every movement his body makes, I see no promise of sex later. He's grilling me, and I'm ultimately failing.

"Just trying to get to know each other." He shrugs and takes another drink.

"You're doing it wrong," I mumble.

Thankfully, the waiter picks this time to take our orders so I'm able to think about his request after I order. It's a strange request, so he has to have a reason behind it. Maybe he wants to understand why I feel the way I do about him, or maybe he's just trying to figure out how to spin his next interview. If he knows how the public sees him, then he'll be apt to change his image a little bit. Hopefully.

I should just tell him that I'm not certain he can do this because he hasn't proven to society that he's worthwhile in the boyfriend or husband department yet. I should tell him as much as I'd love to be able to deepen my relationship with him, I can't because I don't want to end up hurt. I should tell him, and I will. I'll tell him as soon as the waiter is finished taking our orders. When I glance up at him after the waiter walks away, though, he starts talking before I'm able to get any words out.

Just Go   M. Dauphin

"I'm new at this, forgive me. I don't typically play the 'get to know you' game with the women I'm with. Why don't you try telling me a little about yourself?" His gaze isn't lifting to mine this time when he talks to me, but I'm okay with it. I feel like I'm about to break down, my heart is beating faster than it does when I run and my hands are clamming up. Why does tonight feel more like an interview and less like the date I thought it was?

This I can do. This is easy compared to telling a man you are growing strong feelings for that you can't be with him because he's an asshole cheater.

"Well, you know my father so I'm sure you have a grand idea of my upbringing. Moved here from New York before I was a teenager. Just finished up college. Live in a not so wonderful part of the city, but it's all mine. Pretty typical early twenties girl." I shrug. I'd rather not go into the details of how sad my life has become this last week. If he can be vague and not talk about himself, I can play the same game.

"What do you do for a living?"

"Work for my father's company right now. I'm waiting to hear back from schools that I applied to for positions this fall, but no one is hiring right now. My dad offered me a job in his offices as a branch manager and I took it."

"How do you like it?" his eyes narrow at the mention of me working for my dad but I don't pay much attention to it. He seems like a moody type of person, always on the lookout for someone out to wrong him.

"Honestly?"

"It's the only way I play." His eyes narrow and I know he's hinting at something else. Maybe he knows I'm holding something back from him. He's good at reading me, so I'm sure he knows that's not all I know about him. Heck, he's not dumb. He has to know that everyone in this city knows about him.

"I hate it. There's a few employees on my staff that truly have it out for me. I'm trying to feel comfortable there, but it's not what I went to school for so it's not where my heart lies," I answer honestly.

"You're having employee problems?"

"Just one in particular. She's being a huge pain in the ass, but I think it's because I took a spot that she was certain she deserved."

"Your father doesn't just throw people into positions. He's a smart man and does everything for a reason," he says then takes a sip of his drink.

"You're right there. How do you know my father anyway? You talk about him like he's an old friend."

"He's been helping out my company and myself personally for years."

"I'm sure he thanks you for your business," I smile at him.

"We are both of aid to each other," he says cryptically. I wonder what he means by that, but I feel like he wouldn't tell me even if I ask.

"That's great," I say instead.

Our food comes and I dive in. I've never been a girl afraid to eat her weight in food. I've always been active, either with dance, gym, or running. Hitting the gym is just second nature to me, and my metabolism has never been a problem, so eating a huge Italian meal isn't going to kill me. When I look up, I see him watching me in awe.

"What?" I say incredibly unladylike while chewing my food. "I'm not sorry. This food it way too delicious."

He laughs and smiles, the first real smile I've gotten out of him since we left the apartment, then shakes his head.

"You amaze me, Annaliese," he laughs. "First girl ever to eat like that in front of me and not be ashamed."

"I have nothing to be ashamed for," I say after taking a drink of water.

"You are absolutely correct." His eyes pin mine and I'm unable to look away. I feel the heat beginning to pool again, the draw to him becoming stronger, and I'm amazed that he can do this to me with just one look. I need to calm myself down. I'm strung so tight and have been through so many emotional loop-de-loops tonight that I'm afraid I'm going to burst out in tears the next time he gives me one of his intense stares.

"Would you excuse me, please? I need to use the restroom," I say as I stand and head towards the bathroom. The one place I will be able to collect my thoughts without his gaze landing on me.

"Absolutely," he smiles and my panties melt a little more. Jesus, this man does all kinds of things to me.

I walk quickly, nervous that I'll fall again since these heels aren't anywhere near my normal type of shoes, but I really need to get away from his gaze. Tonight feels so much different than the last few times we've been together. Though the last few times we were together were based on sex, and not really trying to build a friendship. This is harder than I thought it would be. My mind is throwing me for loops every few minutes. One minute I think I can see myself with him, the next I'm mentally slapping myself for even thinking that. He's way too much for me, and I'd never be able to trust him after what he did to his wife. The sex and chemistry between us is undeniable, but I can't put myself through that. Anyway, I'm still having a hard time believing why he would want a girl like me. Mousy brown hair, curls that are untamable, giant eyes that are too big for her face. My long and lean legs are pure brilliance, but the rest of me is just like any other normal girl.

I'm staring at myself in the mirror when an older lady walks in and smiles at me. She's beautiful for her age, the look of a pure mother. Like someone who spent their whole life taking care of others. Someone comfortable.

"Hello," she says to me, a warm smile spreading across her face.

"Hi," I answer.

"You're the young lady with Adam tonight, aren't you?" How in the world does she know that? We're sitting in a corner where no one can see either of us.

"Um, yeah," I answer, confused.

"I'm Elle, Paolo's wife. He wouldn't stop talking about the young beauty that Adam brought in. So proud of that young man." Her smile is so sweet, I hate to break her heart about the type of person Adam really is. One that's lying, cheating, and will do anything for money. I'll just make sure to leave out the fact that he's the best sex I've ever had, and probably will have. And the fact that I can't stop obsessing over him. "You seem lost." Her voice breaks into my thoughts.

"Oh sorry. I'm Annaliese," I hold out my hand to shake hers when she pulls me into a hug.

"You're wonderful, Annaliese. Adam is a lucky man. He deserves something good in his life."

"Really?" I realize I said it out loud as soon as I see the look on her face change to a serious look.

"Oh yes. I still remember the day he found her. Poor man, poor, poor man." She shakes her head and pats me on the shoulder. "Take care of him, and treat him well. He might look tough on the outside, but we're all worried about him." She walks into a stall, leaving me stunned and alone, staring at the bathroom wall.

What did she mean by that? How strange would it be if I continued to talk to her while she was going to the bathroom? Really freaking weird, Ann. Don't be that person. I wash my hands quickly and head back to the table, slowly walking to gather my thoughts. If he found her, that would mean he didn't cheat on her, right? And if that's the case, then my entire belief that he isn't cut out for a relationship is crap.

"Hey, you were gone for a while. Everything okay?" He asks worriedly as I sit back down.

"No lies, right? You said earlier you only play by the truth. Right?" I blurt before my head has a chance to catch up with my thoughts. My hearts beating out of my chest. This could change everything.

"Uh, right…." His eyebrows furrow. "What happened?"

"Did you cheat on her?" If I waited any longer, I probably would have chickened out, so I let the ball drop and see his facial features relax. He smiles, a very relaxed smile. A smile I haven't seen on him yet tonight. Then, he leans in towards me, elbows resting on the table. Looking me square in the eyes, he clears his throat before he talks.

"Annaliese Ryder," he starts and I get chills from his gaze. "I never cheated on my wife."

"But—"

"Do you always believe everything you read in magazines, Annaliese?"

"I don't—"

"What about the Internet? Are you a believer that everything you see online is true?"

"No, but—"

"So why is it that you believed so strongly something about me, something so personal that only I would know the truth, just because someone in the media told you?"

I'm stunned. Shocked. His eyes are pinned to mine and I don't know what to say. This changes everything, and now I feel like a terrible person for judging him like I did, before even getting to know him.

"My father told me," I whisper.

Our dessert arrives but Adam never takes his eyes off mine. The waiter speaks to us, and Adam replies, but I can't hear anything over the ringing in my ears. Why would my dad lie to me like that? I don't follow gossip magazines, and only every now and then watch shows about celebrities, so I never had a reason to second-guess him before. Plus, my dad never lies to me. Ever.

We sit in silence, staring at each other for what feels like lifetimes. His jaw ticks, and he shakes his head and chuckles to himself, finally breaking eye contact.

"So that's it? Your dad told you, and that's what you believe?"

"Sounds crazy, but that's why I believed him. My dad has never lied to me, Adam. I've had no reason to second guess him." Now I wonder how many times he's really lied to me and what secrets he's keeping.

"And now?" His gaze meets mine again. It's such a loaded question.

"I don't know," I whisper, shifting my gaze to the table. I know it means that my dad lied to me. I know it means that Adam isn't the cheater that I always thought he was. I know it also means that my belief that Adam isn't good relationship material has been thrown completely out the window. I don't know how to tell him all of that yet, though, because I'm not sure how I feel about that. This means that he might actually want to be with me, and only me. I'm not sure I'm strong enough for a relationship with him, though. He'd crush me.

"Do you still believe him?"

"No," I whisper then move my eyes back up to him.

A smile breaks across his face and warms parts of my body that react to him so well.

"Good."

Chapter 12

Adam

My phone won't stop buzzing in my pocket but I ignore it. Annaliese's eyes are huge, waiting for me to say something. I'd love to proclaim my feelings for her right now, but that'd really push her away. She's so timid when it comes to me, and so outgoing with the rest of her life. I at least know why she's like that now. She's thought this entire time that I'm a cheater, all because her damn father lied to her about me. I thought that Vick and I were on good terms, but it seems that I'm going to have to have a little chat with him next time I talk with him. He's been spreading lies about me, and that I'm not okay with.

"Try it," I say taking a piece of the chocolate dessert that was delivered to us on my fork and holding it up to her. She opens her mouth and lets me feed her the warm dessert, moaning as she closes her mouth around the delicious piece of chocolate heaven. I made sure that Paolo knew to send their best foods out to us tonight, and her reaction to her meal and desert has not disappointed. Hell, I couldn't stand up right now if I needed to, since I've been sporting full wood since I first laid eyes on her tonight. Even with the intense discussion topic, my dick never stood down like it knows what it's supposed to do around Annaliese. Just watching her mannerisms and facial expressions make me want to take her over the table right now—my cock is already nodding its head in agreement. I can't do that, for so many reasons, but my brain and my dick aren't friends right now.

"You like?" I growl as she licks her lips of the chocolate left behind and smiles at me, her eyes glowing, but still worried.

"Delicious. Thank you."

"So, Annaliese." I hear my voice, but I can't stop the words from coming out of my mouth. My heart's beating and I feel like I'm sweating. I've never been this damn nervous before—even on my wedding day. I've never felt anything like what I feel for her. It's mind boggling, knowing what she does to me when she has no clue she's doing it.

"So, Adam." She's grinning at me. Grinning! She's been on edge all night, and for good reason. She knew I was upset, and I had every right to be. She has every right to be upset right now, too, but not at me. At her father. The man who caused all this drama tonight.

"You ready to get outta here?" I need to get her back to my place. I need to show her how much she means to me. Annaliese is not just another 'fuck.' She's the real thing. I want to keep her with me, I want to be the one that makes her smile first thing in the morning, and the one that makes her sigh last thing at night. The thought used to piss me off when other women would try to force themselves into my life, but it all feels so natural with Annaliese.

There's just one problem with this whole thing.

Her father.

"Sure, that sounds great," she says, then puts her hand over her mouth as she tries to hide a yawn. The cutest damn yawn I've ever seen. I smile and her eyes go wide when she realizes she just yawned on our date. "Oh God, I'm sorry. I'm not bored, I promise. I just... haven't been sleeping well since this job started." Her voice falls and I can't tell if she sad, embarrassed, or both. I'm slightly pissed off that she's having to work for her father, and even more so that she hates her job. As much as I'm a workaholic, I love my job and my company. I try to make it worth my employee's time to work for me, and I try to make it to where they enjoy their job as much as I do. To hear that someone like her hates what she has to do for a living, because she can't work in the field she loves, is enough to piss me off. Not at her, but at society.

"It's okay, don't worry about it." I smile at her and she relaxes. "Come on, let's go." I stand, holding my hand out for her to take. When her small hand comes around mine my dick jumps just from her touch. Every time.

We thank Paolo and he makes her promise that he'll see her again, and though her agreement just seems polite, I see another visit for us here in the future. If I have it my way, we'd eat here every week. And I'm a man that almost always gets his way. My phone buzzes in my pocket again for the fifth time tonight and I sigh, pulling it out to glance at the screen.

Shit.

"Hey, I need to take this. I'll be right back," I tell her as I kiss her forehead and walk to the side of the building, leaving her waiting in the alley with Paolo for our car. I hate to leave her there, but I'd rather not have this conversation around her.

"What?" I snap as I put the phone to my ear.

"You aren't here," his voice comes through the phone, trying to intimidate me.

"No, and I may not be for a while, Vick."

"Mind telling me what the sudden change is? We had a lot riding on your bets." That sentence right there tells me everything I need to know. It has to be coming from the inside. There's no other option.

"Why don't you tell me? I'm tired of my fighter being put up against people double his size. I'm tired of the damn looks your men have been giving me. And I'm tired of the phone calls and threats, Vick."

"No one is threatening you, Adam."

"So you know about this?" I'm about to jump through the phone and strangle him. Vick Ryder has gone from someone I respect to someone I'd like to beat the shit out of in a matter of an hour tonight.

"Of course. There's nothing I don't know about, Adam." The line goes silent but I know he's still there. "Nothing."

Shit. There's no way he can have eyes on Annaliese at all times. There's no way he knows about us, or he'd be…. Oh shit.

"It's you, isn't it?"

"She's off limits, Adam. I thought we knew that." Holy hell. He is talking about my girl.

"Why go to these lengths, Vick?" And why does he think me losing a little bit of money would make me stop seeing her? None of this makes sense.

"You need to learn, Adam. Things don't always go your way."

"You're threatening my fighter and his family over her!" I scream at him, my voice echoing down the alley.

"You don't know how to play by the rules, Mr. Chicago." He emphasize the last syllables, like he's mocking me. I didn't give myself that damn nickname and I hate hearing it.

"Goddammit, Vick, she's a grown woman."

"She's my daughter, Adam. Stay away from her," he growls then hangs up.

Son of a bitch.

My mind is racing and I can't think straight. I can't let go of her; I just got her. Hell, I barely have her. He's nuts if he thinks I'm going to bow down to him. I have so much dirt on him he would rot in jail if authorities ever got wind of it. He should be afraid of everything I could to do him. Instead, he's threatening me, like he has the upper hand. We'll see about that.

"Everything okay?" Her voice rings down the alley and cuts through the ringing in my ears. I can't believe this is all because someone messed with his daughter. Someone had the nerve to fall for his daughter, and fall hard. Shit.

"Yeah, great. Sorry about that. Trouble at work." I turn off my phone and shove it in my pocket, then walk towards her and pull her into a tighter hug than I originally planned. I can't let this girl go. She makes me feel more than I've ever felt. She makes me feel real. "You ready?" My voice is gravely and emotional, full of hatred for the man that raised her.

"Where to, ma'am," I smile when I see her grinning at my forced twang. Every now and then it slips, when I forget where I am. Most times it goes unnoticed, but I like her grin, so I'll let it slide with her.

"Can you pull over?" She looks at me anxiously.

"What?"

"Just… stop driving, okay?" she pleads. I slow the car and pull into the first parking spot I see.

Once I'm parked, I turn and look at her. She's worried about something, that much I can tell. Her hands are clasped, her face is tense.

"What's wrong, Annaliese?"

She sighs, then looks up at me with glistening eyes and a sad smile on her face.

"Adam, I'm not sure about… this," she whispers, damn near close to tears. "It's all so crazy. A few hours ago I was dead set on believing you wouldn't ever be capable of being a decent human being—"

"Thanks for that, by the way," I interject and she cocks her head at me. I know she was just believing what she was told, but to assume that much bad about me, without ever actually talking to me about it, still stings.

"I'm not saying what I believed was the truth, but at the time I thought it was. Imagine building a picture of someone in your head and believing it for a long time, then come to find out suddenly it's all been a lie."

"Oh, I can imagine that quite perfectly, actually." Her father put himself on the top of my shit list tonight.

"So now what?" Her eyes are big and her lips are shiny. She's so damn beautiful.

"Now... we see where this goes," I say hesitantly. I'd rather tell her that now we start planning our future, because I'm damn sure she's the girl for me, but I'm not certain she knows the same truth just yet.

"I'm afraid." Her voice is barely a whisper as she moves her gaze somewhere outside the car. Somewhere away from me.

"Of what?"

"Everything, Adam," she says then returns those piercingly beautiful eyes to me. "You're famous. Women throw themselves at you daily, you have more money than I've ever dreamed of having, and your business is huge. How would I even begin to fit into your lifestyle? I've been hurt before by men, Adam, but...." she trails off and the sad look in her eyes makes me want to kiss all of the hurt away.

"But?" I push gently, wanting to hear all of it.

"Most of all, I'm afraid you'll hurt me, and I won't make it out in one piece," she whispers. Ashamed. Her lips press together and her face shows more emotion now than I've ever seen come out of her.

"Hurt you? Annaliese, I'd never hurt you." How can she think this? I could have anyone, but I chose her. I want her.

"Not on purpose, maybe. But something's bound to happen."

"You can't think that way. This is new to me, too, you know. We take baby steps, and we do this together." She can't. I won't let her. I'm not saying I'm not scared, but I'm not going to let it stop me from taking this chance.

Sometimes that one person comes along that makes you want to take every chance. Annaliese is my chance. My chance at being better.

She's looking down again, thinking way too much about this. I reach over and gently lift her chin enough so her eyes meet mine. Looking into her eyes right now, I feel like I can see into her soul. She's scared, she's curious, but she's also excited.

"We've got this, Annaliese." I slowly move towards her, across the console of the car, and gently kiss her soft lips. "Give me a chance." *Please*, I think but don't say. I'm not to the point of begging yet, but I'm not above it. Screw her dad.

She sighs and opens her eyes.

"Just one." She's hesitant but there's a smile playing on her lips. She wants this more than she's letting one.

Yes.

"That's all I need." The smile that breaks across my face feels foreign, but so good. I'm certain I've never felt this level of happiness before. I lean across and kiss her harder than earlier. A kiss that tells her I'm all in, I'm here with her, and she's with me, and nothing can stop us.

Then her phone rings.

"Sorry," she smiles as she reaches for it. "My dad. He worries."

I take a breath to calm the nerves that are running through my system. He's going to make this incredibly difficult.

"Hey, Daddy," she answers as I silently count down from 100 to calm myself and not pull the phone from her and tell him how I really feel. "Yeah okay," she looks worried then glances over at me and smiles. "I gotta go, Daddy. I'll take care of it in the morning." She waits a moment longer, then sighs. "Fine." She clips, then presses 'end' and puts her phone back in her purse.

"Everything alright?" I want to know everything he said to her, but that'd be a little too intrusive.

"Yeah," she sighs. "He's just protective. Sometimes too protective." She groans. "I have to get home." Dammit, I was hoping she'd end up at my place. I still can't get the thought of being inside her again out of my head.

"You sure? It's still early," I say hopeful. She gives me a sad shrug and smiles.

"There's stuff with work that came up. My dad needs it done tonight. And apparently I have a meeting with him in the morning about an employee of mine." She rolls her eyes and shakes her head. "I'm sorry."

"Don't be, you're just doing your job. I'll get ya home." I take her hand in mine and move it to my mouth, laying a gentle kiss on her knuckle. The minute my lips hit her skin I feel a warmth spread throughout my body. I want her, and from the look in her eyes she's on the same page as I am, but she's also a dedicated worker, and I respect that.

The drive back to her place doesn't take too long, but I don't let go of her hand the entire time. I need the connection to her. She's so real, and everything else in my world seems so fake. Plus, her hands fit perfectly in mine. By the time we pull onto her street, my mood has taken a dive. I don't know how to do goodbyes like this. Because I want to see her again. Soon.

I pull in front of her apartment building and kill the engine. She makes a move to get out of the car but I stop her. I'm determined to show her I'm more than a rich, smug asshole. Walking around to her side of the car, I take note of the things that are less than stellar about her living conditions. How in the world would Vick let her live in a place like this, but be so protective of other aspects of her life? Something seems terribly wrong about this.

"Thank you for tonight, Adam. It was wonderful." She smiles and her face lights up. Just one smile from her, that's all I need to get my heart racing again. One smile.

"When do I get to see you again?"

"I've got a few late meetings this week, but text me. I'm sure I can fit you in," she grins then winks. I pull her to me and wrap my arms around her. Her brown eyes look up and me and she smiles. "Sorry I'm calling it an early night. I really was looking forward to a... second dessert." The grin on her face tells me exactly what she's talking about, and if she doesn't watch it she's going to be feeling just what she's missing out on.

"Mmm... sounds delicious." I kiss her and hug her tighter, not wanting to let go.

"It is. I've tried it before, and it just makes me want more," she whispers then pushes away from me. "Next time, Mr. Chicago. That's a promise."

I smile and chuckle as she walks to her apartment building, leaving me standing in the dark, on the side of the road, grinning like a fool. Once I see she's safely inside, I return to my car and lock the doors. It's not even ten yet, so I grab my phone and call Benton.

"What, dude?" he groans sleepily.

"Were you sleeping?" I laugh. "Old man."

"Shut up. What do you need?"

"B, we got a problem." I say. Changing my mood to serious business in three seconds flat has always been a talent of mine. Not that I'm not still over the moon that Annaliese is mine, but I have other pressing issues to deal with now that she's safe inside her apartment.

Like her father.

Chapter 13

Annaliese

It's only Tuesday, but so much has already happened this week that I feel like it should be Friday. Now I'm running on three hours sleep, four cups of coffee, and it's only five am. I laugh to myself then realize I'm laughing all alone in a dark and empty office at five am. I'm not even sure why I'm here this early, but my father requested something from me, so here I am. Always trying to please him.

I'm not certain when it became my life goal to make him happy, but there have been so many times I did something just to satisfy him that I've lost count. Going to school to be an educator or administrator was something I did because I love it, and it was my way of telling him I'm done living my life just to please him. I want to live for me. Ironic, really, since here I sit in an empty office building, before the sun comes up, waiting for him to get here for a meeting he called last night after dark. All because I wasn't able to make it in this world without his help.

Then, to add to that depressing thought, last night, my view of my father was blown out of the water when I realized he's been lying to me about Adam this whole time. I figured they knew each other from the way my father talks about him, but now that I know he lied about him, I can't help but wonder what else he's lying about.

My phone rings and I pick up before the second ring.

"Annaliese Ryder," I say, holding back a yawn.

"Hey." Adam's voice soothes my nerves and makes me smile.

"Hey, you. What're you doing up this early?"

"Business meeting out of town today, getting a head start on traffic."

"Ah, good thinking." The yawn creeps out and I hear him laugh.

"I'm beginning to think I bore you, Annaliese. Always yawning around me."

"Sorry. This job is just so… ugh." I typically don't bitch to others about things, but I'm over this job and it's only been a week.

"Glad to hear it's not me." I hear his smile. There are a few car horns in the background and a door slams and makes everything silent again. "When do I get to see you again, Annaliese?" His voice is low and gravely, like he's trying his hardest to keep this conversation to himself and not let anyone else around hear him. Just the thought of seeing him again has my stomach in a bunch of nerves.

"I'm free on Friday," I answer as I see my father walking into the office. "I've gotta go."

"I'm putting you down for Friday."

"Later," I say, smiling as my dad as he walks in and sits down. "Hey, Daddy."

"Annaliese. You look tired, are you getting enough sleep?" he sounds worried, but he's the one that forced me to be here this early today.

"I'm fine, Dad. What's up?"

"Did you finish the paperwork from the transfer?"

"I did, but it didn't make any sense. Why am I losing three drivers? And where are they going?" I don't really care, but I need to sound like I care about my job a little bit. All I care about is finding a real job. One that I love doing, not one that I dread going to because of terrible hours and terrible employees.

"Annie, you've had... complaints. People aren't taking to working with the boss's daughter too kindly." He shakes his head and sighs. I don't want to be talking about this. I want to be talking about why he lied to me about Adam and what else he's lied to me about.

"That's their own fault. They just aren't used to actually having to work," I mumble then glance at my father's shocked expression. "So who am I getting as a replacement?"

"Joe's moving over to help you out until we get new people in here," he answers shortly, then stands and makes his way towards the door. Turning like he forgot something, he looks at me and cocks his head. "How was your night last night, dear?"

I furrow my eyebrows at his strange question, wanting to come back with a smartass comment. Instead I smile and cock my head at him curiously.

"Fine, thanks," is all I give him. He doesn't need to know about my relationship with Adam. Not yet, at least. I'm certain he won't be happy about it, so I need to try to figure out a way to warm him up to Adam before announcing that we're together.

By three o'clock I'm beat. Being short drivers has made scheduling insane. Hopefully my dad gets people in here soon, or I'm going to have to start carting these rich people's asses around myself.

Joe's been a huge help in figuring out schedules. I can't help but feel something for the man every time he comes near me, but knowing that Adam is insistent on being with me and only me, I can't exactly make a move on Joe. Not that I really want to, knowing what waits for me with Adam. Jesus, just thinking about Adam and everything I want to do to him has me wet and ready. I'm not certain I'll be able to wait until Friday for him. Deciding to see what his plans are tonight, since I'm off in an hour and cancelled dinner plans with my parents, I grab my phone to text him, just in case he's not busy.

ME: Hey. Are you free later on?

I hit send and wait. Sitting at my desk there are so many other things I could be doing right now, but I don't want to do any of it. I want to stare at my phone and read his message as soon as it comes through. Knowing him, though, he's probably busy and won't be able to get to his phone for a while. He's important, he's rich, and he's busy. He told me Friday; I just should have waited.

Then my phone dings.

ADAM: After 11, yes. What's up?

Well, that's a nice surprise. He's prompt, and he's free. It's late, but I couldn't care less. He's making time for me and I need to see him. I want to see him.

ME: Don't wanna wait 'til Friday. ;)

ADAM: I was hoping you'd say that.

Damn he's fast. My stomach starts to flutter at all of the ways I want him to take me. Mostly, though, my nerves are a wreck.

I know it's not just sex anymore. It's a relationship. With the wealthiest man in the city.

And he only wants me.

I throw my stuff into my bag and head out of my office. Passing a practically empty office, I smile at Joe as I head towards the doors.

"Where you headin'?" he asks as my hand reaches for the door. I sigh and look back at him.

"Home. You cool with that? I've been here since before the sun came up. I'm exhausted."

"Absolutely, I've got this. Get some rest." I open the door to leave and he calls for me again. "Have a good night, Annie."

"You too, Joe," I give him my most sincere smile, though my brain is telling me not to, since he could very well mix that into something I'd rather him not.

The entire drive home I'm worrying over Adam. Am I making the right choice in being with him? What's my family going to say? Will I still have a job when my dad figures out I'm sleeping with one of his clients? Shit! I don't want my dad to know I'm sleeping with anyone. Those thoughts plague my head until I get home and finally fall asleep, texting Gabby to be incredibly quiet when she gets home. Actually threatening bodily harm to her if she wakes me. I need my rest for Adam. Something tells me he'll be keeping me up all night.

***

Just Go   M. Dauphin

"Annaliese," his voice drums into my dream and I smile.

Sure, Adam. You can take over my dream any night.

"Annaliese," he whispers, then nips my ear. Jesus, that feels so real. So hot. "Wake up, Annaliese." His lips land right under my ear and I gasp, feeling the heat and wetness between my legs start to pool.

"Mmm," I moan as his hands push the hair out of my face.

"Hey, my Sweet," he says, this time in a sweeter tone than before.

"Hey," I mumble sleepily, then my eyes shoot open and see him. Fully clothed, propped up on his elbow, grinning at me.

"It's after eleven," he smiles and laughs at me as I'm still trying to wake up.

"That's... I laid down at five!" I sit up and look around at my dark room. Jesus, I must have been more tired than I thought. My stomach rumbles, reminding me I haven't eaten yet, and I groan. "No. I had things I needed to do tonight!" I moan and lay back down on the bed, throwing my arm over my eyes, not caring that Adam's currently seeing a not so flattering side of me.

"Eat would be one of them, I'm guessing." He chuckles when my stomach grumbles at me again, protesting the fact that I haven't fed it in almost twelve hours.

"That... and shower... and work... and... shit," I sigh, removing my arm to see him smiling down at me. "What're you smiling at?"

"You're cute when you're pissed."

"I'm not a morning person."

"Not a middle of the night person, either, apparently," he laughs and I shove at him, barely making him move. "Hey, don't shoot the messenger! Let's get you up and feed you."

"Wait," I sit up, staring at him. "How'd you get in here?"

"Your roommate let me in. I'm fairly certain she hates me."

"She doesn't hate you." I smile sleepily. "She just strongly dislikes the man she sees you as."

He raises his eyebrow at me and I laugh.

"You know, playboy deluxe. Never giving a shit what women want." I shrug and grin. "You did it to yourself, you know. She's just worried you're gonna crush me. That if you break me...." I trail off and his gaze locks with mine. "If you break me, I won't come back from it."

He sighs and rubs his jaw, then sits next to me again. Taking my hand in his, he stares at our connection as his thumb traces over my knuckles.

Silently thinking about my words, we sit there for what seems like hours before he speaks.

"Is that how you feel, still, Annaliese? Like I'm going to crush you? Like I'm too much for you?" His voice is tired, but his eyes are anything but. When they lock on mine I feel the pull in my heart that I've started to feel around him. A warming sensation that makes every nerve in my body on edge, almost tingling.

"No," I whisper. "I used to, before I got to know you. You're a good man, Adam. I was all wrong about you."

He isn't smiling, but he's not sad. He's serious. Is he telling me what I think he is?

Before I can get another word out, though, he leans in and kisses me. His lips are gentle, and I feel a slight tremble in his hands as they cup my face. His fingers thread through my hair and he pulls back just enough to rest his forehead on mine, taking a deep breath, then whispering so low I almost don't hear him.

"Please don't crush me," his voice is raw. Needy.

I kiss him, moving over to straddle him. His hands rest over my thighs and his lips push back, his tongue slipping past my lips, tasting me. I feel his arousal start to grow in between us and smile into the kiss, pushing myself down to grind on him. He moans and his hands come around to cup my ass, then he swiftly flips us onto the bed, so he's hovering over me. When he sits up on his knees, I watch in awe as he strips off his shirt. The muscles underneath rippling as he pulls his shirt and tie off and tosses them across the room. I laugh, since those two pieces of clothing probably cost more than my share of the rent, but it doesn't seem to bother him. He grins and my heart starts beating a little faster.

I reach for the button of his pants but he takes my hands in his gently.

"My speed tonight," his eyes are pleading with mine. "Please."

I take a breath and look into his dark eyes and see an emotion in his expression I've never seen on him before. My whole body starts to tingle as his lips land on my collarbone, moving up the side of my neck and nipping my ear.

"Just relax, Annaliese." He trails his tongue down my neck and chills course through my body. Gently, his hands reach the hem of my shirt and he removes it with skill I never have seen in another man. Shortly after that, he has my shorts off and I'm trembling with need. He stands and removes his pants, freeing his rather large erection. I grin, looking at his size, and sit up to meet him. Silently, he kisses me, then lays me back down, not letting my hands go where they want to go. I want this so bad. I need to feel him. Instead of entering me, he lowers his mouth to my nipples and nips gently, making me buck up from the sudden pain. He laughs deep and moves his hands down to my core.

"So wet already, Annaliese," he growls and brings his fingers up to taste my juices.

Jesus, that's hot.

I moan when his fingers find my core again, then push in gently.

"Dammit," he grunts. "I can't wait." He sits up and grabs a condom from my nightstand, applying it with ease.

Hovering over me, his muscular arms brace himself on each side of me and his eyes connect with mine. He looks like he's about to say something, but I bring my legs up and wrap them around his waist. Instead, he enters me fully in one sweet movement. Our eyes are still connected as he starts moving slowly. I'm not used to this kind of intimacy during sex. Never have I looked into someone's eyes and been able to tell their every emotion. There's so much fear, so much vulnerability in him.

"Shit," he hisses as his movements get harder. He closes his eyes and bows his head, resting it on my forehead. The emotions flowing out of him match what I'm feeling perfectly. So enamored with each other, so connected. He lifts his head and kisses me hard, then lowers himself to his elbows and gently nips my neck. "You taste like perfection," he hums as his lips find mine again. "Pure perfection," he says as his eyes connect with mine and I see more than lust in them.

No man has ever looked at me like Adam's looking at me right now. And all I can think is *please don't ruin this*. It's too soon for feelings like that, isn't it?

I feel my release building and know he can sense it too. His movements become more ragged and hard. His head lowers to the crook of my neck as he slams into me, releasing his orgasm at the same moment mine peaks and my world around me turns into a haze. I yell out, not caring who hears, and clutch on to him as my orgasm explodes and rips through me like never before.

"Dammit," I hear him hiss as he continues thrusting into me, beads of sweat forming on his shoulders. "Shit," he grunts.

I smile at him, too weak still from the mind-blowing orgasm to say anything. My toes are tingly, my arms are weak, and all I can do is smile. I'm fairly certain this man just stole the rest of my heart. The part that I was trying to keep locked up so when it is crushed, it's not my entire heart being crushed. Once his eyes connected with mine, though, and I saw the raw need for me in them, I knew. I knew he'd be the one that those walls break for.

Just then, there's banging on the wall by my TV and I hear Gabby screaming form the other side. "Quiet the fuck down, you two assholes! Some people have to work in the damn morning!" she yells and I laugh.

"Next time, we'll go to my place." He smiles and leans down to kiss me before pulling out and disposing of the condom.

When he returns to bed, I have to hide my shock. Sure, he came here for me, but he also is a man who has round the clock business meetings and early mornings. There's no way he's going to stay here tonight, is he?

"My Sweet," he whispers and pulls me into him. Wrapping his arms around my front, I can feel every hard inch of his body. We lay there for a while, lost in our thoughts.

He's staying to be with me.

"Why'd you do this?" I ask, tracing his tattoos on his arm with my fingertips. He adjusts his head and clears his throat.

"I was young," he replies. "I needed a way to be myself. A tattoo was the perfect solution."

"Why so many, though?"

"I like the feeling of them, for so many reasons. Each one means something, or was inked at a certain point in my life that meant something to me. It's a way of me showing the world that even though I may be rich and wear suits every damn day, I'm still a human that can think his own way." He sighs and shifts to kiss the top of my head.

"That's deep, Adam."

"I'm a deep man, my Sweet," he whispers.

We lay there in silence, just enjoying each other's company. I don't know when he falls asleep exactly, but I can tell he's sleeping by the rhythmic and even, breathing, and relaxed arm that's wrapped around me.

He's nothing like I was taught to believe. I was told he was a ruthless businessman, who fucks women all day, every day, never the same woman twice. I was told he didn't care about his ex-wife, and he cheated on her multiple times. All of this I was told, but what I'm learning from actually being with this man is that he's nothing like the man my father makes him out to be.

He's intense. He's loving. And he's all mine.

Chapter 14

Adam

It's been three weeks of enjoying time with Annaliese. I never thought that I'd feel something so strong for someone in such a short amount of time, but when love hits, it hits hard. I had to leave Annaliese's house early this morning due to a meeting with her father. One that I hate to have, but one that I know has to happen. Something's going on with him and I'm not one sit back and let my money dwindle away. The fights have been slowing down. Benton hasn't won but one fight in the last three weeks and I'm getting tired of not betting on fights. I miss the rush of winning, but I'm not stupid enough to throw away my own money. The phone calls and threats have slowed down to about three times a week, but they are still there, and the one time I did attempt to bet, Benton got the shit beaten out of him. Something's going on, and I plan on getting to the bottom of it.

It's almost seven when I get the call that he's waiting for me in the conference room. I take my time, letting him know that he no longer has any control over me. I have so much dirt on him, that I could have him turned in and arrested in no time flat. He needs to fear me. He needs to know that I hold all the cards here.

"Reese, hold all my calls for the rest of the day," I smile at her as I walk by her desk. I plan on taking a half day and surprising Annaliese at her work, maybe going out of the city for a while this evening. Something to help me feel connected to her. Being in this city sometimes makes me feel like it's swallowing me whole, like I'm not the man I want to be because of it.

The day that Annaliese and I went to my grandparents' farm was one of the most relaxing days I've had in a long time. I need to make it a point to get back there more often, and I need to make sure to bring her with me.

I open the door to the conference room and see Vick sitting at the table alone with a smirk on his face.

"Nice of you to meet with me, Adam." He stands and shakes my hand, which I grip tighter than typical. I'm not going to let him intimidate me this time.

"Glad you could make it, Vick."

"So what has you calling me in here on an off week?" He sits and smiles at me. It's a creepy smile and when he leans back in his chair, relaxed yet still powerful, I start to feel like maybe I don't hold all the cards.

"Ah…. I'm not certain how to tell you this, Vick, so I'm just going to come out and say it. Someone in your ring is rigging the fights against me. I've received threats, my fighter has received threats, and I've lost thousands because of these threats and rigs. I'm about to pull my man out of the ring and find somewhere else to enjoy my hobby if this isn't cleared." I lean forward and clasp my hands on the table in front of me, watching his stone-faced expression.

He doesn't look surprised at all.

"Adam, there's something you need to know about me," he starts, then sits up and leans forward, mimicking my position. "I'm a man of much more power than you think. Much more than you, son."

I narrow my eyes at him, wondering where this conversation is going.

"It's not about power, Vick," I growl. "It's about the safety of me and my fighter. It's about the money—bottom line."

He laughs and shakes his head at me. "I'm not stupid, Adam. You had one rule starting out. One measly rule that you couldn't even follow."

Shit.

"I'm certain you have to be mistaken, Vick."

"Really? Because," he pauses to pull out an envelope from his pocket and spread its contents across the table in front of me. "These prove me right." The slimy grin on his face does nothing to help the sinking feeling in my gut.

Spread out on the table in front of me are photos, all black and white, most taken from far away, and all of me and Annaliese.

Son of a bitch.

"Vick, what the hell?" He's been following me?

"I believe I should be asking you the same question, Adam. The one reason I brought you into this underground scene was because you promised to stay away from her. Now, three years later, and instead of staying true to your word, you go behind my back and do this?" His face is expressionless.

This meeting isn't going anywhere like I thought it was going to go. Why the hell would he have his daughter followed? It's either that, or he's having me followed. Neither of those sit well with me. I feel like I'm going to hurl from the nerves running through me. I came in here so confident that I could scare him into getting the threats to stop, but instead here I sit, staring at pictures of me and his daughter, when I did promise him that I'd never touch her. To be fair, at the time, I'd also never laid eyes on her. How could someone like me promise to never touch someone like her in all honesty? She's the most beautiful woman I've ever laid eyes on.

"Vick—" I start, but he holds his hand up to stop me from going any further

"You listen to me. You stay away from her or this whole business game of yours is over. I have enough dirt to take you, and everyone that works here, down. You stay away from her, Callahan, for everyone's safety." His face is stern, his hands still clapped in front of him

What the hell kind of dirt could he possibly have on this business? I could see having the fighting info on me, and all of the bets, but that's not enough to take down the company

"I'm not sure what you're talking about Vick," I growl, pissed that he's threatening me in my own offices.

"Oh, Adam. You're not that blind, are you? What do you think your ex-wife has been up to all this time? She's not just being a good little vice president, ignoring that fact that the man she was married to screwed her over in the divorce?" His smile is so slimy I can barely contain may rage for the man. The only thing holding me back is my curiosity for that statement. That, and my love and respect for his daughter.

"What the hell do you mean by that statement, Vick?" I feel like I'm on the edge of a cliff and one wrong thing is going to make me jump. From knowing that he found out about Annaliese and me, to learning of this new development, my nerves are about shot.

"You might want to ask her. I've never liked to be a rat." He stands and looks at me again before leaving. "And I mean what I said, Adam. Stay the hell away from her. Oh, and the fight tonight's been cancelled," he adds, then he walks out of the room, slamming the door behind him, leaving me in a complete daze.

What the hell just happened?

I give myself a minute to compose my emotions, things I didn't even know I had until Annaliese came into play, and then I walk out to Reese.

"Get me Benton James. Now." I growl, then walk into my office and slam the door, then darken all the glass around me. This whole day is going to shit, and it all started off so promising.

Last night with Annaliese was amazing. I almost told her I loved her before I made love to her, but the words got stuck. I saw the fear in her eyes, like she knew it was coming. I don't want to see fear in her eyes when I tell her, but I will tell her. It's insane, but I know already she's the girl for me. She makes me feel things I never thought I'd be able to feel after my divorce. Things that I didn't think I wanted to feel, and now I couldn't imagine a life without her.

Minutes later, the door opens and Benton walks in without knocking.

"No chicks this week, A team. What gives?" Benton plops down on my office couch like he owns the place. I mean, he might own a portion of it, but not this office.

"Just haven't felt the need," I shrug and make myself look busy. These last three weeks with Annaliese have been so fucking amazing, and I want to scream to the world that she's my girl, but she wants to keep things on the down low until she has a chance to talk to her father. Knowing now what I do, though, I'm not sure what the hell I'm going to do. I need her, but I need this business too.

"Right," Benton narrows his eyes at me. "Got something ya wanna tell me." He crosses his arms and gives me a look like he knows what's up, but I can't tell him. I press my lips together and shake my head.

"Nope," I clip. "Nothing, other than the fight tonight's being cancelled."

"What the fuck, man? What's going on with him?" He leans forward and rests his arms on his knees. "Dude's gone off the deep end," he says shaking his head.

"You don't need the money still, do you? I thought the adoption was almost finalized."

"It is, but I wasn't planning on stopping 'til the baby comes. That gives me at least two more weeks."

"Well, looks like you might just be going into early retirement," I laugh at his face and stand from my chair. "Look, Vick's going through some shit right now. Don't worry yourself about it." I'll tell him if it comes down to it, but he's got enough on his plate right now to worry about the company.

"He threatened you, A," he growls and stands.

"Yeah... about that. Have you heard from Dianne lately?" I ask, feeling him out.

"Nope. She's been working out of our Aurora offices lately, so I haven't seen her. Good riddance," he scoffs then looks at me. "Why? What's up?"

"Nothing really, just curious how her projects are coming." I lie. I need to talk to her, and as much as I don't want to, it seems to be the only way to figure out what's going on.

"Great. Then I'm out, dude, I've got shit to do today. Some of us actually work during the day," he glances at me again. "What're you gonna do about Vick, then?"

"I'll take care of Vick, you just get that wife ready for the baby. I hear sex stops once you have a kid. Good luck with that, man."

"Ha! And with your lack of sex lately, we're both going to be horny old men pretty soon."

"Very funny. Now get out, I have a meeting."

He stands to leave and stops at the door. "Oh, I meant to tell you. The law firm is happy with their recent choice of assistants. They are thinking of moving her up to practicing lawyer once the test is passed and expanding their offices." He smiles, knowing full well that was his deal originally, so that means more money in his pocket.

"Great, B. That's good news. Now leave."

He salutes me with a grin, and closes the office door behind him.

I sit back down at my desk, looking around, not able to focus on anything but the scene from last night playing through my head. Annaliese is a force to be reckoned with in the bedroom. She brought me things last night, let me do things to her that no other women have let me do to them. It was pure ecstasy, the feeling of filling her ass, hearing her moans and screams when she came around me. Shit. I'm getting hard just thinking about it. I look at the clock, and by now she should be on her way to work, so I decide to shoot her a text.

ME: Morning my Sweet ;)

The winky face conversation has come up a few times now. I actually told her about the first time she sent me one, and now she won't let me live it down, so I leave them everywhere I can. I know it makes her laugh, and I like to make her laugh.

SWEET: Hey babe. How's ur day?

ME: Boring without you.

SWEET: I know the feeling. We still on for tonight? ;)

ME: Absolutely. I'll see you after work.

SWEET: XOXO

I smile reading her response. My fingers itch to reply with those three words I've been waiting so long to say, but I don't allow them to type it. It's about damn time I tell her just exactly how I feel. I just want to show the world how amazing my girl is, but now I need to get this shit with her dad figured out before anything. How I'm going to do this without telling her about it is going to be tricky. I never informed her about the fighting because rules are rules: don't ever talk about it outside the fight ring. Obviously she didn't know, or else that night she picked me up from the fight she wouldn't have asked about it. I can't tell her about the threats from her dad, because she would eventually find out about the fights, and the betting, and a part of me is worried that if she knows about all of that she won't stay with me.

I've lied to her. I've kept things from her. I don't want to do that anymore, but I'm not sure how to fix this without hurting her.

I know where to start, though. Once I figure out what Vick meant about Dianne, I can start trying to figure out why he seems hell bent on no one ever being with his daughter. One step at a time. Picking up the receiver, I call over to the Aurora office myself to try and get to the bottom of whatever's going on with Dianne.

"Carson and Lewis, this is Audra," the friendly voice answers. I remember hiring her a few years back and smile. I love a good company with low turnover.

"Audra, Adam Callahan here. I need to speak with Dianne, immediately."

"Mr. Callahan, I... uh...." she stutters.

"Audra, is everything okay?" I ask, suddenly wishing I would have made a visit in person. I can read people so much better in person rather than over the phone.

"Yes. Fine, sorry. I'll go get Dianne. I mean... um... Ms. Barkers." She immediately clicks me to hold and I sit, listening to the terrible waiting music they have on loop. Making a mental note to update the company's hold music, I wait for no longer than a minute before Dianne's voice comes through the phone, making my anger rise just from hearing her.

Typically, Dianne and I get through a week without any phone calls to another. It's such a big company, that emails are the best way to discuss topics, so that's just what we do. I wish she'd just leave the company, but she won't do that just to spite me.

"Yes, Adam?" she sighs into the receiver, obviously pissed that I actually picked up the phone to call her. I'm not too thrilled about it either.

"Dianne," I greet then get down to business. "I have on good authority that you're up to something that could ruin the business. Now either you inform me what's going on, or I hire an investigator and take you to court. Your choice," I growl. Just saying it out loud is absurd. She's smarter than to pull something that would damage her baby, no matter how much she hates me.

"Oh, Jesus, Adam." She curses again then I hear the hold music again without any warning. She's never been a very personable woman. "Okay, I'm back. Listen, it's nothing you need to worry about," she tells me in the same voice she had when she told me not to worry that she was cheating on me. My stomach feels sick and I'm about to throw the damn phone across the room.

"What's going on, Dianne?" I'm close to screaming at her, but that wouldn't get me anywhere at this point, so I hold it back.

"I just... Adam you drained me!" I hear the tears in her voice and press my fingers on the bridge of my nose, holding back my anger for her. "I have all these bills... and all the payments I have to make. It was just a little bit, and I plan on paying it back," she whines into the phone. My ears start to ring and I fight through the rage building inside of me.

"How much?" I growl.

"Uhhh... I.... Ummm...." she stutters.

"How much?!?" I scream at her, losing all control over my emotions.

"A mil," she whispers and I see red. Slamming my fist on my desk, I lose all sort of control of my composure.

"You did what?!? You took a million fucking dollars, Dianne?!?"

"Adam, you ruined me!" she cries. I have no remorse for pulling the pre-nup on her though. I didn't ruin her. She did that herself. It's not my fault she didn't keep a copy of it, and totally forgot to tell her lawyer about it. It's not my fault I conveniently kept it hidden until the final signing of the divorce papers.

"Dianne, you were left with a hundred grand. A hundred grand! How do you spend all of that in only a few months' time? It's not even been a goddamned year!" I never thought I could feel this much rage, but at this point in my week, I'm certain everything I ever thought is a joke.

"My... my car. The house. My credit cards." She hiccups and I know she's forcing the tears. I've seen it a million times before with her. This is all just a show.

"You didn't adjust your living style at all, did you?" I growl.

"I didn't think you'd actually cut me off! I had to do something. They were going take my car, Adam!"

Jesus Christ.

"You're out of the company, Dianne. Thanks for making this massive mess for me to clean up. I'll have my lawyer contact yours about the lawsuit," I growl. I hear her start to beg me as I hang up the receiver, but I don't stay on the line to hear her out. She's had enough chances.

"Reese," I say into the intercom. "Please come into my office when you get a chance."

Not a minute later, she's standing in my doorway, iPad in hand, waiting for notes.

"I need you to call security over to the Aurora offices. Dianne no longer works with this company. Then I need you to contact Benton and get him in here ASAP."

"Got it. Anything else?"

"Yeah, send flowers to Annaliese Ryder's apartment with a note that says 'Sorry I couldn't see you tonight. Miss you." She gives me a funny look, then grins and nods.

"Great, consider it all done." She's the only person I'd ever consider having do my dirty work, since there's never any questions that come out of her.

"Thank you, Reese," I say as she shuts the door.

Now to figure out why Annaliese's dad is so against her being with me.

What the hell is he up to?

Just Go   M. Dauphin

Chapter 15

Annaliese

"Hello," I huff into my phone, carrying groceries up the stairs. Our elevator's been broken all week, and it isn't getting any cooler as summer rages on and our AC is way too weak to keep our old building cool.

"Hi, may I speak with Annaliese Ryder, please?"

"Yes, this is she," I say.

"Hi, this is Angela Warden from Allmeyer Middle school in St. Louis. I'm calling regarding an opening we have available in one of our fourth grade classrooms."

"Oh, great."

Shit, why now?

"Yes, hi. How can I help you?" I try not to sigh into the phone while my brain attempts to remember even applying for a job so far away.

"Ms. Ryder, we've taken the steps already and spoken to your professors from DePaul. They all had wonderful things to say about your professionalism and behavior with the students and teachers you've worked for." She pauses and I feel my heart beat escalating.

Is this really happening? Am I about to be offered a real teaching position?

"Ms. Ryder, I know you are located in Chicago at the moment; however, we are quite desperate, and have heard wonderful things about you. The school year starts in a week, and we'd love to set up a phone interview with you tomorrow to see if you are a good fit for the current position we have available."

"Yes… yes, absolutely." I'm trying to sound a little upbeat about this, but it's hard to find any excitement over this news

This is what I've been waiting for. Why am I not as excited as I should be, though? I should be over the moon excited that I'm finally getting my break. I could finally get out of my dad's office and get into a career that I love. A career that I went to school for. A career I want to retire in.

I should be stoked, but I can't help but feel a sinking feeling in my gut.

"Great, how's four work? I will have another administrator on the line for the interview as well."

Another administrator. A real phone interview. For a real school. I should be excited for this, but it's so far away. From everything.

From everyone.

"Yeah... yes. That's great. I'll talk to you then." I hang up the phone and stand there, groceries sitting on the floor in the hallway of my dingy apartment.

Looking around, I sigh and take in everything that I've been overlooking since we moved in. The peeling paint, the burned out light bulbs that never get changed. Even the smell isn't very welcoming. My family wasn't happy that I moved in here, but I didn't care at the time. Now, seeing how the other side lives, seeing how I could have been living right now if I didn't force my father's influence out of my life. I was so convinced that I could make it on my own, and I proved them right, even if it meant living in this apartment, shopping at Target instead of Macy's, and hitting clearance wherever I can.

"Hey, whore, you waiting for the food to spoil?" Gabby's voice brings me out of my thoughts.

I look up and smile, cocking my head at her. "Take these, bitch," I say handing her a bag. We walk inside and she silently starts putting away the groceries. About a minute into emptying the bags, she stops and looks at me, hands on her hips, head cocked and eyebrow raised.

"So, you ever gonna tell me what's got your mind all sorts of out of it today? Too much sex with hotness making your brain useless?" She grins and I can't help but laugh.

Her nickname for him is *hotness*, but he hates it. The fact that he hates it has made her more open about using it in front of him. The two get along fine, I guess, but she still doesn't trust him. Gab has a tough time trusting many people, though, so it's not surprising he hasn't gained her full trust yet. The fact that she can stand him at all is still surprising to me. Maybe working at such a big law firm has helped get her used to being around arrogant pricks.

Not that I'm calling Adam a prick, but he can get a little arrogant at times.

Like yesterday when he told me I needed to just quit the job I'm at and live at his house if I was so miserable in that office. Well yeah, I'm miserable, and the employee situation hasn't gotten any better since my first day, but I'm also making my own way, which is huge for me. I'd rather not have to rely on someone else for an allowance, and become the needy stay at home girlfriend. Jeez, who even does that?

"Hello? Annie?" I blink a few times and realize I've been staring at the block of cheese in my hand this whole time. Gabby's staring at me like I'm insane and all I can do is smile weakly as I place the cheese in the fridge and grab more items to put away. "Oh my

God, you love him," she gasps which makes me fumble and almost drop the yogurt in my hand.

I stand up straight and glare at her. "Excuse me?" What would make her say that?

Am I that easy to read?

"You've been daydream central lately, Annie. Hell, you just stopped putting the cheese away and stared at it like it was going to give you your next big orgasm. You can't stop thinking about him, Annie. I see it. He's always here or you're always at his place. The smile hasn't left your face since you guys got together, and you 're not bitching about your job as much as you were the first week now that you've got him to keep you company. I see it… you love him," she says, then grins at me and continues putting away the groceries.

So what if I can't stop thinking about him. So what if every time I think about him, my heart flutters and my face turns up into a goofy grin. So what if I've already fallen completely head over heels with him in less than a month. He's not ready for that, and I'm about to get a job five hours away from him.

"Well, that's it." I sigh and toss the reusable shopping bags into the pantry.

"So you're not gonna talk about it?" Gab clips.

"I'm not sure what you want me to say, Gabby," I look at her and see that she's upset with me. I know she wants me to talk, but I can't say the words out loud. If he loves me, he's not the type of man that would hold something like that back, and I'm not going to be the girl that declares her love for a man just to be pushed away.

"I just want you to be happy, Annie. That's all."

"Well," I start to tell her about my interview, when my phone rings. "Sorry, it's my dad." She shakes her head and slaps my ass on the way to her room.

"Hey, Daddy," I answer cheerfully. No reason to let him in on how down about things I am.

"Hey, baby girl. How are you today?" He sounds stressed about something but I've never asked before so I'm not about to start now.

"I'm okay. What's up?" I sit on the couch and look out our picture window to the city skyline. I love this city, and I'd rather not have to leave, but if I can't find a job here, I don't really have a choice.

"Listen, I need you to do a run with Joe tomorrow night. There's some sketchy areas he's listed for, and I'd rather not have him alone." What?

"Why?" This makes no sense.

"Don't question me, Annaliese. I'm your boss, and I'm telling you to do a ride-along tomorrow," he growls at me, and my mood suddenly changes. Why do I get the feeling he really doesn't need me to do this as much as he wants me to for some reason?

"Fine," I sigh. "I'll be there."

"Good girl." With that he hangs up and leaves me staring at my phone in a stupor.

What the hell just happened? There's no reason that I should be needing to ride along with anyone tomorrow night, but apparently my father has other feelings on it.

"Gabby!" I yell, storming into her room. She's sitting on her bed texting someone and when I walk in, she quickly puts the phone away and looks up at me, smiling.

"What's up?"

"I need to bitch," I say plopping down on her bed. "I feel like nothing's in my control anymore, Gab. I got an interview for a teaching position in St. Louis." I look at her and her eyes grow wide.

"That's... I didn't know you wanted to leave," she whispers and I feel my heart breaking.

I don't want to leave, that's the thing.

"Gabby, I never applied for it. I wouldn't ever apply to a school that far away. School starts next week and they are apparently desperate, so they called and already talked with my professors, and really seemed interested. It's so weird...." I trail off, wondering why my dad would send me out of the city just for a teaching job. I'm doing a good job at the company, even if I hate it every moment I'm there. He wouldn't send me away without other motives.

"Maybe he just wants to see you happy, like all of us that care for you," she says then gives me a weak smile.

"I am happy though," I sigh and lay back on her pillow. "I just hate my job." I laugh and she follows. "I don't know why he'd send me so far away. If he wanted me to get a teaching job so badly, I feel like he'd try in the city first or somewhere in the suburbs, not five hours away in a city where I know no one."

"I don't know, Annie. Maybe you should talk to him." She shrugs and gets off the bed. "Now get up, I'm about to pass out if we stay on that bed any longer. Time for me to tell you all about the new guy I met today." She grins and walks out to the kitchen. I smile and sigh, figuring the conversation with my dad can wait. Hopefully.

As I walk into the kitchen, there's a knock on the door.

"Weird," Gab says walking to the door. I stay behind in the kitchen, getting out a bottle wine and some crackers and cheese to munch on. We both skipped dinner, but it's already too late for a full meal so this will have to do. When she returns, my eyes fly open and jaw drops.

"What the shit is that?" I say, astounded at the outrageous arrangement of flowers she's carrying in. I hear her laughing, but I can't see her face from the massive floral mess she's carrying.

"Jesus, Annie." She laughs and I shake my head.

"You know I hate that name, Gab. And I've heard it way too many times tonight." She sets the flowers on the counter and laughs then plucks the card from the flowers before I'm able to read it.

"My dearest Sweet," she says and I smile. "I wish I could see you tonight, as I miss everything about you, but something came up that will keep me in the office all night. I miss you. Love, Adam." Her eyebrows raise and she smiles at me. "Love?"

"Stop. Give me that!" I snatch the card out of her hand. It's typed, meaning he didn't really write it. "Gab, this was probably done by his assistant. Anyway, just because it's signed 'love' doesn't mean anything," I say, not wanting to believe my own words.

"Alright," she says skeptically. "I still think you're in denial of your feelings towards him. Life's too short, Annie." She grins and takes a bite of cheese.

All I can do is stick my tongue out at her, like a spoiled child, because she's right. I'm in denial of my true feelings because no matter how much he tells me to trust him, I still am scared that I'll end up the one being hurt. The flowers are beautiful, though, and he is thinking about me. I pull out my phone and send him a quick text, sitting down on the couch to relax for a bit before I get my brain ready for the interview tomorrow.

ME: Thank you. They're beautiful. Tell Reese she did well.

I add in the final part, letting him know that I know he didn't do this all on his own. Shortly after, I get a text back from him.

ADAM: In meeting. I'm sure she'll be flattered. ;)

I laugh, then decide to mess with him.

ME: A meeting, huh? I'm all alone...

ADAM: Don't do this, Annaliese.

I smile to myself, able to hear the growl in his tone. This could be fun. Instead of replying, I stretch my bare legs out across the couch and snap a picture of them, making sure the lighting makes them look perfect.

ME: Miss you....

I hit send and smile, hoping that makes his meeting a little more bearable. Not thirty seconds passes and I get another text.

ADAM: Jesus...I can't wait to be between those legs again, my Sweet.

ME: Oh yeah?

I quickly snap a photo a little higher, almost showing him what he wants to see. Grinning, I send it and wait for a response. Just playing like this has me hot and wet for him, and I haven't even heard his voice yet. It's not long before my phone dings again.

ADAM: You're killing me, Annaliese. I'm so hard for you that I won't be able to stand up when this meeting ends.

I grin and send him one a little higher, making sure he sees my fingers pushing aside my shorts and playing with the edge of my panties.

ADAM: Jesus...Touch yourself for me.

I smile and move my fingers under my panties, feeling the wetness that this conversation has created. I moan then close my eyes, playing with my folds while imagining it's his hand. My phone buzzes next to me and I read the screen in a lustful haze.

ADAM: Now stop.

God, how does he do that? I pull my fingers out as another text comes through.

ADAM: I want all of your pleasure. After tonight, you won't tease me like this again. No release until it's by my hand. Understood?

ME: Yes sir.

I grunt and attempt to pout, but just reading the final text of his has me hot all over again, and not getting the release I need is really going to put me off my game tomorrow.

ADAM: Mmm...I like that. Go to bed, my Sweet. XOXO

I read the text and smile.

If I can't get an 'I love you' out of him, the next best is the xoxo, I guess.

But I do really want those three words, even if I can't admit it out loud yet.

***

The next morning I dress for work slowly and head into the office. I didn't get much sleep last night with the lack of release that I desperately wanted but didn't give myself. I want to please him, and doing what he tells me to, sexually, pleases him. Neither late nor early, I walk in right on time for the crazy day to start. Phone calls, meetings, and scheduling conflicts fill my morning, and before I know it, it's lunchtime and I'm starving. As if he reads my mind, Joe knocks on my office door and lets himself in.

"Hey there," he says and smiles as I smile back genuinely. He's been huge in helping my group work together. They may not all like me, but they all like and respect Joe. He's my right hand man, and I couldn't be happier about it. If I have to hate my daily job, I may as well enjoy at least one of the people I work with.

The fact that he's beautiful to look at makes it easier too.

"Hi, Joe, what's up?" He sits and places a bag of food in front of me.

"Oh God, Chinese again, Joe?" I take in the aroma and moan.

"Wow, had I known it would've gotten that type of reaction, I'd bring it more often." The lopsided grin he gives me makes me feel more for him than I should. I'm with Adam now. I shouldn't feel things for other men.

"Well, I will have to run a little extra this week, but I'll forgive you since you brought my favorite."

He smiles and we dig in, eating faster than normal since the day's been so hectic. Making small talk, we make it through lunch with no other awkward topics brought up like my moaning.

"Oh hey," I say as he stands to walk out of my office and get back to work. "My dad wants me riding with you tonight."

The look on his face says he wasn't privy to that notice.

"Are you sure he said me? And not another driver... maybe John?" He looks confused and I can't help but wonder why he would care if I drove along with him. It was fun last time.

"Nope, he specifically said you," I say then shrug.

He runs his hands through his hair and sighs.

"Alright. Be here at nine. Front door. And don't wear anything too revealing. Tonight's a different crowd than last time, Annaliese." His eyes narrow at me and he shakes his head then silently leaves my office.

Just Go   M. Dauphin

What the hell was that about?

Chapter 16

Adam

The game she played last night had me hard all night for her. I tried rubbing one out in the shower while picturing Annaliese the entire time. Even after I finished, my dick still wouldn't stand down. It's like my cock is holding out for the real deal—Anna's sweet pussy.

Me too, boy.

I'm still reeling from the deal with Dianne. The board thinks she's going to retaliate, and try to hurt the company in other ways. They aren't a fan of how I dealt with her, but I couldn't care less. She needed to go, and with what she was doing, the faster the better before she had a chance to take more money. I've been on the phone with investors and some of the businesses that she was looking over, assuring them that it won't affect them at all. What they don't need to know is that the money to replenish those funds she took from is coming out of my pocket until we figure all of this out, so that pisses me off even more. I've got enough to cover it, but it shouldn't have happened at all. All because she's a selfish bitch.

"Hey, man," Benton barges in, yet again, like he owns the place.

"Dude, don't you know how to knock?" I growl, not bothering to look up at him.

"Man, this whole 'not getting laid' thing is making you an asshole." He laughs and sits on the couch. "Got a call this morning. The baby was born this morning," he says, smiling wider than I've ever seen.

"Shit, B... that's fantastic!" It really is too. They've been through hell and back just to try to start a family. He deserves something good.

"Thanks.... Thanks. I'm so... I just...." he trails off and smiles at me. "It's everything I've ever wanted."

I smile and nod, not knowing exactly how he feels, but I have sort of the same feelings for Annaliese. She's everything to me.

"So when is it official? Do you get to take her home from the hospital?"

"Yeah. She's a couple weeks early so they wanna check her out a couple days just to make sure she's healthy, but so far so good." The smile won't leave his face, and it's actually helping me get out of my funk.

"You ready for this? The diapers, the poop, the crying?"

"Shit yeah, man, I've been ready," Benton sighs and shakes his head. "It's so unbelievable." He looks at me and his smile fades. "Thanks, man. I know you didn't need to do what you did."

"Anything for you two. You and Carly deserve this," I say honestly.

My phone rings just then, putting our conversation on hold.

"Yes," I grind out.

"Mr. Callahan. Mr. Ryder is on the phone for you."

"Send him my way." I sigh and wait for her to move him to my line.

"Vick's on the phone," I tell Benton as I wait for the phone to beep. When it does, his ears perk up and he leans forward to hear my conversation. I hit the speaker button and hold my finger to my lips, signaling to B to stay quiet.

"Vick. How can I help you?" I say as nicely as I can.

"Tonight. Bring your boy. Same time, same place."

"That's no notice at all, Vick. I'm not sure...." I pause while I see Benton's face light up. He starts nodding and mouths "one last time" at me. "Alright," I sigh. "We'll see you tonight."

"I'm putting you down for your usual 2?" Vick asks.

"I'm not sure, Vick. Who's he fighting?"

"Elliot Sangra, he's fought him before and won both times."

Benton nods and smiles.

"We're in. See you tonight."

I hang up and look strangely at Benton.

"You sure about this, B? Your baby was just born today."

"I know, and I know after we bring her home, Carly's not going to have me going out late at night to these fights. This is my last chance, man. I gotta do this. I'm doing this."

"She's not gonna be happy with you," I warn.

"I'll deal with my wife, Adam. You just get whoever it is that's messed with your head straightened out before your balls are blue for life." He laughs and stands. "See ya tonight." He raises his eyebrows and slips out the door quietly.

The rest of the day I spend taking notes on different employees that would be able to step in to fill Dianne's shoes. As the day goes by, my attitude towards her betrayal changes from hate to pity. She never had a chance. There are plenty of employees here that could easily fill her shoes, which makes me positive I'll find a good fit by the end of the week.

My cell phone rings at about five, and I smile when I see the photo I snapped of Annaliese while she was sleeping pop up on my screen.

"Hey, beautiful," I say, smiling.

"Hey. Uh... What're you up to right now?" She sounds worried, which immediately puts me on high alert.

"What's wrong, Annaliese?"

"Nothing's... just... Can I stop by? Are you home?"

Shit. Why's she being so weird?

"No, I'm still at work. Talk to me, Annaliese. Please," I say, begging for her to open up to me. I don't like this feeling that I can't help her, and I can't... not until she opens up to me.

"Adam, I'm sorry... I can't right now. I have work to do. Shit, I didn't want to do this over the phone," she whispers the final part and I hear her take a deep breath.

"You're scaring me, Annaliese," I growl.

"I'm sorry. I just... Adam, I had an interview today," she says, void of all emotion.

"That's great!" Why would she be worried about telling me this? "For what school?"

"Uh... Elmhurst Middle School...." She trails off so I push on.

"Where's that? I haven't heard of it." That's not saying much, though, since I know nothing about grade schools in our area.

"Um... St. Louis," she whispers the last part, but I still hear it enough to make my heart start racing.

St. Louis?!? That's... that's five hours away from me! *That's so fucking... no!*

"Oh," I manage, trying not to let her know how much I hate the idea of her not being in the same city as me. "How'd it go?" I ask, barely able to form the words.

"Um. Great?"

"Uh huh...." is all I'm able to get out. I'm fuming right now that she didn't tell me about this.

"Adam, they offered me the job." She sighs and I see red. Fucking red.

"Oh?"

"And the school year starts next week."

Mother. Fucker.

"Right. So... congratulations, I guess," I say, trying not to sound as pissed as I feel. "When do you move?" I'm so mad she didn't tell me about the possibility of her leaving me. I thought she was here for good. I thought Chicago was her home. Why would she take a job so far away from all of her family and friends? It's just teaching. I could have found her a job in the city had she asked. She didn't ask though, which means she doesn't want my help, which means she doesn't want me in her life as much as I thought she did. Right?

"I haven't given them an answer yet, Adam." She sounds tired and it breaks my heart to hear her like this. Like she's trying not to be happy.

"What're you waiting for? It's what you want, right?" I practically growl.

I'm so pissed that I let myself fall in love with her.

All so she could break me.

"I... uh... I'm not sure," she stammers and I laugh harshly in her ear. "Adam, I never applied for this job. It kind of just fell in my lap last minute." Right, like I believe that. Schools don't hire people that don't seek them out.

"You know what, Annaliese? This week has been shit. Complete shit. Your fucking father stopping us from being more than we are and threatening everything I love, my vice president screwing me over, and now you leaving me for a fucking job I could have gotten you in the city. Fuck all of this, Annaliese. If you want to leave everything you have here, just go. No one's stopping you," I spit at her. It's probably the worst thing I could've said to her in that moment. I wanted to be begging her to stay, but I'm so pissed I can't even see straight right now.

I should've told her I love her. I should've told her I don't want her to leave. I should've said everything I've wanted to tell her for weeks now. Instead, I tell her words that will hurt her enough to not have to choose between me and a career she's been working towards her whole life.

"What are you talking about, Adam? What does my father have to do with this?" Her voice is barely a whisper.

I know I've ruined her.

Good, because she fucking destroyed me.

"Go, Annaliese. It's what you want," I grind out, not answering her question, then looking down at my phone right before throwing it across the room and watching it shatter on the glass wall. I stand, looking around my office, and nothing looks normal. I'm in a haze of anger, and I'm not sure how to deal with this.

"Everything okay, Adam?" Reese's head pops in the door then her eyes get wide at the sight of me. I'm breathing heavy, the phone is shattered and laying on the floor next to my door, and I'm sure my face is bright red. At least I feel like it is. I feel like I could spit fire I'm so mad. I look at her and don't move.

"No. Cancel everything today, I say then storm out of my office and head to my car. Reese calls out after me, but I choose to ignore her, afraid I may say something I regret to her. I can't lose her today, too.

I know exactly who did this. And I'm going to be teaching him a little lesson tonight on who not to fuck with in this city.

Men from New York always think they can waltz into Chicago and take over our city. Vick Ryder is no different, but he's about to learn a very hard lesson.

"Call Benton," I say to my car as I start it up. After three rings he picks up.

"What?" he growls, sounding about as pissed as I am.

"I'm guessing she didn't take it well?"

"No. She got in her car and sped off. I'm not certain what the fuck she's doing, but I have to fight tonight."

"Good, because I need you there for some extracurricular activity."

I then proceed to confide in him everything that's been happening with Annaliese.

Absolutely everything.

And by the time I'm done, he's ready to beat down Vick's ass all by himself.

Chapter 17

Annaliese

"You didn't listen to me, Annie," Joe sighs as I get in the car. He's glaring at me like I shouldn't be here and I'm still not certain why.

"Excuse me? I was here at quarter 'til just so I wouldn't make you run late," I say looking at him like he's crazy.

"Not to be blunt, but I can see your fucking bra through your shirt. Jesus," he sighs and shakes his head. "Don't get out of the car tonight and you should be fine. We don't have time for this. We're going to be late."

Great, I've already managed to piss him off, and I have to now spend the next few hours in the car with a man who's pissed at me, not able to get out for fear of... something. I don't even know why tonight is any different than the other night I drove with him. I looked over the maps and it's nothing out of the ordinary.

At least that's what I think at the first pick up, when we pick up two men in business pants and button down shirts. Good looking men, chiseled jaw, nice cut hair. Men wearing wedding bands but looking at me in the mirror like I am fresh meat.

"Who's the chick, Joe?"

"Ah... Vick's daughter," he chose to answer, which pisses me off. I shake my head and stay silent, watching the men in the backseat stare at me the whole ride.

The minute we start heading north, I know something's not right about the schedule. Why's he going this direction?

"Joe—" I start but he cuts me off quickly.

"No. Just ride along, Annie. Please, for the love of God, don't ask any questions. I'm not sure what he was thinking having you here tonight, but just... don't ask any questions," he grinds out, hands gripping the wheel like it's a lifeline. He won't look at me anymore and I'm getting a bad feeling in my gut about this.

I've already been sick for hours since Adam was so harsh with me. I'm not taking the job. I already decided that before our phone call, but I wanted to get a feel for it from him. Apparently he wanted to jump to conclusions, though, and not let me talk. I just need to talk to him in person, and I plan on doing that as soon as I get off tonight, no matter how late this night runs. I need him to understand I don't want to leave him, and from today's conversation, he sounded more hurt than anything. Sure he was mean, but I get it. I'd be upset too if he pulled something big like that on me. We promised the truth—no lies, nothing hidden, and open books. And I didn't give that to him.

Pulling up to our destination, I look around and it all looks very familiar. This is the building that we picked Adam up at the night he called Joe for a ride. My breath quickens and pulse speeds up. I look over at Joe, panicked that I'm really not supposed to be here, and he lays a hand on my knee. The warmth that spreads over my body soothes me.

"You're fine, Annie," he whispers. "Just stay in the car." His eyes pin mine and all I can do is nod my head. Joe doesn't know about the fight Adam and I had. He doesn't know about the job offer in St. Louis.

I watch as Joe opens the door for the two men in the backseat, and hear them tell me that they'd see me later before closing the door. Joe knocks on the front door of the old warehouse building and looks around nervously as the three men wait. The door cracks open and Joe leans in to say something to the person on the inside. I have a bad feeling about all of this so I stay put in the locked car. The door closes, just to be opened a second later, just enough for the two men to slide quickly inside. Joe looks around then jogs back to the car. He gets in, buckles up, starts the car, and drives off. All without saying a word to me.

"So... where to next?"

He sighs and looks over at me. His hand comes across the car to mine and he grasps it.

"I can take you home, Annie. Tonight's... it's gonna be like what you just watched. All night. And the later it gets, the rowdier they get."

"Orders from the boss. I stay." That, and I really do want to find out just what this operation is.

The next hour goes exactly as the first drop had been. Each time Joe reassured me that everything would be fine, each time the strange behavior was recorded, and each time he sped away from the building before anyone could see us.

I have to see what's in there.

After making a drop of three older men, ones that stared at me blatantly the entire drive to the warehouse, I knew something was up. All men. All wealthy. All being dropped off in the same spot. And all the while, the books back at Ryder Inc. state that the cars tonight are driving people to and from multiple functions. Someone's messing with someone, and my dad's going to be pissed.

"Where are we going?" I ask as Joe moves the car to a nearby empty lot and puts it in park. He sighs and lays his head back on the seat. His hand reaches over and rests on my knee, a movement that gets me warm in areas that I shouldn't be warm in when with him.

"You know I'd do anything for you, Annie. This... this isn't what it looks like."

"What does it look like, Joe? Please, enlighten me." I'm starting to get irritated that all this shit's being hidden from me.

"I know you're thinking that it's something terrible, but it's not."

"Then why can't I get out of the car? Why can't I see what's on the other side of that door, Joe? And why do I get the suspicion this is all being hidden from my father?!" I'm pissed now, and the anger keeps getting worse the longer I sit here.

"Annie, I can't—"

"Fuck that, Joe! You've been keeping this from me and I'm not doing this anymore."

I open the car door as quickly as I can and book it across the parking lot. Running every day helps me get to my destination faster than Joe can, but it doesn't help me figure out how to get into the building. I hear him coming up from behind me, but don't expect his next move. His hands come around my shoulders, pushing me hard against the side of the building. His body is hard against mine, and his breathing in my ear is turning me on in a frantic time when I should be scared of this man.

"What the fuck are you doing, Annie," Joe growls in my ear, not letting loose of me.

"I'm trying to figure out what the hell is going on, Joe. Since no one here is going to tell me anything, I plan on finding out myself." I try to fight my way out of his grip but it's to no avail.

"What the fuck's going on?!?" I hear a familiar voice yell, but the way Joe has my head pushed to the wall, I can't turn to see who's witnessing our struggle.

"Go. I've got this," Joe grinds out, obviously pissed that he's been caught.

That makes two of us.

"Let her go," the voice says, closer now. I know that voice. "I said let her go!" he yells, then a cool burst of air hits my back and the pressure is gone. Instead of sticking around to see the shit get beaten out of Joe, I do the only other thing I know how to do. I run.

I run until the streets don't look familiar. Until the dark alleys are hauntingly scary. I run until I'm all alone.

Or so I think.

When I hear the footsteps behind me, I gasp and turn, looking into the eyes of a man that have been haunting me for weeks.

"Adam," I whisper, more like a question than anything, then I run to him and throw myself into his arms. I'm not sure if it's the adrenaline or the fact that

I already miss him so much, but I can't think of any other place I'd rather be right now. His arms come around me and he squeezes like he never wants to let go.

Please don't let go, Adam.

"Annaliese, what were you doing back there?" he whispers into my hair, a muffled sigh escaping his lips.

"I... I have to know, Adam. And...." I pull back and look at him. He's dressed in his suit and tie. The same outfit he left for work in this morning. "What the hell were you doing there?" I ask, it suddenly dawning on me that he was inside the building we had been dropping clients off at all night. "What the fuck?!?" I yell and storm away from him, pissed that he's in on this too.

"Stop, Annaliese. Hear me out," he pleads as his hand comes around my arm.

"Oh that's funny, just like you heard me out today on the phone? Really, you're going to ask me to listen, when you couldn't even listen to what I had to say about my future?" I spit at him, yanking my arm out of his grasp and keep on walking.

"Please, just listen." He doesn't touch me again, but his pace is consistent with mine, so he's not falling behind at all. I'm not sure where I'm walking, and I'm certain I'll end up getting us lost, but I have to burn off some of my anger before I do something stupid.

"Adam, this isn't how relationships work. You're the one that said no lies, yet you've been so secretive with things. This building, whatever happens inside, will end up ruining us!"

He sighs and stands in front of me so I have to stop walking.

"I know," he says. "I know, and I need to tell you everything. I want to tell you everything. But not here. We need to go back to my place."

He looks around anxiously and I get the feeling he knows we're in a bad area. Pulling out his phone, he dials a number and tells the person on the other line where we're at, then hangs up.

"What's going on, Adam?" I ask wearily.

"Jesus... there's so much I have to tell you. Just wait, okay? We need to get off these streets." He looks around again and a minute later the car pulls up.

The car I was riding in with Joe.

"Adam, I'm not getting in his car," I say shaking my head. What happened with Joe is enough to make me never be able to trust him again. No way I'm getting back into a car with him.

"It's not Joe, doll." He smiles and the door opens. A man in his early thirties gets out of the car. He's got a bloody lip, a swollen eye, and dried blood on his forehead.

Jesus Christ. What's going on here?

"Annaliese, this is Benton. Benton, Annaliese," Adam introduces us and we both look at each other strange. Like we're both a big part of Adam's life, but have yet to hear each other's name muttered, even in passing. "Listen, I know this is strange, but can we please get the fuck out of here before someone shanks us?" He sounds nervous, but Benton laughs and smiles, walking towards the car.

"I'm not your damn chauffer. Open you own damn door," he grunts getting in the driver's seat.

Chapter 18

Adam

I find it hard to laugh in a situation like this. I'm about to tell Annaliese everything about... well... everything. I'd rather not have it this way, but after Joe's insane behavior, I have a feeling her dad has more reasoning behind not wanting me to be with her than just protecting his little girl. Something was weird with him tonight, he was more reserved and distracted than normal. My plan was to get to him after the fight, after the crowd dispersed. When Benton and I saw the scuffle on the side of the building, he went running. Naturally, Benton always runs towards trouble. I had to follow, frustrated that he'd get involved in something in this neighborhood.

When I saw her face, though, my rage exploded. B had to pull me off and show me that she ran. I'm not sure what Joe ended up looking like, but whatever it is, it's not half of what he's going to endure next time I see him.

"Get in, Sweet," I say watching her waiver with her decision.

I just want to take her in my arms, tell her it'll all be okay, but I'm not even certain of that anymore. She looks at me, pissed, but also weary. That's good, I can work with that. Sighing, she walks towards the car and opens the front passenger door.

"Back, Annaliese," I growl and hear Benton laugh from the driver's seat.

She turns and looks at me, then cocks her head.

"No," she simply states, getting in the car and buckling her seatbelt immediately.

Shit. She will be the end of me. I thought I'd be able to let her go. I thought I'd be able to watch her move to St. Louis, five hours away from me, because she'd be doing something she loves, but I can't.

I can't let her leave.

Shaking my head, I get in the back seat of the car that we took from Joe. I was using him as a ride home tonight anyway, so it's really not stealing. Even if Vick gets pissed, I couldn't care any less right now. His driver had the woman I love pushed up against a brick wall in the worst part of the city, and that woman happens to be Vick's only daughter left. He should just be happy we didn't kill the man. I think. Maybe B did kill him; he was pretty pissed.

On the entire drive to my place, I hear Annaliese talking to Benton, but I can't tell what they are saying. I wish I could be holding her right now. I need to feel her warmth under me to know that I didn't royally screw things up with her because I couldn't rein in my anger earlier. Jesus, I was stupid. The drive sucks worse than normal having to watch her interact with Benton and completely ignore me. When she ran to my arms in the alley I was convinced I hadn't lost her, but now seeing her reaction to me in the car I'm starting to think differently.

Why do women have to give off so many mixed signals?

For the rest of the drive I try to take my mind off the beautiful woman ignoring me from the front seat and make mental notes of everything I need to tell her. Everything I need to apologize for. Maybe if I start with the apologies, then tell her about her father, then go into more apologies it won't be as bad.

Who am I kidding? There's nothing good that can come out of this conversation, but I'm going to try my hardest to make it okay. *It has to be okay.*

By the time we make it to my place, I'm so nervous I feel my hands shaking. I know she needs to know, and I know I'm the only one in her world that's going to tell her, but that doesn't make it any easier.

Just Go   M. Dauphin

We ride the elevator in silence. She doesn't look mad, but she's not all over me either. My spirits are lifted a bit when she lets me hold her hand, and just the heat from that small connection has my dick screaming at me to pause the elevator ride and screw her, but I can't. This has to happen tonight, and we can't be in a post orgasmic haze when it does. We need clear heads and clear hearts.

Even though my heart will forever belong to her.

"You go on in. I need to take Thor out," I say unlocking the door.

"Hey!" my sister yells from the couch, curled up with a sleeping puppy.

What the hell is she doing here?

"What're you doing here, Bug?" I growl. Running my hands through my hair, I stare at her but she doesn't see me. The only thing she sees is Annaliese, who recently ripped her hand away from mine and is wide eyed and pissed beyond belief.

"Hi." My sister smiles widely and gets up, holding Thor, and walks over to Annaliese. She holds her hand out but Annaliese just stares at it.

"Wonderful," Annaliese whispers in disbelief, and I suddenly realize why she looks so mad. It's not because my sister is here, taking over our alone time. It's because she doesn't know that the beautiful specimen—crazy as she may be—standing in front of her is my sister.

"Shit, sorry. Annaliese, this is Cara." I smile as Annaliese stares her down. "My sister."

I watch the anger on her face morph into pure embarrassment, and the reddening of her cheeks makes my heart swell. I laugh and my sister chuckles and shakes her head.

"You probably didn't know this asshole had a sister, did you?" she asks Annaliese, still laughing.

"No. Apparently there's a lot I don't know about him." Her glare moves to me and I'm suddenly scared for what's about to come.

"Well, just so you know, his teddy from childhood is in the guest bedroom, but he only puts it there every morning after waking up from snuggling it all night." She grins and pets Thor. "So, Adam. I'm guessing you want some privacy?"

"Please," I growl. "We'll visit the fact that you're at my place at almost midnight randomly another day."

She smiles and shrugs.

"Okay. I'll take Thor with me. You look like hell, Adam. Annaliese, you're beautiful. Let me know if I need to throat punch my big brother."

"Out, Bug," I growl, growing impatient with her as the seconds tick on.

"Nice to meet you, Annaliese," she whispers then waves lightly as she takes my puppy and leaves.

Typically, I'd be worried about where she's going or why she's here, but all I can think of is how to get Annaliese on my good side again. Especially after what I have to tell her.

"So let's hear it then," she bluntly states then sits on the single chair across from my couch.

"You want a drink?" I ask, my mouth suddenly parched.

"No. I want you to tell me what the hell's going on, Adam." She crosses her arms and it takes all I have not to stare at her gorgeous tits.

I sigh, "Well, I'm getting a water. I'll be back, then you can ask me anything you want."

I grab a bottle from the mini-fridge in my wet-bar in the living room and sit on the couch, as close to her as I can get. She crosses her legs away from me and raises her eyebrows, expecting me to start talking.

"So, where do you want me to start?"

"How about what all of that was about tonight? How about the fact that Joe pinned me to the building, Adam! Just because I tried to find out what was inside the building!"

"Joe shouldn't have done that," I grind, remembering my rage when I saw him pressed up against her.

"No, he shouldn't have, but you're not answering my question. Look, if you're gonna keep this from me, fine, but I'm not staying here tonight with you lying to me." She goes to stand and I take her hand.

"Please stop. Sit back down. I'll tell you everything."

She sighs and sits hard, back in the same chair. It'd be easier to do this with her next to me, touching me. Instead, I lean forward and reach over to take her hand in mine. She looks up at me and my heart breaks a little for the hurt and sadness and anger I see in them.

"Annaliese, I met your father a few years back as you know. About a month after meeting him and using Ryder, Inc. as my driving service, I learned how he really makes his money."

I pause and watch her take a deep breath. Her hands tighten in mine and her eyes narrow at me, but she sits still, quietly waiting for me to continue, so I push on.

"I was accidentally dropped off at the building we were at tonight. When the driver realized it, she was already five city blocks back, enough time for me to throw a huge fit that she got it wrong. Huge enough for your father to be called outside the building and take me in before anyone called the cops. The poor men at the door hadn't ever been screamed at like that before." I shake my head at the memory. "When he took me in, I saw a whole new world open up in front of me."

"Get to the point, Adam," she whispers.

"It's not as bad as what you're thinking, Sweet." She glares at me and I try to smile. "Annie, we don't kill anyone."

"Don't call me that," she growls. "Don't."

"Fine. But it's not horrible. Annaliese, he runs an underground fight ring. The biggest in the city. High roller betting, fights almost every night. Your dad gets a cut of all the bets, and bets aren't allowed if they're under one grand."

She narrows her eyes at me.

"Fighting? My father runs a fight ring? What kind of fight ring, Adam?"

"A human fight ring?" I chuckle at her question but she apparently doesn't find it funny. "It's MMA style, but no rules. The man you met tonight, Benton, he's my fighter." I sigh as she takes her hand from mine.

I see it the minute she realizes what that means.

"Your *fighter*?" She stresses the word 'fighter' like it's poison or something. She stands and paces the room in front of me. "How much do you drop a fight? Huh? How much money have you been practically supplying our family with for years?"

"It's not like that, Annaliese," I say, trying to keep my calm.

"Then please explain it to me," she growls, hands on her hips.

Damn, she's sexy when she's mad.

"I don't pay your dad directly. He's just the middle man, between the winners, the losers, and the schmucks that think they can outsmart him."

"How much, Adam?" Her eyes narrow at me. Shit.

"A few grand a week," I say then pause. "On a slow week." I hear her laugh then she shakes her head.

"A few grand a week?!? That's insane! How much does my dad get?!?" she screams.

"I'm not certain. Winnings are different every fight, but most nights the winner goes home with ten to twenty grand in his pocket, and that's not including the fighter that won or your dad's cut." Jesus, I already feel defeated and I haven't even started in on my apologies, or my groveling, or telling her the rest of everything I still need to tell her.

"Son of a bitch," she sighs and sits again, this time in a chair further away from me. "So all this time I thought my dad's business was just that good, but in all honestly, he's just been running illegal shit in the basement of a run-down warehouse." She shakes her head. "Wow."

"I'm sorry for not telling you," I whisper, waiting for her eyes to meet mine, but they never do.

My heart starts to hurt from fear that I've lost her, but I have to go on. It's now or never. "Annaliese, that's not all."

Her head moves up to look at me and I see the unshed tears in her eyes.

"Baby, no," I say, standing and moving to her before I'm even sure what my body is doing. I kneel down in front of her and place my hand under her chin, gently raising her eyes to mine. "I..." I want to tell her I love her. I want to tell her that nothing else matters. I want to, and I almost do, but I have to get the rest out so instead I lean in and kiss her gently. Her lips soft, she gently kisses back and I pull back before it gets out of hand. "I'm sorry, but there's still more," I say. "Can you just... please sit with me," I say, taking her hand. She puts up no fight walking over to the couch and sitting down, and I'm scared she's already gone numb to her feelings tonight.

"Just get it out, Adam. I'm tired and need to get home," she whispers.

No. She's not leaving here tonight. I don't care if she sleeps on my couch, I'm not letting her walk out of that door upset with me.

"Baby, listen... when I met your dad, and learned about the fight ring he has going on... well he only let me in under one circumstance."

"Let me guess... he told you never to look at me, never to fuck me, and pretty much never to talk to me?"

What?

"Uh... yeah. How'd you—"

"He's been warning people off from me my entire life Adam. I get it; he's protective, but he's harmless."

"He threatened me, Annaliese. He's been rigging fights and I've lost thousands because of it. He threatened my company, and he threatened Benton. Don't tell me he's harmless. I feel like I know him better than you do at this point," I snap, and hear her gasp. "Shit, I'm sorry. I'm sorry for all of this, Annaliese, but I just couldn't stay away."

"I know the feeling." She smiles and looks at me, her eyes still glistening. "So what now?"

"Well...." I start, then my phone interrupts us.

"Aren't you gonna get that?" she asks as it continues to freak out from my pocket.

"It can wait." I have to get these words out. Three measly words that are eating at my insides. I have to tell her.

"You're the 'most important man in the city'," she uses air quotes to mock me and I smile. "Answer your damn phone. I'm not going anywhere," she says, then lays her head back on the couch. I pull my phone out and see it's Benton.

"Hey, B—"

"She's gone, Adam." His voice is void of any emotion, and my stomach drops.

"Benton, what're you talking about?" I manage, though my gut feeling tells me it's exactly the horror I'm imagining.

"Carly... she's... oh God, Adam," he starts sobbing and I stand and curse under my breath.

"B, where are you?" I ask, but there's no answer from him. "Benton!" I yell into my phone.

"I'm home," he sniffles. "I'm here... she's not here. Adam, she's... I can't...." Shit just listening to this is making me tear up.

"B, what happened?" I wait for what seems like hours for him to calm down enough to answer, and when he does I feel like vomiting.

"She was in an accident," he manages through his tears.

Son of a bitch.

"Don't go anywhere, B. You hear me? Don't go anywhere," I say then look over at Annaliese. She's sitting up straight, concern etches her face. "I'm coming over."

He doesn't reply through the tears, so I hang up the phone and curse again. I run my hands over my face, as if the motion would bring her back. Carly's gone, and Benton's never going to be the same. The man relied on her to breathe. If there were ever a fairytale romance, that was them. To the T.

Just Go   M. Dauphin

"What's wrong, Adam?" Annaliese stands and places her hand on my shoulder. Her touch calms me slightly, but not near enough I need it to.

"I need to go," I manage through my raging emotions.

"I'll go with you," she says.

She doesn't ask for permission. She doesn't ask where we're going, or why it's so sudden. She doesn't push, but she wants to be here with me. For me. She wants to be here for me, and I'm okay with that.

"Okay," I mumble as I walk towards the front door. Each minute that passes since the phone call, I feel more of my body going numb from the overwhelming sadness. Sadness for so much. Carly was bright, happy, forgiving, and everything a man would want in a woman. They were each other's firsts, and Benton loves her more than his life. Sadness washes over me with the thought of him living alone, raising a baby without her, without a mom. I feel my eyes start to swell, and know the tears are close, and I don't even care anymore.

"I'm driving," she says as we reach the garage. I glance at her, but the look on her face it determined, and I have no energy to fight it. "I need the address," she says gently after we've buckled into the car. I rattle off his house number and lay my head back on the seat.

I'm certain the car is moving, as the lights through my closed eyelids keep changing and flickering, but I can't feel anything. They were supposed to last forever. They just adopted a baby.

"Oh God," I moan, feeling sick to my stomach.

"You wanna talk about it?" Annaliese lays her hand on my knee. It's a comforting touch, so I wrap my hand around hers and shake my head.

It's the middle of the night, so traffic isn't terrible. We make it to Benton's in fifteen minutes and there's a cop car parked out front of his building. They're probably inside with him, hopefully stopping him from killing himself. I've never heard him so upset. He's devastated. How's he going to manage a baby, a newborn, without her?

"You ready?" Annaliese gently smiles at me.

"Don't you want to know what happened?" I ask, curious why she's being so nice to me.

"I'm sure I understand most of it. You don't need to tell me anything if you don't want to talk about it right now," she smiles again and my heart warms.

I can't lose this one.

Walking into the apartment wasn't anything like I pictured. It's eerily calm. The officer at the door nods at us and lets us in to the living room. There are two more officers sitting at the kitchen table, drinking coffee talking quietly, but there's no sign on Benton anywhere. When the officers notice us, one stands and greets us.

"Sir, Officer Keaton. Very sorry," he looks towards Benton and Carly's bedroom. "He's in there," he says quietly.

My hand is still holding tightly to Annaliese. She's been a silent partner since we got here, and when I move towards his room, she holds back.

"What?" I whisper, turning to her.

"I'm not… you go. I'll be okay out here. He needs his friend now, Adam. Not me." She gives me a weak smile and kisses me before walking to the couch and pulling out her phone.

I stand there for a moment, staring at the closed bedroom door, wondering how in the world he's going to get past this. Slowly, I make my way to the bedroom and knock gently. When there's no answer, I open the door to a dark room. Shit.

"B?" I say as gently as I can.

I don't hear his voice, but I hear him sniffle and know he's at least alive in here.

"Can I come in?" I ask, opening the door a bit more, finally able to see him sitting on the edge of the bed.

He raises his head from his hands and looks at me. There's nothing left in his eyes. They're completely void of… everything.

"Close the door," he whispers while staring at me.

I do as he asks, then walk to the bed, unsure of how to approach him.

"How…. I'm sorry, Benton."

"It's not your fault, man. It's mine. Had I not fought tonight, she wouldn't have left pissed at me."

"Don't do that, B." I shake my head and sigh. "Shit's gonna happen if it's meant to be."

"Easy for you to say," he scoffs. "Last fucking thing she told me was she hopes I get my head out of my ass before the baby comes home, or else I'm gonna be the worst dad ever." He takes a deep breath. "And now…. Shit, man."

I sigh, not having any words for him. I know being here with him is all he needs, but I'm a problem solver. I thrive to be able to fix things, and make things better. This is something I can't make better. I put my arm around him when he starts to cry and shake my head. I can't even imagine the hurt he's feeling.

If Annaliese died like that…. God, I'd be ruined.

No.

"Did they say how it happened?" My gut keeps screaming at me that it wasn't as much of an accident as everyone is saying. My gut is making me want to vomit from the thought of my Sweet's father being involve with this, but I can't tell anyone until I know for a fact. This ruins everything. If I stay with her, I could end up being the one in Benton's shoes right now. I wouldn't ever put anything past Vick, even injuring his own daughter.

"Just a tragic car accident. No witnesses, no other person at the scene. So fucking dumb," he curses and hangs his head again.

Oh God, I feel like I'm going to throw up.

I can't be ruined. I don't want to end up like him, do I? I don't want to be the one mourning over the loss of a life too young. Holy shit, I have to let her take the job. I have to let her go.

I don't want this hurt.

"Keep that one out there, A," he whispers. "Don't ever let her go."

"Benton—"

"It hurts so fucking bad." He sighs and curses. "Jesus Christ."

We sit in silence for two hours. At some point in that time I pull him in for a side-hug that he doesn't fight. It feels awkward as hell, but it's the only way I know how to console him at this moment, because there's nothing I can say to make him feel any better. He's hurting, and it's not hard to see. I'm not sure he's said more than three words in the last hour, and he just keeps staring at the corner of the room. From being in here once before, I remember that corner of the room is her wardrobe. He's staring at her fucking clothes probably wishing he had her back. Now every day he's going to be reminded of her and the hurt and the pain that was caused by an accident.

Am I strong enough to live with a pain like that?

No. I don't think I am.

I've only ever lost my grandparents. I was raised privileged, not sheltered, but I have felt the pain of loss, and I still remember how it hurt when they passed. I also remember the pain my grandma went through when my grandpa died before her. I saw it in her eyes, but I didn't understand. I understand now. That's the look of complete devastation from losing the person you love so dearly it hurts to even think about living without them. That's the look that Benton has right now.

I'm not strong enough to lose someone I love.

"Shit," I whisper. "B... what can I do, man?"

"There's nothing you can do, dude."

"Anything, B. I have to do something. Arrangements, phone calls. Anything," I beg. I'm getting antsy just sitting here, and I need to try to make him better. To piece him back together.

He raises his head and looks at me, finally.

"Your girl out there still?"

"Annaliese? I'd think so."

"They told me she's gonna need... an outfit," he whispers. "I can't... A, I can't do it...."

"Okay. Alright, I'll... is it cool if Annaliese comes in?"

He nods and I get up and peek into the living room. She's sitting there talking to one of the cops and smiling, a coffee cup in hand and legs tucked under her. She's so beautiful; it makes my heart hurt that I'm going to have to let her go and follow her dreams, but that's what I have to do.

No way do I want to feel this heartbreak.

"Hey." She smiles and stands, walking over to me. "How's everything going?" She asks like she's honestly worried. Could she really be that kind to worry and care for someone she just met tonight?

"Uh... he's not doing so hot, actually," I say, rubbing my neck. She wraps her arms around me and hugs, helping ease some of the tension that's set in my body.

"What happened?" she murmurs into my chest. Obviously tired, but not complaining that we've been here so long.

"Car accident," I say, then feel her body tense. The minute I speak the words, I remember her sister and the tragic accident she died in.

"Oh." She takes a breath and pulls pack. "What...how can I help?" I feel a slight tremble in her hands but she's holding together.

"Well... he needs an outfit. For her."

"Right. Yeah... I... I remember that," she whispers and wrings her hands in front of her.

"But if you're not comfortable, I can go find something, Sweet. I know you—"

"Stop. That was a long time ago. I'll be okay, Adam." She gives me a gentle smile and takes a deep breath. "So where do I start?"

She doesn't bitch that she never knew Carly, nor does she bitch that she's been out here alone for hours just waiting. There are simply no complaints coming out of her, and it's blowing my mind that she hasn't asked to go home yet.

"Um... in here," I say, leading her to the bedroom. "Hey, B, we gotta turn the light on, okay?"

"Fine," he mumbles.

When the light comes on, I notice how terrible he really looks. It's amazing how much darkness can hide. His eyes are bloodshot, his hair messed, face puffy from the tears shed over this tragic event.

"Hey." Annaliese smiles. "I'm being told you need a little assistance?"

"Yeah... uh... her clothes. I need... they need clothes," he says as he look at the floor. "Over in the wardrobe." He nods his head and she glances to the corner he was staring at earlier.

Annaliese turns and gives me a quick and sad smile, and walks across the room to start going through Carly's clothes. About three minutes into her looking through the options, Benton curses and leaves the room. Annaliese turns as he leaves and shrugs her shoulders, smiling sadly.

"It's gonna be hard on him for a while, Adam," she says when she notices me grimacing at the doorway.

"I know, I know. I just... it's so unfair," I say, running my hands through my hair. "How are you doing over there?" I ask as I watch her try to match dresses and sweaters. There's no way I would be able to do this for a loved one.

"Did you know her? Personally? I just... I want to pick something that she'd wear. What do you think of these?"

She holds out a few different outfits and they all look like something Carly would wear to me, probably because they are all her clothes and I've seen her in them at one point or another. I pick one that I think is classy enough, something that'll show her beauty.

We spend the rest of the night sitting with B in his living room. The police left when Benton left the bedroom, I guess they were just making sure he was okay and had someone to sit with him. I guess there's too many times spouses can't handle the loss and decide to take their own lives instead of deal with it.

Annaliese falls asleep on the couch, curled up with her head resting on the armrest, and I cover her with a blanket then grab a few beers for Benton and I.

We spend the rest of the night in pretty much silence. Every now and then he'll start talking about something, but I don't push the subject of any of the arrangements or anything in that nature. Tomorrow's a new day and will bring its own challenges.

By the time we go to sleep, I've tried my hardest to harden my heart to the fact that I'll never be able to live with a loss like this. Harden it to the thought of telling Annaliese she needs to take the St. Louis job because I'm not big enough man to handle what Benton's going through right now.

I've hardened my heart so when I break it, it won't fully shatter.

Chapter 19

Annaliese

The next few days are a whirlwind of events. From arrangements, to phone calls, to will meetings, Adam and I are there for everything. My heart hurts for this man that absolutely loved his wife as much as he did. I've heard talk about an adoption, and Adam and Benton have had some serious, stressed, heated discussions about it, but I'm staying out of it. I don't know this man at all hardly, so I don't feel I have a say in anything. I want to be here for Adam because obviously he's hurting too, so that's what I'm doing.

We've put our discussion of our future on hold. I know we eventually need to talk about it, since I'm not totally over the fact that he lied to me about pretty much everything. I haven't talked to my dad at all about everything, but I suppose that'll come with time. Right now I'm focusing on being there for Adam. When someone you love is hurting, the only thing that seems important is making them feel better. So that's what I'm doing. We've made love, we've talked, and we've sat in silence for hours. I can tell something's on his mind, but I'm not pushing him. Obviously he and Benton are close, which only means he was probably close to Carly as well. I couldn't imagine what Benton's going through if Adam is this torn up about it.

The funeral was three days ago and we are sitting at Benton's house, staring at the TV but not really paying attention to it. Each day Benton looks a little worse, and each day we spend trying to help him out of the depression that's setting in. Today's the same as the last few days, and the down mood is really starting to wear on me.

"Hey, babe, I think I'm gonna head out for a bit," I say to Adam when Benton walks out of the room.

He looks at me and smiles gently.

"I understand. I'll talk to you later," he says almost coldly. I try not to be offended by his lack of affection lately, but it's really hard.

I kiss him gently and stand. Benton walks back in the room and stops when he sees me leaving.

"What's up?"

"I'm heading out for a bit. I've got… uh… work stuff to do. "

He gives Adam a weird sideways glance then tries to smile at me.

"Thanks for everything, Annaliese," he says, then gently and awkwardly hugs me.

I step outside, closing the door behind me, and take a deep breath. I keep telling myself that he's just been weird these last few days because his head's in a bad place from his friend's death, but I can't shake the feeling that he's pulling away from me.

My phone rings on my way back to my apartment and I hit the Bluetooth to answer without looking to see who it is.

"Hello."

"Mrs. Ryder. This is Angela from St. Louis. We've been trying to get a hold of you. Have you come to a decision?"

"Oh my gosh, I'm so sorry. We had a death in… the family. I've been out of it, and am so sorry." Shit, school's supposed to start this week!

"I'm terribly sorry for your loss, but we really do need an answer from you."

"I know. I'm so sorry. I'm…." I want to tell her no, but something's nagging at me. I need a shower and some coffee before I can properly decide about my future. "May I call you after I get home? I haven't been there in days with everything that's going on, and I'm currently driving."

"I need to know today, Ms. Ryder," she clips, obviously not happy with me.

"I'll call you back. I promise. Thanks for understanding," I say, then tell her goodbye before hanging up and sighing.

What am I going to do? I love Adam, I'd love to stay with him, but he lied to me, he keeps things from me when he made it obvious at the start he needed the truth, and all of it. Plus, he's been distant lately. Am I really the type of girl to put her future on hold because of a man?

I get home and open the apartment door. I don't see anyone, but I definitely hear our guests in Gabby's bedroom. Shaking my head in annoyance, I really wish she could figure her shit out. I love her to death, but she's not getting any younger, and these games she plays with both men and women get tiring to me. Especially living with the background noise. I start some coffee and look at the clock. Ten am. I'll give myself a couple hours to decompress, then I'll call Adam. I need to talk with him about everything before I call the woman back about the job.

Once the coffee is done, I take my mug to the couch, staring out the window at the city around us. I really do love this city. I'm comfortable here. Everything and everyone I know lives here. Why would I want to leave and go somewhere less comfortable with no friends?

Just Go M. Dauphin

I hear Gabby's door open and pull a blanket over me to cover my bare legs. No reason to show anyone she's with any goods they don't deserve. A man walks out, fit, tanned, and sweaty. He walks directly to the fridge to grab a water bottle and on his way back he spots me.

"Hey," he says, confused.

"Hi," I say.

"Who... are you her girlfriend?" he asks, pointing to Gab's room. I can't help but laugh.

"No. Just her roommate. Don't worry." I smile and he sighs.

"Good. Whew," he laughs. "So.... what's your name?" he asks and leans against the wall. I can tell he's flexing his muscles just enough to show me what he has, but I'm not interested. There's a knock at the door, but the man standing in front of me isn't taking his eyes off me. I stand up, having to slide past him, smelling the sex he just got done having with my roommate on him, to get to the door. "Mmm...." I hear him moan as he watches me walk to the door.

"Pig," I grunt under my breath as I swing the door open, not checking to see who's on the other side.

"Adam," I say confused as to how he got in the building without buzzing and why he's here in the first place. "What's wrong?"

His eyes go directly past me to the man standing across the room. The half-naked man that's more than likely checking me out. The man that's about to get a verbal lashing from the most influential man in Chicago.

"Oh shit, you're—" dude starts, but Adam stops him.

"Take your fucking eyes off her," he growls, then pulls me to my bedroom, shoving past naked man. I laugh when I hear a growl come out of him on our way past him.

We get to my room and he slams the door behind me.

"Who the hell is that, Annaliese?" He's attempting to regulate his breathing and I have to laugh. I like the jealous side of him.

"Gabby's most recent fuck. The girl's still in the room with Gab," I say laughing at the look on his face.

"She's?"

"Curious," I answer smiling. "What're you doing here?" I ask. He sits on the bed and pats it, inviting me over. I sit next to him, but he doesn't touch me. Instead, he leans forward, resting his elbows on his knees and puts his head in his hands. His weird behavior worries me. He hasn't said more than a handful of words to me since he got here.

"What's wrong, Adam?"

He sighs and sits up, looking at me with sadness in his eyes.

"You need to take the job, Annaliese," he whispers and my heart sinks. Literally, it feels like there's a massive boulder on my chest, and the immediate urge to vomit courses through me as his words sink in.

"What?" I manage through the raging emotions that suddenly took over my body. "You're telling me to leave?"

"I can't do this, Annaliese. You need to live your dream, and I need to focus on the company. Seeing Benton... what he went through... I can't do that. I can't turn into him," he whispers, then stands up, pinching the bridge of his nose.

"Adam, that's not... that's stupid!" I yell at him, standing to meet him. "You're being a chicken shit, Adam. You're a lying piece of shit if you think what we have here isn't worth working for." My body is shaking, and I'm so exhausted I feel like I could cry any minute now.

"You need to take the job, Annaliese." His voice is devoid of every emotion. There's nothing there. "We have nothing, Annaliese. It was fun, but you need to go."

That's it. That's what breaks me.

"Fuck you!" I scream hitting his chest, pushing him back until he hits the door. He doesn't resist, he doesn't look at me; he just stands there letting me hit him. His eyes red, face defeated.

"Annie!" I hear Gabby yell from the other side of the door. "What the fuck, Annie?" she tries opening the door but with him against it, it's not budging.

"Screw you, Adam Callahan! I love you, you asshole. And I know you feel it too. You're stupid if you think throwing this away is going to save you from fucking heartbreak," I spit out. He gives me the saddest look I've ever seen on anyone, ever, then shakes his head.

"Annaliese," he starts but I don't let him finish.

"Go Adam," I whisper through my tears.

Asshole.

"Ann—"

"Just... go. Please. Just get out." I push him aside and open the door for him. He gets one glance at a fuming Gabby and her two partners standing in the hallway, half dressed, and leaves without another word.

"Oh God, Annie, what happened?" Gabby rushes in and wraps her arms around me before I collapse to the floor. "Get out!" she yells at the two people standing in the doorway watching the freak show. "Now!"

They scurry to grab their things. Moments later, we hear the front door close. I'm so numb I can't stand, so I don't even try. We sit on the floor, her arms wrapped around me, and I cry. I let it all out. The anger from the lies, the anger about my father's second life, the heartbreak that Adam could give up so easily on us, when I thought we really had what it took. I was stupid, and blinded by lust when I thought that Adam Callahan could really learn to love someone.

"You're gonna be okay, babe," Gabby whispers, her head leaning on mine. "He's an asshole."

"I love him, Gab," I sniffle, sounding like a child.

"Oh, Annie," she hugs me tighter and I cry harder.

Why does this hurt so bad? I've only known him for a month.

"I need to get up, Gab. I have to call the lady back from St. Louis," I say trying to stand on my own.

"You're taking the job aren't you?" she whispers.

"I have to. I need... I need out. Away for a while." I'd rather not live with the constant reminder of what we had.

"I'll kill him," she growls.

"It'll be fine, Gabby. You can visit, I'll come home for holidays. And if it doesn't work out, then I'll move back." I shrug and take a breath, moving towards my phone.

"Wait. You really love him don't you?"

"I do," I say, defeated. "But he... he's not willing to feel the same. I guess."

"I don't get it, Annie, but I'll support you with whatever you do." She stands and hugs me. "I'll miss your ass, bitch." She smiles sadly and I hug her back.

"I know. Me too,"

I grab my phone and make the phone call. She seems happy that I've decided to take the position, but I can't find that feeling. It takes about an hour to get everything straightened out, but once the phone call is done, I have a one way flight out of Chicago tomorrow afternoon to St. Louis. And so begins my new, lonely life.

That night I head over to my parents' house. I hate to leave on mad terms with my dad, but I'm not turning a blind eye to what he's been doing. To what he did.

"Hey, Annie!" he beams when I walk through the door, acting completely oblivious to my mood.

"Father," I clip, then hug my mother hello.

"What brings you here, dear?" she asks, obviously not privy to the side of my father that's manipulating and mean.

"Uh... I got a job?" I muster a smile and she gasps.

"That's fantastic!

"Congratulations my girl, I knew you could." My father beams, like he didn't force me out of everything good I had in this city.

"It's in St. Louis. I leave tomorrow," I spit out before the words get stuck in my throat. My mom covers her mouth in a gasp and my father's features tighten. I glare at him, barely holding back the words I really want to say

"Ah, I see," he says. "I would have thought—"

"What? That I wouldn't take a job so far away? Why do I get the feeling you set me up for this, Dad? Giving me assholes to boss around, warning men away from me my entire life, even Adam you scared away! Now you push this job on me, and job I didn't even apply for, and you act surprised that I'm ready to get out of town. It's…. you're outrageous. And you make me sick with everything you've hidden from this family." I'm growling by the time I finish. "Oh, and if I EVER find out what happened to Benton's wife… what *really* happened… I'll make sure you never see sunlight again." I spit out, anger coursing through my bones.

Knowing what I now know about my father, I wouldn't put it past him to have her killed to prove a point to Adam.

My mom's crying by now and my father looks like he's going to explode with anger.

Go ahead, dear old Daddy, I dare you.

"I'm sorry, Mom. I can't stay here, in this city, with everything that's been happening behind our backs. I have to go," I whisper, then hug her tightly, not sure of the next time I'll see her.

"I don't understand, Annaliese. What're you talking about?" she manages through her tears. I look at my father and raise my eyebrows at him.

"I think that's something that you and Dad need to talk about, Mom. I'll let you guys know when I land safely tomorrow. I have to go pack," I say, kissing my mom goodbye and pushing past my dad.

The entire drive back to my apartment I let the tears roll, making a promise to myself that by the time I get home I won't shed another tear over this. He isn't man enough to live up to his word, my father is an asshole who's been lying to my family all these years, and I'm about ready to uproot everything I know and move to a city to start a job I'm not certain I even want anymore.

By the time I get home, Gabby has the boxes out and has already started packing. She's blaring music and has a bottle of wine and tub of ice cream sitting on the counter, both already started.

"Hey," I say closing the door and setting my things on the side table nearby.

"You don't have to do that. I'm leaving most of it with you anyway, Gab." I say walking over to where she's started packing my things. "I'll be back in a few weeks for my car, and I can get the rest then."

"I know, I know. I just... I have to help somehow. I have to do something. Sitting here in silence waiting for you to get back was depressing. So I broke out the good shit and started packing." She shrugs and takes a drink of her wine.

"Well, good shit it is," I smile, taking her glass from her. "Come on, we need to pack my closet. I can't show up in shorts and a tank top on my first day of teaching."

"Oh God," she whines as we start picking out my clothes to pack. "You're not gonna turn into one of those teacher styles, with cardigans and pants are you? Oh, Annie," she whines and starts to laugh. "God, I can't picture you as that! Please, bring skirts, and dresses, and, for the love of God, please take your heels."

I laugh as she lists off all the things I have to bring along, and before I know it she's taken over packing my three suitcases full of the necessities. She grimaces when I tell her not to worry about the sexy underwear though.

"A girl needs to feel sexy, even if her pussy isn't getting any." She laughs and throws them in the bag.

Great, just what I need.

Chapter 20

Adam

Three Months Later

"Jesus Christ, A. Why don't you just go after her already? You're such a fucking idiot," Benton grumbles sitting on my living room couch. Everywhere the man sits he acts like he owns the fucking place. He puts his feet on my coffee table like it didn't cost me two thousand dollars, and kicks back, making himself at home while his daughter sleeps in the bouncer next to him.

"Knock it off, B. I told you, it wouldn't work," I warn him with a sideways glance that I'm not about to talk to him about her.

Just Go   M. Dauphin
I can't talk about her. It hurts too bad.

To say he was pissed when he finally realized what I did is an understatement. It was about three weeks after Carly died that he finally put two and two together, and I wore a nice shiner for about two weeks after that.

Did I deserve it? Probably. I was an asshole to her, and a pussy for telling her to leave.

Do I love her still? Absolutely. Just thinking about her hurts. It's like there's a hole in my chest where her love for me resided, and when she left, the hole started growing, like a black hole. Taking all of my energy, passion, and care for anything. She fucking told me she loved me and I just stared at her. I still remember the massive blow to my heart when she spat those words at me. God, I can still feel her anger, her sadness, and each time I think about it, I fall deeper and deeper into this depression.

I couldn't tell you what's been going on at Carson and Lewis. I've showed up for work, locked myself in my office, and played with stocks and under the table betting all day, every day. I've lost some money in the process, but it doesn't bother me. I can't find anything I'm passionate about anymore because the only thing I had true passion for is five hours away, living her dream.

"Dude, seriously. You're miserable to be around. I fucking lost my wife and don't look as bad as you do," he says in all honesty.

He's right. It took him a couple months, but he's finally back to his old self for the most part. Maybe it's the fact that he has a tiny baby to take care of now, or maybe the fact that the doctors finally put him on Prozac to help his mood swings, but I see a glimpse of the old Benton more and more recently.

The baby starts to cry and he goes to her while shaking his head at me.

"I don't get you, man. You'd rather put yourself through misery every damn day, just so the chance of something happening to you like happened to me doesn't come up. It makes no fucking sense." He picks her up and starts gently bouncing her around to calm her. I smile at his actions. He's got this fathering thing down.

"One of these days your daughter's gonna catch onto that language, you know," I say as I watch him walk her around the room. "She's gonna need to come to Uncle Adam just to get away from it."

That makes him laugh and smile.

"Right, because you're such a great role model. You push away everything you love and enjoy."

"I said drop it, man." I sigh and stand up. "Aren't you supposed to be going out tonight?" I ask, taking Hannah from his arms.

"Yeah. I uh... I'll be out all night. Probably won't be back till tomorrow. My parents are picking her up in the morning. You sure you're cool with her?"

"Absolutely. We need to bond, right?" I ask her. She giggles and smiles at me. "She loves her Uncle Adam."

"Right. So then bottles are in the fridge, warm them up—"

"I know, B. I've watched her plenty of times. Go... have a break from this. You need it," I say, forcing him out the door. He kisses her goodbye and leaves us to ourselves.

Nights like this have happened a lot lately, but I don't mind it. I like the company of a baby, and Hannah's one of the best babies I've ever seen. It took me seeing Benton holding her, looking at her with all of his love, to realize that going through with the adoption was exactly what he needed. The agency wasn't too thrilled with it at first, and his parents are still skeptical, but he's determined to prove everyone wrong.

I put Hannah on a blanket on the floor and Thor comes barreling in the room to play with her. He's surprisingly good with her, and she loves watching him. She's started giggling recently, so watching her laugh at Thor is pretty much what we do when she visits. I never wanted kids, but seeing the bond that Benton already has with her makes me think that it wouldn't be such a bad thing.

The thought of kids brings me back to Annaliese, and how much my heart and mind miss her. I dream of her every night, and can still smell her on my pillows, even though they've been washed multiple times in the last months. I can't stop jerking off to my memory of her because I can't fathom putting my dick in someone else after I've felt what it's like being inside of her. I miss her so much it physically hurts, and there are days I don't even get out of bed. I thought it'd get easier after time, but it seems to be getting harder and harder as the days go on. The one photo I had of her on my phone was deleted when I heard she actually left town. I was pissed, but I had no right to be. She did just what I told her to do.

I still remember the words I told her: *There's nothing between us.*

It hurts just thinking about it, so I don't. Instead I watch Hannah every chance I get, I go out with my sister on the other nights. I'm certain she's getting tired of me, but I need something to do, and fucking women randomly just doesn't feel right.

My heart still belongs to Annaliese.

I want to fix it; I wish I could, but too much time's gone by. I said too many irreversible things to her.

All I can hope is that she's happy, because at least then I'll feel like I made the right choice.

"Hey, asshole," my sister's voice echo's through the apartment.

"Sorry, Hannah, you're surrounded by foulmouthed adults," I say to her in the baby voice

I've adapted so well these last few months. She smiles and laughs which brings a hint of a smile to my face.

"Dude, again?" my sister asks, walking to grab a drink before coming to the living room. "Don't you watch her every weekend?"

"Yeah, but I don't care. I love this little baby," I scoop her up and feel a small amount of warmth in my chest, knowing it's the love I have for Hannah and nothing more. When her dad picks her up, the black hole will be back, I'm certain of it.

"She at least makes you smile," she grumbles taking a drink of her beer.

"What's that supposed to mean?" I'm fully aware of my mood lately, but I've been trying to act normal around my sister. Apparently it didn't work.

"You've been an... a... a meanie." She gives me a smartass grin and cocks her head. "Ever since you let Annaliese go, you've been a different person. Someone who's crazy depressing to be around."

"So why do you keep coming around, then, Bug?" I ask, exasperated that this conversation keeps coming up with my friends and family. "I'll be fine without you."

"Whatever, jerk-face. You wouldn't last a day without me or Benton here to bust your balls. And honestly, Mom and Dad put me on suicide watch, so you're stuck with me," she says and grins as I throw one of Hannah's baby toys at her.

"Not funny, Bug. I'm not suicidal," I grumble, though at times I think it'd be easier than living with this regret every day. I'd never actually do it though.

"Right. You sure have us fooled," she scoffs.

"Well believe it. Nothing's gonna change, so you better believe it and start having a life again. I'm not going anywhere," I tell her, then head into the kitchen to make a bottle for Hannah.

Feeding her, I watch her little fingers wrap around mine and smile.

"You would've made a great dad, Adam," my sister whispers as Hannah finishes her bottle. "You've been staring at her this whole time, like there's nothing else in the world. You could've had that." She shakes her head and mumbles something about me being stupid.

"I still can, you know," I whisper, not believing my own words.

"Right. I know you. You don't love often, Adam. Both times you've sent them away."

"Both? I never sent away Dianne. She did that on her own."

"I'm not talking about her, and you know it."

I do know it, but I choose not to think about it. Ever. It used to hurt, knowing the woman I broke up with to move to the city to start my own company ended up married, happily, with kids and never looked back. Now that I know the hurt I've caused myself with Annaliese, though, that pain doesn't seem too bad anymore.

"How do you know all of this, Bug?" I never told a soul about her.

"Little sisters know things, Adam. I spent my childhood admiring you, watching you, and learning from you. I know love when I see it, and I never saw it again until you met Annaliese."

She smiles sadly at me and shrugs.

"I know, Bug," I sigh. "I know."

"So what're you gonna do about it?!" she yells, which makes Hannah jump in her sleep and I give my sister the death glare before standing to walk Hannah back to sleep.

"Nothing. There's nothing to do little sis."

"Bull. It's never too late, Adam." She stands and kisses Hannah's cheek on her way to the door. "I wish I could help you, big bro, but this is something you need to fix on your own. And you better damn well fix it. I'm tired of watching over your moping ass."

Then she makes her grand exit, leaving me with a sleeping baby and my own thoughts. Typically on alone nights, I drink myself to sleep to help numb the sadness, but not being able to do that tonight is going to suck. Majorly. I put Hannah in her pack and play and turn on the TV, trying to watch mindless shows to take my mind off of Annaliese.

It's stupid how mad at myself I am, and even more stupid how stubborn I am. I should've followed her. Hell, I never should've told her to go, but I did. And then I had the audacity to be angry when she actually left. The week after she left, I almost bought a plane ticket to go see her, but I didn't. I couldn't. She probably hates me.

Most nights I fall asleep wishing for one more chance to make it right. But she's already given me all my chances.

***

The next morning around ten, Benton's parents come to pick up Hannah. Before the funeral I'd only met them a time or two, but ever since we've become pretty close. They're actually down to earth—real people. Talking to them isn't anything like talking to my own parents. Benton's parents show real concern for a man that isn't their own son. My parents just want me to get out of my 'funk' already.

"Adam, you look tired. Was Hannah up all night?" B's mom asks.

"No, she slept great. I just... I don't sleep well anymore," I muster a smile for her and notice her sad glance she gives her husband.

"Adam, can I tell you something without you being offended?" she asks. I nod and smile, waiting for her to give me too much old person advice I'm really not into.

"You're being an idiot, dear."

"An asshole's more like it," her husband grumbles.

"Excuse me?" I ask, shocked they'd go there.

"We know you care dearly, and strongly. You love our granddaughter like she was your own. You care for Benton like he's your brother. Why would you put yourself through this agony of losing the one girl you love?"

"It's not like that," I whisper staring at them like they've grown three heads. Why is everyone trying to get involved in my business lately?

"We know it is, son," Benton's dad chimes in. "I did the same thing when I was younger."

"What? Did what?" I'm curious what they think I did to make myself so miserable.

"Push someone I loved dearly, with my every breath, away because I was afraid."

He smiles and looks at Benton's mom and I shake my head.

"He did, you know," she smiles at me. "But I wouldn't let him be that stupid."

I take a moment to register what they just told me.

"So you left her?" I ask his dad and he nods. "And you wouldn't let him get away with it because you knew he really loved you?" I look at his mom and she smiles and nods. "It's still not the same. I really hurt her," I say. I'm not sure why I'm opening up to them, but it feels like therapy, finally able to get it all out. "I miss her like crazy, but I hurt her. Badly. She left because I told her to go. Because I told her we didn't have anything together, when all I wanted to do was pull her in my arms and hold her. I wanted to tell her how much I love her, but instead I was afraid of ever losing her and going through what Benton went through that I ended up pushing her out of my life completely. And it...." I take a breath, forcing the lump in my throat down. "It really sucks," I say, in half a laugh.

The all-powerful Adam Callahan has completely ruined himself over a girl.

My how the mighty can fall.

"It's not too late, Adam."

"Yes, it actually is." I put my hands in my pockets and shrug. "Thanks for the talk, I appreciate it, but it's been too long. I'm sure her hatred for me has just grown by now."

"Promise me you'll talk to Benton about this, Adam. He's worried about you," she says and I nod.

"Will do. You two have fun with this baby," I say, escorting them to the elevator.

I wish it wasn't too late. I also wish people would stop telling me I still have a chance.

I don't. I used all my chances.

Just Go   M. Dauphin

Chapter 21

Annaliese

"Okay class, ten minutes of silent reading, then we're moving on to math," I tell my fourth graders. A few of them struggle to understand the concept of 'quiet,' which makes me have to pull out the 'mean teacher' voice, something I've had to pull out too many times to count in my three months at this job.

I thought teaching would be more fun than this, but it's so much paperwork, so much politics and making sure your paperwork is up to date and properly on display, that time spent teaching is shadowed by time spend preparing and worrying about being fired.

Maybe that's just my mood lately, too. Before Adam, I would have probably loved a job like this, but now I feel nothing for it. Sure, the kids are sweet. They smile, they laugh, they joke around like any other kids I've worked with, but I just don't feel the joy in it anymore. I always thought this was something I wanted to do, but now that I'm here, it's nothing like I imagined. I guess I thought it'd be a lot more glamorous, but it's nothing like I pictured.

"Ms. Ryder," I hear through the school intercom. "You have a visitor. He's very... insistent... on speaking with you," Debbie, our school secretary says with a sigh. "I'm sending Arnie down to fill in for you."

"Thanks, Debbie." I look at my children, all of which are staring at me like I have three heads, and smile.

"You all be good for Mr. Arnie," I warn. Some kids chuckle and others put their heads down. "I mean it, guys."

They've had it out for Arnie since he started here. Why fourth graders think being mean to someone that's different than them is beyond me, but it's so frustrating seeing them tease a grown adult behind his back.

Once my class is settled and Arnie has taken over, I head down the hall and make my way to the office. I haven't had any visitors in the three months I've been here. I haven't left my apartment except to get groceries and go to work. Last week, my father sent Joe to check up on me, and he hasn't left yet. He keeps telling me he's milking my dad for all the paid 'vacation' time he can, but I feel like he has other motives.

I make it to the office and through the glass I see a tall male figure with his back to me. My first thought is Adam, and my heart flutters, until I realize Adam isn't nearly as built as this man. When he turns to talk to the secretary, I almost collapse.

Benton.

I'd remember that face anywhere, even if I only knew him for a few weeks. The pain he went through when he lost his wife is enough for me to never forget his face. It looks better, less stressed now. He looks through the glass at me and smiles. He smiles! What the hell is he doing here? I walk into the office and look at Debbie and she's swooning over the tall, muscular man that's gracing her office. Of course she is. I swear the woman would screw anything on two legs.

"Benton. Hi," I say walking over to shake his hand. He gives me a weird look then pulls me into a hug.

"Hey, you," he says pushing me back a bit to look at me. "You look just about as bad as him. Jesus," he shakes his head and my eyes go wide when I realize what he's talking about. I can feel my heart speeding up and my brain's filtering out a ton of questions I want to ask.

Now's not the time nor the place.

"What're you doing here, Benton?" I put my hands on my hips and back away from him a few steps.

"I need to talk with you. Debbie here says you have lunch break next, early ass lunch break if ya ask me," he looks at her with a raised eyebrow. Probably because my lunch break isn't for an hour. What's she up to?

"I... uh," I stammer.

"She does. Ms. Ryder, you and your guest can visit in the teacher's lounge. If anything arises, we will contact you."

Thanks, backstabber.

I smile sweetly at her and nod slowly.

"Great. Follow me, Benton," I grind out, pissed that all of this is happening at my place of employment. He couldn't wait until tonight?!?

We get inside the teacher's lounge and I close the door tightly behind us.

"What's going on, Benton?" I sigh and sit on the couch, crossing my arms and legs, glaring at him.

"You need to come home, Annaliese," he states it as if he has the final say on things, which makes me laugh.

"That's not your call to make," I tell him, still laughing. "You don't know anything about this situation, Benton. I'm still trying to understand why you're here, and how you even knew where to find me?"

I'm on overload right now just seeing someone from my old life. I told Gabby that I'd visit, but it's been three months and I can't bring myself to make the five-hour drive. If I saw him with another woman, I'd be ruined. Not that I'm not already ruined, but that would be the nail in my coffin.

"I know it's not my call to make, but you have to see how miserable you are. Right? It's not just me, right?"

He can tell that from just a few minutes with me?

"Is it that obvious?" I whisper, angry that I've let myself get this depressed.

"One look, Annaliese. He's just as bad. You two need each other. Why can't you guys stop being so stubborn and realize that?" He sits at the table across from me. "You know, I knew the Carly was my one. I knew it the minute I laid eyes on her. Thinking back, I remember the first day Adam met you. He had that look, but I wasn't looking for it. You made him a better person, Annaliese. Sure he's an asshole, but that's to be expected from someone like him."

"He told me to leave, Benton. I'm not sure how me doing exactly what he wanted is me being stubborn," I huff. "Anyway, I can't leave now, the school year's already started."

Just Go   M. Dauphin

"So you make the trip to see him. You guys do the long distance shit. Something. You look terrible, no offense, but Adam... he looks... like hell... horrible. He barely smiles anymore, and has been an asshole to work with. He's hurting, Annaliese."

"Good," I mumble. If I'm hurting, at least I know he's right there with me.

"You really hate him don't you?"

No.

"That's a strong word," I whisper.

"Then why don't you give him another chance?"

Chance. He asked me for one chance. I gave him more than that.

I gave him my hear, and he stomped on it like it was a small, annoying bug.

"He doesn't want one, Benton. He was very clear about that." My voice threatens tears and I close my eyes.

"I call bullshit. We both know he didn't mean it, and he's just a pansy that didn't want to take the risk of ever being hurt. He was hurting from the loss of Carly, Annaliese, and I wasn't there to talk him out of the most idiotic decision he's ever made. I'm sorry, but please. You gotta see how much you need him."

He stands and looks at me. I have no words. I want Adam more than I want sleep at night. I dream about him, I have nightmares that I'll never see him again, I wake up in tears because he's not next to me. Nothing in my life seems right, because he's not in it. I stare at Benton, unable to form any words to respond to him. He walks to the door and turns to look at me, sadly.

"Thanks for taking time out of your day, Annaliese. Think about it okay?"

"Wait," I stop him before he opens the door. He looks at me and waits. "How'd you know where to find me? I mean, it's not that I was hiding, but I haven't exactly made it known where I am."

"I'm not the only one in Chicago that's noticed how pitiful you two are without each other. I'm not the only one left in that city that cares for my best friend…." He trails off and smiles at me. "I'll be seeing you, Annaliese," he says, then salutes me and walks out the door, closing it behind me.

Fucking Gabby.

I sit there in silence, stupefied that all of that just happened. Benton was really here, in my Podunk school, telling me… no, begging me… to come back to Chicago. All because Adam's apparently miserable. If he's so miserable, though, why wouldn't he reach out to me? Why wouldn't he tell me it was all a mistake?

The logical part of me is telling my body to get up and move back to my classroom, pretending like nothing happened. The part of me that's still madly in love with Adam is telling my body to book ass out of here and get the first flight to Chicago.

Unfortunately, just like Benton said, I'm insanely stubborn.

If Adam misses me, he's going have to really prove it, and not send his best friend here to talk me into crawling back to him.

I take the long way back to my classroom, ignoring the stares from the ladies in the office. I'd rather not have to explain to everyone why I'm not the 'ray of sunshine' that one of my professors from DePaul called me. I'd rather not have to relive everything that happened to practical strangers.

By the time the school day is over, I'm more exhausted than I've ever been working here. I spent the rest of the day worrying about Adam. If he's really as torn up as Benton said, how's the business fairing? How's his health? I know I've been sicker these last three months than normal, just because when I get depressed I tend to get sick easier.

I throw things in my bag, not even paying attention to the things I'll need to grade over the weekend or the lessons that need written, and mindlessly make my way back to my apartment, forgetting about anything and everything. At least, trying to. Adam's face keeps popping up in my mind, though, and it hurts every time.

By the time I get back to my apartment, I completely have forgotten that Joe's waiting for me to get ready for dinner tonight.

Shit.

"Hey, you. Everything okay?" he asks from the couch, where he was playing on his laptop.

"No, Joe. Everything isn't okay. I...." I take a good look at Joe and something clicks.

My father sent Joe here. Alone. With no other reason than to 'check up on me.' Now he's allowing Joe to stay in my apartment with me. Alone. That goes against everything my dad ever did.

"Joe." I narrow my eyes at him. "Why are you still here?" I ask.

He gets up and walks over to me, putting his hands on my shoulders and gently squeezing.

"For you, baby doll." He smiles and hugs me, tighter than he's hugged ever before.

He knows I know something's up.

"Right." I pull away and look him in the eyes. "But what did my dad tell you to come down here and do?"

He looks like he's been caught, and his mouth falls open.

"Annie, I'm... I'm not sure...."

"Tell me, Joe," I grind out. "Goddammit, Joe, I swear if this is all a scam over something. Another one of my father's lies… that's it, isn't it? He's…. Fucking Christ, Joe, just tell me!"

He sighs and rakes his hands through his shaggy blonde hair.

"Shit." He shakes his head and walks to the couch. Pulling out his phone, he ignores my question and dials someone, holding the phone out in front of him on speakerphone. I cross my arms and wait to hear what I'll never be able to un-hear.

"Is it done?" my father's voice comes over the phone.

"I can't, Vick," Joe tells my father.

My heart is racing and my mind is screaming at me that something's terribly wrong. I stand in silence and listen to their conversation.

"What do you mean 'you can't'?" my father growls. "I've had this deal with your father for years, Joseph!" his voice booms.

Deal? Oh god, I'm getting dizzy.

I walk over to the dining room table and sit, listening to their conversation, holding on to each word like it's my last.

"I know you two did, but I have a conscience, Vick. I can't do this." He sighs and I put my forehead on the cool table, trying to calm myself down before I go irate on both of them. What the hell is happening?

"Listen here, Joe. I've kept your ass with this company all of these years because of this deal. You renege on this deal and you're fired. Completely." My father's voice is like one I've never heard. Full of hatred.

"Then I guess I'll be starting over, Vick. I'm done. I'm cutting the deal."

"Your father would be very disappointed in you, Joe."

"Believe me, Vick, I already know that."

He hangs up the phone, and after a moment, I hear him get up and walk into the dining room.

"So...." he says, sitting at the table. "There's a little bit of a back story I guess you should know."

"You're damn right about that, Joe. You're going to tell me, then you're getting the hell out of my life for good," I grind out, trying to hold back all emotions. I'm sure I'm going to need them once he finishes his story.

Then I'm going to have a nice talk with my father.

Chapter 22

Adam

I've been staring at my computer screen for an hour but I honestly can't remember what I'm supposed to be doing. Each day that passes is harder. Not having Annaliese in my life is ruining me, but she's doing what she wants to do. She's happy and safe.

I had to let her go.

I tell myself that about three times an hour, but it never makes me feel better. I was an idiot for letting her go. Hell, I practically pushed her out of my life. Why? Because I'm a pussy. Because I didn't want to possibly get hurt. If I could take it all back now, I would.

"Earth to Adam." I hear Benton's voice from the doorway and look up to see him leaning on the doorframe.

"Oh, wow, sorry, man." I run my hand over my face to try to get out of my funk and stand up. "You ready?" I ask grabbing my keys. Today we're meeting with a new branch venture. B's set all of it up, so all I know if that it's potentially a good thing for the company. Hell, if it wasn't for him, this company would've plummeted by now.

"Yep. I'm driving." He smiles and shakes his keys. "You're just along for the ride with this one, dude."

"Fine." I sigh, giving in much easier than I would have a few months ago. He knows how much I used to like control over all things. Now I'm just numb.

The drive is short, and spent talking over the basics of the company. It's an out of town company that's trying to make it big in the bigger cities. They focus on independent bookstore owners and act as a PR agency for them. None of this interests me, and really bookstores are a thing of the past, so I'm not certain why Benton thinks investing in a company like this is a good idea, but he's never steered me in the wrong direction before so I'll trust him for now.

By the time we get to our lunch meeting I'm starving and pay more attention to the menu than I do the poor people sitting nervously in front of me. One's a girl, blonde, good tits, someone I would've fucked had I met her before Annaliese. Now I look at her and all I think about is how much better, how much sexier, my Annaliese is.

Shit, Adam, stop thinking like that. She left. Get your dick back in the game!

"Adam," Benton clears his throat and looks at me expectantly.

Crap, did they ask me a question?

"Would you excuse us for a minute?" Benton smiles politely and pulls me from the table.

"What?" I ask, smoothing down my suit jacket that he wrinkled from yanking me from the table.

"Stop staring at her tits, Adam," he growls. "You need to at least show interest in these people as a business, and not as someone you'd like to take back to your place."

"I know. Jesus...." I sigh and pinch the bridge of my nose, trying to stop the headache that's forming. "I don't see a bookstore business bringing in any revenue, though, B. It's all a joke to me. I'm not even certain why you brought me here," I sigh and look over at the table. The girl is looking at me like she could devour me. A look that used to make me hard, now just makes me depressed.

"Just play along, okay, man?" He starts back to the table and I follow, putting on my best game face.

Benton leads the discussion, trying to rope me into their gig, but I'm just not feeling it. I've made it to the top of this city by knowing what's good and what crap is. So far, all they are giving me is crap.

"So, where did you guys start out?" Benton asks, taking a drink of his water.

"Oh, we have our main hub in St. Louis." The girl smiles and twirls her hair.

Stop flirting with me.

"St. Louis. Interesting." Benton smiles at me and it all clicks. That motherfucker did this on purpose. "I'm sure if we were interested you two would be willing to spend a few days showing us how it all works, right? If we were to... say... come to St. Louis some time... soon?" He looks at me with his eyebrows raised and I shake my head at him.

He knew exactly what he was doing.

"Oh of course! We'd love it if you two would take a chance with our company. Having you down, seeing everything that we do first hand, would be fantastic." The man says, clasping his hands together.

Chance.

There's that word again.

Annaliese took a chance on me, and I blew it. I think it's time for me to take a chance for her.

"You know what, I think that sounds like a fantastic idea, Benton." I smile at him. A true smile, one I haven't felt in months. "You need to set that up. How's tomorrow sound?"

"Oh, Mr. Callahan—"

"If you are truly willing to be a part of this company, you will know that I expect excellence at all times. Short notice trips are exactly the way I run things," I glare at the girl who's stopped twirling her hair. Her mouth drops a bit and her eyes are wide with shock. "If it's a good enough business, you don't need any notice to fix things up before I see it, right?"

From the looks on their faces, they weren't expecting that, and from the look on Benton's, neither was he. Honestly, I couldn't care less if this company is running right or not. I'll probably never put my money in them, as bookstores are a dying art, but it's a reason to get me to St. Louis.

It's a reason for me to be close to her again.

My mind is running a thousand miles a minute and by the end of the meeting I can't even remember what we talked about.

All I can think about is what I'm going to say to her when I finally see her again.

What I'm going to do to her when I finally touch her again.

The thought of her having a boyfriend isn't okay with me, so he's out of the picture the minute I'm back in it. And tomorrow can't come fast enough.

***

The plane ride is the longest hour and half ever. We used the company jet, but it doesn't fly any faster than commercial flights. Unfortunately, the entire flight Benton spends staring at me and smiling like a damn fool.

"You know that look makes you look stupid," I grumble trying to seem upset that he set me up for this.

"I know your weakness, Adam. That girl is your life. You just needed to stop being so damn stubborn," he says, smiling.

"I'm not stubborn. And who says I'm doing this because of her?"

"You are. I see it in your eyes. You don't even care about this little company we're supposed to be seeing, do you?"

I look at him and shake my head.

"Not a bit." I smile. "You asshole."

"You're welcome."

By the time we get into the car, it's almost lunchtime and Benton smiles.

"You know, I never thought I'd get you here."

"What the hell does that mean?"

"You let her go so stupidly, man. Because of what? I'm not certain I've ever grasped on to your stupid ass reasoning behind you forcing her out of your life."

Shit. I never told him I suspect her father in Carly's death. I never told him because there's no evidence behind my claims, but I know it had to be. He threatened too much for it not to be him. I've got people looking into it, but I'm certain nothing will ever come from it. He's not a stupid man. He would have covered all of his tracks if it were him. The fact that every threat and all contact with him has stopped since that night pretty much sums up my claims. I don't use him anymore as a chauffeur service, and from what I gather, the fights have stopped as well. I'm not certain what happened there, but I can't help but think it has something to do with Annaliese.

"She needs to be happy, Benton. Teaching is her passion, so I forced her to it." I've been telling this lie to myself for months, but it feels so terrible that I'll never believe it.

"Can I let you in a little secret?" His eyebrows raise and I have a feeling I'm not going to like where this is going.

"What'd you do?" I growl.

"I may have visited her," he says so matter-of-factly that it takes a minute to register what he did.

"You did what?!" He saw her. He got to see my Annaliese without telling me. "What the hell, B?"

"I came to see her. The night you kept Hannah, I drove down here. Alone."

"Why the fuck would you do that, Benton?" I growl, feeling like I've been played and not liking it.

"You're miserable, Adam. She's miserable too, just so you know. Neither of you are doing yourselves any good by staying away from each other."

My God, he really did. He came down here.

"How would you know she's miserable, Benton?" I grind out the words, hating to hear that he thinks she's not happy. I let her go because I knew she wanted to teach. Well, that and the fact that I was scared of something happening to her and me dying on the inside. I let her go because... I.... "Benton, she's really miserable?" I ask, brows furrowed. "I thought this is what she wanted to do. I thought this was her life?"

He shakes his head sadly and shrugs. "You two can't live like this forever. Something has to change."

My head is spinning. There's too much to focus on right now to make sense of any of it.

All I know is that my Annaliese isn't happy, and that needs to change.

I know exactly the way to change it too.

"Where is she?" I ask, feeling my heartbeat rise.

"Work. Listen, there's one more thing I need to tell you." His face looks like he's going to be in trouble for this one.

"What?" I snap.

"So, I went by her apartment...." he trails off and I look at him, waiting for him to finish the sentence. "She had that dude there."

"What dude?" I'm going to puke. I can't live with the thought of her being with someone else.

She loves me. Well, she loved me. Jesus Christ, what've I done? I forced the woman I love out of my life because I was a pansy. Fuck! And now she's sleeping with someone else.

"The one from the night after the fight. The one that I beat to shit. He answered the door in his boxers."

"Was she there too?" I growl, pissed that she let him into her bed that easily.

"No, dude, she was at work."

"Take me to her apartment," I grind out and Benton smiles.

"Already headed there, man," he says and laughs.

"What the hell, B?"

"This was never a business trip, Adam. That was all a rouse to get you here," he's smiling like he just won a fucking marathon.

Shit. I've been played.

"You're serious, aren't you?" I whisper, amazed that he'd go through all of this for me. For Annaliese.

"You two need each other, Adam. If I could do my life over again, knowing the outcome of everything, I wouldn't change a thing. Even knowing I'd lose my wife too suddenly, I wouldn't change it. She was my world and I wouldn't be who I am right now without her. Why you'd give up on your world just because you're afraid is beyond me, but here's your chance to make things right."

He nods out the window and I've noticed the car's stopped in front of a brick building.

"It's a lot nicer of a place than her old place. Shit down here's cheaper than the city." He smiles and shrugs.

"How the hell... you know what, I don't want to know," I say, shaking my head.

"Good luck, man."

I nod at him and get out of the car to be met with the cool breeze of a fall day in St. Louis. The city noises here are nothing compared to Chicago, but from what I hear, the crime rate has skyrocketed recently. Looking around her neighborhood, it looks nicer than where she was living in Chicago, but looks can be deceiving.

I knock on the door, wondering what the hell I'm doing not having a key or anything, but when the older woman that opens the door smiles at me, I know it's already been taken care of.

"Mr. Callahan. So glad you could make it. I'll take you up to her place. My name's Rita, the landlord here," she says sweetly, walking me up a flight of stairs. I'm either going to owe Benton a punch in the face or a new car after today.

When she opens the door, I'm immediately hit with Annaliese's scent.

"She's normally home around five," she says then smiles sadly at me. "She's a sweet girl. Sad, quiet... but sweet." She pats me on my arm and leaves to go back downstairs, leaving me in Annaliese's apartment.

I have five hours to figure out how I'm going to apologize for being the biggest asshole on the planet.

Chapter 23

Annaliese

"Oh, Annaliese, what a nice surprise!" My mother's voice rings from the living room, but I barely register it through the hatred seething out of me towards the man that answered the door.

The man that calls himself my father.

"Hello, mother. I need to have a word with dad, if you don't mind," I say, not taking my eyes from his. The man should be scared, but he doesn't look like he has a remorseful bone in his body.

"Oh," my mom whispers. "Yes, yes that's fine." She slowly walks out of the room, leaving me and Vick to hash this out together.

"This is a surprise, Annaliese," he says, sitting down in his worn brown leather chair. A chair I used to curl up with him at night when the nightmares got to be too bad to handle.

"You knew it was coming, don't act surprised." I snap crossing my arms.

"I wouldn't have expected anything different," he sighs.

"Tell me why, Dad." My words are forced, the emotions rolling through me are so hard to handle right now. I want to scream and hit things, but I need to try and stay calm.

"Why what, dear?" he asks, raising his eyebrows. Condescending asshole.

"Everything. Why the fighting, why'd you push me out of town with this job, and why Joe?" His name comes out a whisper at the end of a very hard to speak sentence. I feel terrible that Joe was caught up in the middle of my father's drama. I feel guilty that I didn't see through my dad's lies earlier, before Joe fell for me. Most of all, I feel sick just thinking about my recently ruined relationship, all because of my father.

"Annaliese, that deal with Joe's father has been in the books since you were ten years old. I've been using his money all these years, all with the promise that you'd marry his only son. The Ryder and Hoertel names would be combined when you two married to create one of the most powerful families in the city. Moving you out of town seemed to be the only way to finish that deal once you started seeing Adam. Of course I didn't want you with Callahan. He's not worth your time, honey. Joe's a much better candidate. You can do better than Mr. Chi—"

"You stop," I growl clenching my fists. "Adam is a better man than you'll ever dream to be. He helps people every day. He makes sure his employees are well taken care of, and he doesn't bend and manipulate people's lives to how he thinks they should be living them. You've spent your last night dictating how I live my life," I spit. He looks stunned that I'm speaking to him like this, but I'm finally letting it all out. "I've spent my entire life trying to be good enough for you, and you know what, dear old dad? I don't care anymore! Nothing I do will make me good enough for you, and I just don't care. It's time for me to start living for myself, and not for some poor, pathetic asshole like yourself." I'm seething, staring at his smug face and fighting the urge to punch him.

"You could've married Joe. That would've been enough Annie."

"Oh fuck you, Vick!" I scream, hearing a dish crash in the kitchen. "You're the lowest piece of shit I've ever encountered. Selling off your daughter for a few G's!? Who the hell are you, anyway?!" I'm furious. Beyond furious. "I pray to God that mom leaves you. I pray she gets out and gets as far away as she can before you ruin her life as well." I start to walk out of the room, leaving him in the chair without a care in the world. "Oh, and one more thing," I say. He turns his head to look at me and I take a second to try and see any semblance of remorse in his eyes but there's nothing. "Don't expect to be involved in any part of my life. Ever again. Marriage, kids... nothing. I never want to see your face again," I manage to say, then storm out of the house, slamming the door behind me.

Getting in the car, I allow myself a few minutes of tears for the future memories I've lost because of the man in that house, then I start the car. Moving back downstate to my lonely little life.

***

I hate Mondays.

Especially Mondays after a weekend from hell.

Seeing my father this weekend helped put some closure to everything that's been going on lately. His words crushed me, but not as much as the reminder that no matter how hard I tried, I was never enough for him. Believe me, there were days that I wish it was me instead of my sister in that car years ago. I feel like she never would've been as big of a disappointment to him as I've been. I'm certain my parents are getting a divorce after this weekend. If I were my mom, I would. I won't ever forgive him for ruining everything, and I'm certain she won't either. Now all I can do is attempt to rebuild in a new city with barely any money, no friends, nothing I love, and no family.

Seems easy, right?

I sigh, rolling my neck, trying to work off the frustration from the weekend and look up at the clock when the bell rings.

Finally.

I remind my class of their homework and check agendas on their way out the door. When the last one leaves, I shut and lock the door behind them. All I need to do is get my things together and I can head home. Home. I chuckle to myself, since the place I want to call home is so far away now, that I'm not sure I'll ever go back. Moving back to a city full of liars and cheats and men that don't want you in their lives would be worse than living alone in a city with no friends or family.

No thanks, I'll stay right here. Maybe I'll get a cat.

I stop on the way home and grab a pizza. Takeout for one. It's Monday and I'm single. I can do what I want. The thought should make me happy, but it's actually more depressing the more I think about it. I haven't been laid since the last time with Adam. Joe tried, but I never let him. I can't see myself with anyone else but Adam.

Joe told me he loved me right before I kicked him out of my life. Too much damage had been done in the past, too many lies, to even think about keeping him around. Even as a friend.

I get the door open to my apartment building and smile at Rita.

Just Go   M. Dauphin

"Hey, Rita," I say as I close the door behind me, trying to balance my pizza box and drink in one hand.

"Oh, Annaliese." She looks up and smiles from her apartment door like she's been caught. Caught from doing what? I'm not sure.

"You cooking something? It smells fantastic," I say taking a whiff of whatever she's got on the stove.

"Oh, um... nope. Not me. Must be the other tenant upstairs." She smiles and sighs. "Beautiful day, huh?"

"Yeah... sure. Okay, so... I'll be upstairs if you need me." I smile again and head up the stairs. The scent of spaghetti sauce hits me hard when I get to the top of the stairs and I look over at my neighbor's door. They just moved in a week ago so I haven't had a chance to get to know them yet, but I really should if they can cook. Pizza and takeout every night is going to kill my wallet.

I unlock my door and swing it open, just to be hit with the scent stronger than before. Walking slowly into my apartment, I freeze when I notice the candles.

All the candles.

"Hello?" I call out, nerves running through my body.

My first thought is Joe, but I know better than that. He's back in Chicago. Gabby saw him yesterday and said he looks like shit.

Who would...?

"My Sweet." His voice purrs from across the room and I gasp.

How did I not see him? How is he here? What's going on?

"Adam?" I whisper, my heart beating wildly for the beautiful man standing mere feet away from me.

A man who's haunted my dreams since the day he let me go.

"Annaliese," he whispers in a voice rough and full of emotion.

That's all it takes.

I drop everything, not caring about the food, or my bags, or shutting the door behind me. I drop it, and run. Straight to the man I love.

His arms come around me and he lifts me to him, wrapping me and holding on for dear life.

"Oh God, baby," he whispers into my neck as my legs wrap around him and I cling to him like my last breath. "My God, I've missed you, Annaliese."

There are tears pouring down my cheeks and I can't even tell if I'm crying or laughing.

He's here. He came for me.

"Adam, what're you doing here?" I ask through my sobs.

"I... I need you, Annaliese."

He sets me down but takes hold of my hands.

"I... Shit," He pulls me in for another hug, this time kissing my forehead. "I need you." It comes out a whisper and I can feel the wetness from his tears hit my shoulder.

"I'm here, Adam." I shake my head like he's lost it and smile. I can't stop smiling, and the tears are still rolling.

What's he doing here?

"I know. Shit," he smiles at me and my heart flutters back to life. "You're here. You've always been here."

I smile and wipe the tears from my face. He sighs and sits down on the couch with me right next to him, never letting go of my hands.

"I've been an asshole, Annaliese," he starts. When I try to speak, he puts his hand to my mouth and shakes his head. "I'm not done. Hear me out. Please," he whispers the last word, his eyes begging me. I nod and listen patiently. "These last three months have been hell. I was stubborn, I was stupid, I was scared, and I pushed you away." He takes a breath before he goes on. "I made the biggest mistake of my life when I told you to take this job. Not a day has gone by that I didn't see your face. Not a second of my life has passed without me regretting those words I said to you. None of them were true, my Sweet," he whispers. His hand comes to my cheek and his thumb caresses my lips. "Jesus, I'm so sorry, Annaliese," he whispers, then leans in and kisses me gently. I sigh into his kiss, leaning towards him, not wanting the connection to break.

He pulls back and grins at me. "I've missed that," he whispers.

"I've missed you," I manage through all of the raging emotions running through me.

This last week has been absolutely insane, and now that he's here with me, I don't care about anything but us.

"I know. I'm so sorry, Annalise. So goddamned sorry."

"You ruined everything, Adam," I whisper. As much as I want to go running back to him and forget all of this happened, it can't happen. I need answers. I need time. "I took a chance on you, and you ruined me."

I start to cry again and he pulls me to him, hugging me and kissing the top of my head, whispering his apologies over and over.

"I know. I know you did, and I know I messed everything up. But I promise you, I'm going to fix this." His eyes lock with mine and I know he means it.

"How, Adam? I work here now. And you work five hours away," I whisper, my gaze still locked on his.

"I love you, Annaliese Ryder," he says then sighs and smiles, shaking his head. "We will figure this out. Weekend trips, I'll start doing more business down here. We can do this." He watches me and his face falls when I don't say anything. "Annaliese?"

I'm trying to form the words.

I told myself I was over him. Every day that I woke up and he had no contact with me, I made a promise to myself that I wouldn't go crawling back to him. This isn't crawling back to him, though, right?

"I...." I don't know what to say. I want this, but I'm more scared than the first time because I know how badly my heart will be crushed if it doesn't work. His eyebrows pull together when I hesitate.

"No... no, Annie... don't," he frantically whispers. His hands cup my face and his eyes search mine. "Don't say anything."

"Will you stop?" I laugh. "I love you too, you asshole," I say, smiling the biggest I've smiled in a long time. "God, you're so serious all the time. So old for being so young," I joke with him. "Did you really think I stopped loving you, just because you were being stupid?"

His eyes are big and his mouth is grinning. He's trying not to laugh, but he's not doing a good job at it.

"I... I guess. You hesitated. Why'd you hesitate?"

"I can't let you think I'm gonna cave that easily, mister. You still have a lot of making up to do." I move towards him and put one leg slowly over his lap, pulling my skirt up enough for my legs to wrap around him.

He groans when my hands go to the back of his neck and pull him in for a kiss. His hands immediately find my ass and I smile and grind into him, feeling his hard length growing.

"Jesus, Annaliese." He nips my ear lobe and his fingers play at the top of my dress. "Shit. I made dinner," he says as he continues kissing me.

"You cooked?" I pull back and smile.

"Of course. I can cook, you know. I just choose not to most nights."

I hop up and run into the kitchen and notice all the candles at the perfectly set table. Smiling, I turn to walk back to the living room and run into his hard chest.

"You always did like running into me," he whispers as he wraps his arms around me.

God, I've missed this.

"It's a great excuse to get close to you," I whisper looking up to his eyes. "I'm starving, Adam. Can we eat? This smells fantastic."

"Absolutely, my Sweet." He kisses me and pinches my ass before walking me to the table.

Dinner is absolutely amazing. I'm not sure why he hid from me that he can cook, but someone taught him right. The spaghetti was perfect, and he swears he made the sauce himself, which from what I see is the truth since I find no empty jars in the trash when I look.

We spend the entire time eating and catching up. He tells me about Benton and Hannah, and how much Thor loves to play with her. I have to tell him all about what happened with my dad, too, which is a subject I'd rather never have to approach, but he's opening up so it's only fair I do too. To say he's pissed is an understatement, but he's promised not to do anything too drastic. I did tell him that I've cut ties with my father, though, and he smiles sadly and nods.

"I'm so sorry, Annaliese," he says reaching across the table to take my hand in his.

"I'm not. He's not worth it." I shrug and grin, then change the subject before he notices the sadness in my eyes about it all. "This food is terrific. I've never tasted a sauce like this before," I say shoving more pasta in my mouth and grinning.

He chuckles and sighs. "Jesus, I've missed you."

"Missed you too," I say smiling. I can't stop smiling tonight. "Thanks for getting your head out of your ass."

"You have Benton to thank for that. God, I've been so fucking dumb," he says and then sighs and smiles. "Never again. I promise," he whispers. I can't really believe this is all happening.

The rest of dinner is spent like this, in a light discussion and playful banter. He helps me clean up afterwards and even puts the dishes in the dishwasher. I stand in the doorway, watching him and wonder to myself how I got so lucky. This beautiful man, white crisp button down shirt, slacks, sleeves rolled up to his elbows, is mine.

All I have to do is take another chance on him.

"Hey," he whispers coming over to me and lifting my chin so I can meet his gaze. "Everything okay?" he asks worriedly.

"Everything's just perfect," I whisper, then reach up on my toes to kiss him gently. When I pull back, I see the look in his beautiful eyes and grin. "Come on."

I take his hand and walk past the living room and down the hall towards my bedroom. Opening the door, I go in and drop his hand. Turning to face him, I walk backwards into my room until my legs hit the end of my bed. I grin, and start moving the straps of my dress down my shoulders. He growls and moves towards me.

"You're so beautiful, my Sweet." His hands stop mine from their dance along the top of my dress. "Let me. Please," he begs. I drop my hands to my side and sigh as his lips gently caress my collarbone.

Just Go   M. Dauphin

He finishes what I started, gently pushing my dress down so I'm standing in front of him in a dark blue and black lace set that I had no choice but to wear when I realized I had no clean laundry this morning. He growls his appreciation and drops to his knees in front of me, kissing his way down my body. His hands play at the edge of my panties and I feel the goose bumps rise from his gentle touch. His hands gently help lift each leg from the dress pooled around my feet, then he tosses it aside.

"Lie down, Annaliese," he whispers after standing up to meet my gaze.

I do as I'm told, never breaking our connection, and my hands start playing at the buttons on his shirt as he hovers over me. Once they're undone, I take my time grazing over each muscle, each bulge. Slowly I slip the shirt off him when he sits up, then I show it the same amount of care he showed my dress and grin.

"You're still losing in the clothes department," I whisper, starting to work his pants off of him.

He grins and obliges, quickly standing to pull his pants off, then he's back over me, strong, muscular arms bracing his weight around me. His eyes lock with mine and I feel like I can see into his soul. Our connection is so intense, I'm not sure I could look away right now if I tried.

He kisses me, then trails his lips down to my neck, then my collarbone, and then lower. Making sure to show every part of my body the affection it's been missing these last three months.

"It's been so long, Adam," I gasp when he pulls the fabric of my bra down to kiss my bare breast.

"Jesus, even better than I remember," he growls as he releases my other breast, the fabric of my bra pushing them up for him. His hands cup them, gently playing with my nipples, and when his teeth come around one I gasp and buck up towards him, feeling the wetness between my legs start to pool.

"God, I've missed you," his voice comes out as a whisper as his lips work their way lower. His fingers gently tug at the top of my panties and I lift slightly to allow him to remove them, thanking the heavens I like to keep things neat down there even if it's not seeing any action. "Shit," he whispers.

His fingers graze along my wet slit, then slowly push in with ease. He moans as he plays with my clit, his lips kissing so close. I want more than this. I need him. All of him.

"Please, Adam," I gasp when his lips go around my swollen clit and suck gently.

"Yes?" He smiles as his fingers play me.

"I need you, Adam. All of you," I pant.

He slowly removes his fingers and licks them, his eyes never loosing contact with mine. Holy crap! I forgot how hot that is.

"Condom." He starts to move off the bed, but I stop him and shake my head.

"All of you. Nothing between us," I smile and bite my lip, praying he's okay with it. "I don't want anything between us anymore. Ever."

"God... are you sure? I mean... shit yeah. I haven't been with anyone since you, Annaliese. But... Jesus, I love you," he says, then kisses me as he slides into me.

My arms wrap around his neck and he moves his lips to my neck as I push up to take him all the way. God, he fills me perfectly, and without any barrier I can feel him so much better than ever before.

"You're so tight, Sweet," he growls into my neck, then bites down hard enough to leave a mark as he slowly pulls out.

"There hasn't been anyone since you, Adam," I whimper as he pulls all the way out, just to quickly reenter me and start the slow torture to fill me again.

I can feel the electricity building, my entire body in tune with his. I feel every movement, every hard ridge, everything. He continues his slow movements, making love to me like never before. There's not anything in the world that compares to this, and when he pulls his head up and locks his eyes with mine, I know he means it.

"I love you so much, Annaliese," he whispers as he pushes back in, never taking his eyes off mine. "So much," he grunts and leans in to kiss me.

I start to feel my release building at the same time I can feel him hardening, and his movements becoming less rhythmic. He curses under his breath and speeds up his movements, hitting every part of me perfectly.

"Oh God, Adam," I gasp when I feel the start of the orgasm starting to rip through me. His lips crush into mine as I feel him grunt and release into me, the grinding on my clit the perfect amount of pressure. "Shit!" I clutch to him, my nails digging into his back as he rides his release out and my orgasm explodes around him.

"My God," he pants as he rests his head on my forehead, still trying to find his breath.

I have no words to what we just experienced. It was nothing like anything before.

It was true love making.

"I love you, Adam," I gasp, not able to let go of him.

"I love you, Annaliese. Forever," he whispers then kisses me.

We forget about everything else that night but each other, making up for three lost months without each other. He remembers every part of my body, and explores parts he hasn't yet been able to. Falling asleep in his arms is the best feeling ever. It's hard not to be mad at myself for being so stubborn three months ago while I lay in his arms, finally able to relax for the first time in months.

Just Go M. Dauphin

This is exactly what I need.

He is exactly what I need.

Epilogue

Four months later

"Gabby, which dress?" I ask holding three dresses up in front of her.

I'm back in Chicago for Spring Break and can't wait to see Adam. The last four months I've been able to see him more than expected, but it's still been a week since we've been together and I'm itching to see him again. Tonight he has dinner planned for us at some fancy restaurant that only he'd be able to get reservations at and I can't decide which dress to wear.

Gabby sighs and smiles from the couch, "You know he's going to love all of those. Especially when he rips it off of you." She laughs and smiles, "So wear the one you're least fond of."

"Funny. Don't be jealous," I warn as I choose the light blue one and nude heels.

"I'm not jealous at all, actually. I have my own fun," she says, not making eye contact with me as she picks at her nails.

I worry about her being alone. She puts on a tough act like she doesn't have a care in the world, but I can see past the façade. I wish she'd find someone. Man or woman, I don't care, but she needs someone.

"What time's he picking you up?" she asks.

"In about a half hour. Wanna help with my hair?" I grin, knowing she can't turn down making me look girly for a night.

By the time the knock comes on the door, I smile and she laughs.

"You're hopeless, Annie. I'm so happy for you," she says then hugs me and heads back to her room.

I open the door and see him waiting, relaxed, hands in his pocket. When his eyes rake over my body, I get chills and immediately feel the warmth between my legs. It's been a week since I last saw him and enjoyed him in St. Louis, but it feels like forever when he looks at me like that.

"You look beautiful," he says, then takes my face in his hands and kisses me gently. "Missed you," he whispers, his lips still on mine.

"Mmm," I manage. As much as I want to pull him inside the apartment, Gabby's new one bedroom apartment doesn't leave much privacy and I'm not sure she'd appreciate that.

"Come on. We have reservations, and if we keep this up, I'm going to devour you right here in the hallway," he growls, then walks me outside as we start down the sidewalk.

I feel every tickle of the wind, every ray of the sunshine while walking down the sidewalk hand in hand with Adam. My senses are finally alive again, because I've opened up my heart to the man I love. Being with him makes every part of me more alert. We approach the white limo and smile.

"New driving service, huh?"

He nods sadly, giving me a look like he knows how I feel about his relationship with my father. I've gotten over it through the months, but I still don't like to be reminded of their past. He also knows it's been months since I've spoken to my father, which hurts so much I can't think about it without tearing up. He was my world, until it all came crashing down.

"No reason to keep up with a cheating, lying business."

"That's the truth." I take his hand when we're in the backseat and we spend the short drive to the restaurant in comfortable silence.

When the car stops in front of a sky rise apartment building I look over at Adam confused. He's grinning at me, and when the door opens, he slides out and holds his hand out for me without a word. I take it, feeling my heartbeat quicken.

"What's going on, Adam?" I ask as we walk into the building and head towards the elevators.

"Just wait, my Sweet," he says. I can feel the nerves running through him, and as a result my nerves skyrocket.

What's he got up his sleeve?

We ride the elevator to the top floor, and when the doors open, I gasp at the sight.

Pink and red rose petals decorate a path out of the elevator and on to a rooftop veranda. Gabby is leaning against the banister, a smile pasted on her face and a drink in hand. My mother stands next to her, talking with another older woman who I assume is Adam's mother due to their striking resemblance. Benton's in the corner of the patio, alone, and when he realizes we've arrived his eyes flick from Gabby's area, to us, then back to her. Adam's sister is here, talking to Gabby while Adam's father is sitting at a bar to the left.

"What is this?" I whisper as he slowly takes my hand and guides me to the outdoor patio, fully adorned with candles and rose petals everywhere. A table sits in the middle of the patio, fully set and covered trays with what I'm assuming is our dinner awaits us. He lets me walk ahead and look out from the edge, overlooking the beautiful city that I love. I turn to speak and gasp when I see him down on one knee.

Oh. My. God.

"Adam," I whisper, my hand goes to my mouth, unable to form any words through the threatening tears.

"Annaliese Ryder, I love you. More than anything. You've taken so many chances on me, most of which I didn't deserve, but you did it anyway. We've been through more than most couples ever go through, and I'm so proud of you. For everything. You're the strongest woman I've ever had the chance of knowing." He stands and walks over to me, a small black velvet box in hand. The tears that have formed in my eyes are now spilling down my cheeks. "You've taken chances on me, and I'm eternally grateful for that. I'm asking you now to take one final chance on me." He pauses and opens the box to reveal a gorgeous rose gold diamond ring twinkling from the patio lights above making it shine brightly. "Annaliese Ryder, will you grace me with your love and laughter for the rest of your life? Give me all of your morning hugs and goodnight kisses, my Sweet," he pauses, "Marry me, Annaliese. Make me the happiest man in Chicago. The happiest damn man in the world."

"Oh my God, Adam," I gasp reaching out with shaky hands for him. I take his face and kiss him. Like I can never get enough, because I can't. "You're... this...." I'm speechless.

"So...." He grins and I realize I haven't given him an answer.

"Yes!! Oh my God, Yes!" I yell, and he releases his breath and smiles.

"You had me scared there for a minute." He laughs then pulls the ring from the box.

Sliding it on, it fits perfectly and I giggle, watching it sparkle in the lights.

"It's perfect, Adam," I whisper, then wrap my arms around him, kissing him again.

"I love you, Annaliese. I'll spend the rest of my life showing you how much," he whispers and hugs me tightly.

We make our rounds, accepting the congratulatory hugs and smiles. The ring is huge, nothing short of perfect from *Mr. Chicago*. I've come to accept the fact that women will never stop throwing themselves at his feet, but I trust him. I know he's only got eyes for me.

"Soo... were you surprised?" Gabby asks as I take a champagne flute off a waiter's tray.

"Absolutely. I mean, we've talked about it. I know I'll be moving back up here at the end of the school year, but this.... This is perfect," I smile holding back tears that my father isn't here for me. "He got everyone important together for me."

"Speaking of important people," Adam clears his throat as he walks up to Gabby and I. "This man right here is one of the key factors on this whole ordeal." He slaps Benton's back and smiles.

"Benton James. Nice to meet you again, Gabby," he looks past me and straight to Gabby. I turn to look at her, confused, but the crimson tint to her cheeks tells me everything I need to know. I leave the two of them, taking Adam's hand in mine, giving those two a little time to themselves.

We stop at the banister overlooking the city, and I take a deep breath. This city is mine, I just needed to take it.

"Thank you for taking a chance on me."

"You mean multiple chances?" I grin and he laughs.

"Yes... multiple chances."

Sometimes, all you need to do is take a chance. Or three.

THE END

Just Go

M. Dauphin

Other works by M. Dauphin

Read Adam and Annaliese's first night in the Suits and Shades Anthology: http://amzn.to/1MAwD26

Fight Series

Fight 1: http://amzn.to/1Gf0zli

Fight 2: http://amzn.to/1DY1cYc

Fight 3: http://amzn.to/1FjYlFV

Co-Authored with H.Q. Frost
For3ver- http://www.amazon.com/dp/B00TC1JYA0

Also in:
Once: A Collection of Sinfully Sexy and Twisted Tales (Anthology): http://amzn.to/1SD57Bz

About M. Dauphin

M. Dauphin is a mom, wife, sister, daughter, granddaughter, best-daughter-in-law-EVER, and when all else slows down... a writer. She's a stay at home mom, having an 'early retirement' from teaching at the ripe young age of 27, she now spends her days chasing the tiny ninjas around her house and picking up after them (or else her feet are subjected to sharp as shit Lego pains... and nobody's got time for that).

You should befriend her on her Facebook page. She likes meeting new people.

www.facebook.com/authormdauphin

WRITE A REVIEW!

Readers, in the age of ebooks, remember that you are in control of separating the good from the bad, the wheat from the chaff.

Please take a moment to go back to the site where you purchased this book and leave your opinion, however lengthy or brief, about it.

Make your vote count! Your opinion will help other readers make their future purchasing decisions in regards to ebooks.

Made in the USA
Charleston, SC
20 July 2016